Death of a Billionaire

A Murder Mystery Novel
Tucker May

Tucker May Books

Copyright © 2025 by Tucker May

All rights reserved.

No portion of this book may be reproduced in any form without written permission from the publisher or author, except as permitted by U.S. copyright law. This is a work of fiction; no similarity to any real person or persons is intended or should be inferred.

Other Works By Tucker May

Novels

The Lemon House Murders (Coming Soon)
  The Devil's Query (Coming Soon)

Tucker May Mysteries

Follow @TuckerMayMysteries on Bluesky, TuckerMayMysteries on Instagram and Tucker May Mysteries on Facebook for daily bite-size chapters of mystery short stories.

Subscribe

Visit www.TuckerMay.com to subscribe for updates and receive a FREE mystery novella.

To my wife Barbara, who helped me realize what true courage is and inspired me to chase my dreams.

Chapter One

Barron Aloysius Fisk lay on the floor of his swanky Silicon Valley office with blood pouring from his head. The rug below him, crafted from the fur of a thousand baby alpacas, soaked up the crimson liquid as if eager to absorb as much of the great man's essence as it could. Smart rug. The desk at his side, carved from the trunk of what had been the oldest tree in South America before Fisk ordered it felled for furniture, gleamed in the overhead lights. Behind the desk stood a wall of shelves that showcased artifacts from Fisk's extensive world travels:

A boar tusk carved into the shape of a woman with a bulbous belly and pendulous breasts, gifted to him by one of the few remaining nomadic tribes in Papua New Guinea after he failed to correct their mistaken assumption that he was a god.

A prehistoric flint that Fisk had personally dug out of Olduvai Gorge in northeastern Tanzania and then refused to donate to the Smithsonian.

A chunk of real meteor that had survived its blazing trip through Earth's atmosphere to strike and kill a man near Nice, France, and that Fisk had purchased at an auction for a price nearing the total economic output of Ecuador.

Impressive antiquities all.

A single bullet hole marked the wall at eye level where Fisk had been standing, alive and well, just a few moments before. Fisk's thin lips curled into a smile as his heart gave its final few beats and then fell still. Thus died the richest man to ever live. If it could happen to a world-shaking genius like him, dear reader, it most certainly could happen to a clodhopping nobody like you.

I will not apologize for my harsh tone. I must make clear the magnitude of loss that our world suffered with the death of Barron Fisk. This was a man who had truly done something with his life, unlike you, dear reader, and the hordes of space-wasting, destitute dolts just like you. Fisk was a paragon of vision and character whose unbounded ambition and monumental achievements would, were you faced with a comprehensive list of them, undoubtedly leave you feeling like the penniless swine, the feces-flinging forest ape that you so surely are. Trust me when I say that you would not be fit to lick the bottom of Barron Fisk's brightly polished ostrich-skin Oxfords.

So put down your artery-clogging double McFatass burger, or whatever you poor people shove down your gullets nowadays, and pay attention. I'll be telling this only once, and the incomparable Barron Fisk deserves your undivided attention.

The unwashed masses must learn the truth.

Chapter Two

The morning of June 9, 2028, dawned crisp and clear. The sun's first rays knifed through the expansive windows of Barron Fisk's office to fall upon his cooling corpse. The harried activity around the body contrasted sharply with the usual comings and goings associated with the superstar tech billionaire. Hazmat-clad forensic techs swabbed and dusted every surface. Uniformed police officers canvassed the whole building. Two plainclothes detectives peered down at Fisk's inert body.

"No sign of a struggle," said Detective Benjamin Tanner, a tall, rail-thin man in his mid-thirties. He sported an ill-advised wispy mustache that lent him the appearance of a grade schooler with access to the drama department's costume closet. "Clean job, maybe a professional."

"What kind of professional killer leaves the murder weapon at the scene of the crime?" his partner asked. "The gun is just sitting on the office floor."

"A bad professional killer? I don't know."

Detective Lucinda Reyes rolled her eyes. She pulled out her Fisk-brand ePhone.

"What are you looking up?" Tanner asked. "How fast a body can expel this amount of blood?"

"I'm seeing if any of the grocery stores around here sell Valentina. It's my favorite hot sauce, and I can't find any in my new neighborhood."

Tanner frowned. "Who are you? The Detective Reyes I know would never be on a hunt for hot sauce at the scene of a murder."

"Please. It's not like we lost a saint here. Barron Fisk was wealthy enough to single-handedly end world hunger. Instead, he chose to build a fleet of space rockets so he and his buddies could jerk off in zero-G."

"No way that's what they were doing up there."

"Are you sure?"

Tanner thought about it. "I guess it is one of the first things I'd do."

"Men are pigs."

"Focus up. This is a big case for us. Imagine our names broadcast across the country as the ones who caught Fisk's killer. Not to mention a juicy promotion. So maybe leave the hot sauce for later?" Tanner added, "Sorry, I don't mean to criticize."

"Okay, you're right." Reyes put away her phone. "I'm here. I'm plugged in. What do we know?"

Tanner reviewed the notes he'd taken on his own ePhone.

"Time of death: June 8, 2028, sometime around 10:00 PM. There are no cameras here in Fisk's office, and the security footage from the hallway outside is wiped."

"Suggests an inside job."

"Definitely. The apparent murder weapon was left at the scene of the crime, a Ruger LCP .380. One of the most common guns in the country."

"So the culprit was smart enough to erase the security footage but careless enough to leave behind the weapon? That doesn't add up."

"There's something else strange." Tanner stepped closer to the body. "There's a clear footprint left in the blood here. Why would the killer get that close if they'd already shot him?"

"Robbery gone wrong?"

Tanner checked Fisk's pockets.

"Wallet's here, cellphone too. No keys, but I'm not sure if a billionaire drives himself anywhere. He's got on a couple expensive-looking rings and a necklace. I don't think anything is missing."

"That is interesting."

"Maybe they needed to take a photo? It could have been a hit, and they had to provide proof."

"But then why leave the gun behind?"

"Pretty crazy to take a picture of the guy you killed with a phone from the guy's own company."

"We don't know the killer had an ePhone."

"Everybody has an ePhone. What world are you living in?"

"All right. Let's get the gun to forensics. Maybe we'll be lucky and pull some prints."

A disembodied voice rang through the room, coming from all directions at once. It made Reyes jump.

"I have the capacity to scan items for fingerprints, if I may be of any assistance," said the smoothly robotic voice.

"Mother of Mary, what in the hell is that?" Reyes demanded.

"I am Jennings," the voice replied. "The same artificial intelligence system that runs on all Fisk ePhones. My main console is located here in Mr. Fisk's office."

Detective Reyes glared at the waist-high console in the corner, glowing blue.

Tanner said, "Your voice sounds different than on my phone, Jennings. What's that about?"

"I am not sure what you mean," Jennings said.

"How do we turn that damn thing off?" Reyes barked to the custodian who had discovered Fisk's body. He stood near the office door looking scared.

"I don't know," said the employee, shrugging. "Only Mr. Fisk ever ran it."

"If you do not require my input, Detective Reyes," said the AI system, "you may simply say 'Jennings, power down.' Then, whenever you'd like to reactiva—"

"Jennings, power down," Reyes interrupted the machine.

"Goodbye."

The console in the corner changed from a bright blue to a tranquil green color.

"It's so creepy that it knows our names," Reyes said, eyeing the console with suspicion.

"Hold on a minute, I have an idea," Tanner said. "Jennings, power back up."

The console went bright blue again and emitted a light bloop sound, indicating readiness.

"How may I be of assistance?"

"Jennings, who killed Barron Fisk?" Tanner asked. Reyes scoffed. "What? It's worth a shot."

"I'm afraid I do not know," the AI voice said. "I was able to identify you, Detectives, because you're carrying your registered Fisk ePhones. This, unfortunately, was not the case with the culprit and, as you have already noted, there are no cameras here in Mr. Fisk's office. Thus, I am unable to identify the perpetrator. It could have been anyone."

"So." Tanner sighed. "Pretty much all we know for sure is that somebody knocked off the world's richest man."

"Yeah." Reyes squinted into the middle distance with her hands on her hips. "And I'm going to catch the bastard."

Tanner followed her eyeline. "What are you looking at?"

"Huh?"

"You're, like, staring off into space. What are you doing?"

"No, I'm . . . Damn it, Tanner, I had a cool moment going there. Why do you have to ruin everything?"

"Sorry. Maybe you could include me in your cool moments? I am your partner."

"Get your own cool moment."

"Fine. I will." Tanner struck the same pose as Reyes. "Let's go catch the damn bastard."

Reyes threw her arms out. "Well, don't just repeat what I said."

"I didn't repeat what you said. I added a 'damn'."

"That's repeating it."

"That's not repeating it."

"You're still just repeating me."

"I am not just repeating you."

"Cut it out!"

"Okay, fine, how about this," Tanner said, reassuming the hands-on-hips pose. "Looks like this rich guy's drawn his last breath of billion-*air*." He looked to Reyes for approval.

"You're the worst." She stomped away.

"Hey! Mean!" Tanner called after her.

"Sorry," she muttered without conviction as she disappeared through the doorway.

Tanner turned his attention back to the body, nudging it gently with his foot.

"Yup, he's dead all right," he said to no one. "That is one dead billionaire."

Chapter Three

Alan Benning carefully wiped a spot of grape jelly from the hem of his beige sweater vest and resumed cutting the crust off of his daughters' mid-morning snack. His wife hurried down the stairs wearing skin-tight athletic wear.

"Well, look who's up and about," Alan said cheerfully. "Girls, say hi to Mama." The twin two-year-olds gurgled a response from their matching high chairs. "Good morning, beautiful. Off to yoga?"

Hannah reached across the wide kitchen island. Alan leaned forward to meet her for a kiss, but she simply snatched the car keys resting near his right hand and withdrew. Alan cleared his throat.

"I'm late," she said. "Sergei makes anyone who comes in late set up next to Farty Dan."

"Well, we certainly wouldn't want that. Say goodbye to Mommy, girls."

"Oh. And I need a hundred for lunch at the club after."

Alan produced some cash from his wallet and handed it over. Only then did Hannah grace him with a forced smile. She strode toward the front door. The keys in her hand jingled as she raised her ePhone and spoke into it.

"Jennings, what's the weather today?"

"Today in Cupertino, California, there is an expected high of eighty-two degrees with a ten percent chance of precipitation," her phone answered in a slightly stilted voice. Hannah stopped with a bemused expression.

"Oh, hey," she said. "They gave Jennings a new voice. Huh."

Suddenly, the front door, only a few feet from Hannah, burst inward violently. Small wooden bits of splintered door jamb flew through the air. Hannah screamed and stumbled backward. The door slammed against the far wall as a battalion of black-helmeted, gun-wielding SWAT members swarmed in.

"Cupertino P.D.!"

The girls began to cry.

"What in the world is going on he—" was as far as Alan got before being roughly tackled to the ground.

"Alan Benning, you're under arrest for the murder of Barron Fisk."

"What?" shouted both adult Bennings.

An imposing officer with enormous shoulders displayed an arrest warrant to Hannah. Her eyes ran over it in rapid disbelief. Another officer read Alan his rights as he half-dragged, half-carried the man out of his home.

As the officer shoved Alan into a squad car, he craned his neck to see back through the front door. His daughters wailed their displeasure. His wife heatedly demanded answers from the swarm of police officers. But no answers would be had for quite a while.

Chapter Four

Detective Lucinda Reyes crossed the bullpen of the Cupertino Police Department with purposeful strides. Her dark, arched eyebrows and hawkish gaze told anyone in her way to move, and move fast. Tanner, nearly a foot and a half taller, trailed along behind her. They stopped outside Interrogation Room B down a short side hallway. Reyes spoke quickly.

"We'll hit him right off with the hard evidence, see what we can get out of him before the lawyer shows."

Tanner nodded like a docile labrador. "Right. I'll play the bad cop."

"No. We're not doing that. This isn't some hardened criminal we're dealing with. Let's lay out what we know, and he'll crack."

"You want to be bad cop?"

"We're not doing good cop, bad cop."

"Then what are we doing?"

"We're just interrogating a suspect."

"Right, but what cops are we going to be?"

"Just ourselves."

"Smart cop, dumb cop?"

"I mean. Yes, but not intentionally."

"What does that mean?"

"Nothing. Never mind."

"Just tell me what cop to be!"

"You're you. You're Tanner."

"Oh. That's disappointing."

"You're telling me."

"Hey. Mean."

"Sorry. Let's go in."

"Okay. But I'm doing bad cop."

"No, don't . . . All right, fine, you can be bad cop."

"Score." Tanner pumped his fist as he followed Reyes into the room.

Alan sat on a hard, straight-backed chair and squinted into a bright light. The front of his thinning, hay-colored hair jiggled slightly as his skinny legs bounced beneath the gray metal table to which he was handcuffed. His glasses fogged up from his hot breath each time he exhaled. He turned in the officers' direction as they entered.

"Oh, finally! I've been in here for hours. I need to get home to my daughters."

Tanner smacked the table. "Hey! We're the ones asking the questions here."

"He didn't ask any—" Reyes cut herself off, sighing at her partner. She sat across from the suspect and clicked off the bright light. Alan blinked heavily. "Mr. Alan Benning," Reyes said. "This morning, your employer, Barron Fisk, was discovered in his office with a single fatal gunshot wound to the head."

Alan's eyes darted back and forth between the detectives. Then he broke into a wry smile. "Is this a prank? Did the guys from the office put you up to this? I know they like to tease me, but this is a bit—"

Reyes jumped in. "I would strongly urge you to take this matter seriously, Mr. Benning. This is a murder investigation."

Alan's smile evaporated. "Then why am I here? Do I need to call a lawyer?"

"You haven't called a lawyer yet?" Tanner asked with high eyebrows. Then, catching himself, "I mean, it's time to fess up, you sack of trash."

"Well, I didn't know. I've never been in trouble with the law before. I didn't think . . . This is all a big mix-up somehow. I shouldn't need a lawyer. I shouldn't even be here."

"When exactly did you start working for Mr. Fisk?" Reyes asked.

"I, um, 2022. He brought me on as CFO six years ago."

"You became chief financial officer of Fisk Enterprises six years ago."

"That's right. It was quite the promotion for me, to be honest. Sometimes I think Fisk only suggested me to the board because he thought I'd be a pushover." Alan laughed uneasily as Reyes and Tanner shared a quick glance with one another. Reyes moved on.

"We understand that you and Mr. Fisk have been at odds over a potential business deal, is that right? It became a fairly well-known public feud."

"I wouldn't call it a *feud*. He wants to purchase a virtual reality startup called VigRig. He needs their tech to finish his big project. The Fiskiverse, he calls it. It's meant to be an entirely virtual world for online meetings and games, things like that. But I don't think the acquisition is financially prudent. That's all."

"He made disparaging remarks about you to the press over this disagreement."

Alan nodded slowly. "Mr. Fisk can be, um, a bit brutish if he doesn't get his way. But those quotes were in trade magazines. Nobody even reads those."

"He called you, and I quote, 'a lily-livered coward with a baboon's ass for a brain.'"

"Deep down, he respects me."

"Doesn't sound like respect to me. Tanner, how would you feel if your boss said that about you?"

"I'd feel mad."

"How mad, Tanner?"

"Probably mad enough to kill somebody."

"Interesting."

"Wait a minute," Alan said. "You don't really think that *I* did this. I can't even kill spiders. My wife has to do it."

Reyes faced him squarely. "Mr. Benning, we have good reason to believe that you are responsible for the death of Barron Fisk."

"But that's crazy!" Alan sat in silence for a long moment, searching the officer's face for any hint of levity. He found none. "He's not actually dead, is he?" he asked quietly.

"You tell us."

Reyes pulled a series of photos of the crime scene from a manila folder and fanned them out on the table. Alan took them in.

"Oh, God. Oh, Mr. Fisk, no."

He put his head on the table as his body heaved with quiet sobs. Tanner and Reyes looked to each other in uncertainty at the seemingly genuine show of emotion. Tanner then shook his head.

"The gun we found at the scene is registered to you, Mr. Benning," he said.

Alan's head shot back up from the table, his eyes still rimmed with tears. "What? I don't own a gun."

"According to the state of California, yes, you do."

"It was absolutely covered in your fingerprints," said Reyes.

"That's impossible!"

"Additionally, security footage from the Fisk Enterprises lobby shows you as the final person leaving the building last night."

"Well, that part might be true. We had a meeting scheduled for Monday about the VigRig acquisition. I had to prep the numbers."

"And there was a distinct footprint left in the victim's blood. The tread matches a shoe that our team found in your bedroom closet, Mr. Benning."

Reyes pulled a large plastic evidence bag from a nearby cabinet. Inside rested the pair of dress shoes that Alan had worn to work the day before.

"Are these your shoes? Yes or no?"

"I . . . I . . ."

"Sir, are these your shoes?"

"I think I'd like to call a lawyer."

Chapter Five

I KNOW WHAT YOU'RE thinking, dear reader. Your humble little poor person brain, shrunken and shriveled by years of exposure to what your kind call entertainment, has been rendered as predictable as a subplot on one of your lowbrow TV situation comedies.

You are undoubtedly wondering how your humble narrator came to be in possession of the information relayed to you so far in this story. How could one individual know what happened in the privacy of the Benning household, behind the locked door of a police interrogation room, and at a closed-off murder scene, not to mention all the locales yet to come? Who is the mysterious figure so skillfully weaving this tale of intrigue and interjecting just the right amount of their undeniably correct opinions? Well, rest your weary little head, dear reader, and trust that all answers will come in due time.

The truth is that my identity does not matter. I am sharing this story with you in order to honor the memory of the great Barron Fisk. I knew him well. He had the best yacht of anyone I've ever met and, when you get down to it, is there any greater compliment than that?

I have been waiting a long time to reveal the truth behind Fisk's death. Strap in.

Chapter Six

Alan Benning's annual salary topped out at a humiliatingly low six-digit figure. Even so, he proved capable of posting the bail set by the court, since he was not deemed a flight risk. He even managed to hire a modest team of three defense attorneys. Any self-respecting wealthy person would have at least eight, but that wasn't Alan, who numbered amongst the squalid hoi polloi forced to make do with less. Two days after his initial arrest, he sat at his dining room table and listened to his lawyers' official summary of the situation.

"You're up shit creek."

"Walter," said the second lawyer. "We talked about this. Professionalism."

"I'm trying to give it to the man straight. You don't mind, do you, Alan?"

Alan did his best not to cry.

The third lawyer returned from the kitchen, pressing the end button on his ePhone. "Arraignment's been pushed up to tomorrow," he said. "They're fast-tracking the case thanks to all the media coverage. Apparently even the governor is getting involved. Too much of a headache in an election year. Wants us in court within a month."

"There you have it," the second lawyer said. "We've got a month to hammer out the best deal we can. In my professional opinion, though," he took off his glasses and fixed Alan with a lightly sympathetic stare, "you should take whatever they offer you. A clear-cut case like this, plus all the media scrutiny? They're going to throw the book at you."

The first lawyer said, "You'll be lucky if you're out of the clink before your pubes are gray."

"Walter! What did I just say about professionalism? Pubes? Honestly."

"That's not unprofessional. My doctor uses the word pubes."

"Why is your doctor talking about your pubes?"

"I had . . . I caught . . . Well, that's not important right now."

"Jesus Christ."

The third lawyer chimed in. "Gentlemen, if we could please redirect to the task at hand."

"Hold on, hold on," said the second. "He's said it more times than I have. How am I the unprofessional one?"

"No, I haven't. And I never would have said it at all if you hadn't said it."

"Said what?"

"Pubes!"

"There. Now you've said it more times than I have."

"I'm going to slap you."

"I didn't kill anybody!" Alan shouted. "Can we please focus on that?"

The second lawyer said, "Look, Mr. Benning, you can whine at us until you're blue in the face. But no jury is going to be able to see past what the cops have on you. So unless you can find the security footage from the hallway that you swear would exonerate you . . ."

"It would! I never even went to Fisk's office that night!"

". . . then I'm afraid we can only work with what we've got."

Alan watched with a dour expression as the lawyers packed up and left his home.

Later that evening, he shuffled into his living room to find Hannah and the twins seated on the carpeted floor, rolling a ball back and forth. The girls giggled any time the ball came their way and then pushed it back toward their mother, delighting in the effect their chubby arms had on the small red orb. Tears welled up in Alan's eyes.

"Oh, hell's bells," Alan muttered to himself. He wiped at his eyes forcefully. "Hey!" he then called to his family with false cheer. "Who wants to go get some ice cream?"

"What about the reporters and the photographers out there?" Hannah asked. "Won't they swarm us?"

"If anybody wants to bother us, I'll . . . I'll punch them right in the nose."

She fixed him with a withering look. "You?"

"Yeah, me. I'll sock it to 'em," he said.

Hannah laughed. "Come on, girls. Let's get you ready for bed."

Left alone in the living room, Alan remained still for a long time. He spotted something on the far wall that made his eyes narrow.

He slowly removed his right shoe. Then he strode across the room and, using significantly more strength than was strictly necessary, squished a spider.

Chapter Seven

The following morning, Alan's doorbell rang precisely at eight o'clock. He ignored it.

When it rang the second time, he set down the pen in his hand, pausing his work on a five-star difficulty sudoku in his paperback book of number puzzles. He grunted in irritation and glared at the blank wall across the table from him.

On the third ring, he jolted up from his chair and charged toward the front of the house.

When he flung open the newly repaired front door, his look of anger rapidly melted into one of genuine surprise. Instead of an overly bold member of the vulture-like media mob that had set up camp on his front lawn, he found himself looking at a familiar face from Fisk Enterprises.

Sharla Johnson waited on his porch, shifting her weight and glancing from side to side. Her hair, pulled back in flawless tight braids as always, hung down over a finely pressed burgundy blazer and the usual cream-colored button-down shirt Alan had always seen her wear at the office. She stood with perfect posture. Even now, off the clock for good as Barron Fisk's primary personal assistant, she was impeccably put together.

Alan waved her inside and shut the door behind her.

"Sharla? What are you doing here?"

"I was hoping that I could speak with you. Is this a bad time?"

"I . . . Well, no. I guess not. Would you like some coffee?"

"No, thank you. I don't partake in neurostimulants."

Hannah yelled from upstairs, "Alan, who was at the door?"

"It's fine, honey," Alan called back. "It's a coworker."

"But you don't have a job anymore."

Alan sighed.

"*Ex*-coworker, then. Just stay with the girls, it's okay!"

When Alan returned his attention to Sharla, she had already pulled a small Fisk tablet from the inner pocket of her blazer and conjured up a news feed.

"The papers," she said, scrolling through headlines with worry in her big eyes. "These stories. They're saying—"

"I know what they're all saying. It's not true. I never even visited Fisk's office that night. It wasn't me."

"That's what I thought. You couldn't have killed anyone. I once saw you refuse to cut a birthday cake in the break room because you thought the knife was too scary."

"I wasn't scared."

"Alan."

"Fine. But it was an unnecessarily large knife."

"Do they really have evidence against you?"

"They claim to, yes. Fingerprints, a gun registered in my name, a footprint at the crime scene. Probably more as well, my lawyers tell me."

"So someone is trying to set you up."

"That's what I've been saying! But the police don't take kindly to anyone questioning their evidence. Especially not the accused."

"Well, that's part of why I came over. Can we sit?"

Alan led her to the dining room table. Sharla cast a quick glance at his open puzzle book as they both took a seat.

"Seven goes there," she said, pointing at the half-finished sudoku. Alan grabbed the pen and filled in the square.

"Now," Sharla laced her hands together on the tabletop. "I think I have a lead."

"A lead?"

"You know, like a possible hint for you to look into. About who actually killed Mr. Fisk."

"Sharla. I'm not some grizzled private eye. I'll just give the info to my lawyers."

"No!" She somehow sat up even straighter in her chair. "You can't."

"Why not?"

"When Mr. Fisk brought me on as his assistant eight years ago, I signed a significant amount of paperwork, including several non-disclosure agreements. If it gets out that I shared details about his personal itinerary, his legal team will swoop down on me like hawks."

"Okay. So what are you proposing?"

"If I give you this information, do you promise to look into it yourself? No lawyers?"

"I don't think that's such a good idea."

"What if I help you?"

Alan paused. He scrutinized her face.

"I'll help you look into it," she continued with a hint of eagerness in her voice. "Investigate, I mean."

"Why would you do that?" Alan asked slowly. "We hardly know each other."

"Why? Because I want to know what happened to Mr. Fisk."

Alan's face fell into a disappointed frown.

"What's that look?" Sharla demanded.

"You expect me to buy that?"

"Buy what? I do want to know what happened."

"So do I, believe me. But that's a flimsy reason for you to run afoul of the law. You're talking about interfering in an active police investigation."

"I'm talking about finding the truth," she said firmly.

"Is it possible," Alan hesitated, "that there's something else going on here?"

Her expression sharpened a bit. "What are you implying?"

"Well, I've seen you at the office. You're all work, all the time. Do you have any other mode besides 'go, go, go'?"

"Of course I do. What is this? One minute you're saying that we hardly know each other and the next you're psychologically dissecting my entire life?"

"Let me guess," Alan set his hands flat on the table and fixed Sharla directly in his sight. "You've spent the last few days since Fisk died cleaning your apartment from top to bottom and re-organizing your tax receipts and dipping your toe into a few new hobbies that each held your attention for a couple of hours, and now you're bored. But you can't get a new job until all this Fisk business is settled, so you decided that I would be your new pet project. Is that right?"

"I . . . I wouldn't put it like that, no. In fact, I already have the beginnings of my new career underway. I have since before all this."

Alan crossed to the dining room door.

"Look, Sharla, you're kind for stopping by. I appreciate your concern, I do. But this is my life we're talking about. I can't go toying around with it because you're a workaholic who can't sit still."

"That's not what this is about."

"That's how it looks to me."

"Well, you're wrong."

"Then tell me why you're really here."

"I already told you!"

"I don't think you have!"

"Because I loved him, okay?"

Alan's lips parted, but he made no sound. The admission hung in the air between them as the silence grew long.

"Are you guys shouting down there?" Hannah's voice echoed from up the stairs. "I'm trying to meditate!"

"Sorry, honey! We'll keep it down!"

Alan returned to the table.

"You and Fisk?" he whispered, scandalized.

"Oh, it's not like that." Sharla waved a hand in dismissal. "It wasn't anything physical. He was my friend. Maybe my only one, I'm now realizing." She sighed. "I'm not from around here, you know. I grew up back east. I came here specifically to work for Mr. Fisk, and he kept me so busy I guess I . . . I kind of forgot to make friends.

"Maybe it's silly, but I've worked for him most of my adult life. And he treated me well. Holidays, birthdays, big milestones. We spent them all together."

Her eyes softened. Her gaze shifted upward and to one side as she chuckled to herself.

"We used to do this thing when we were stuck working long hours. Kind of a game. We'd pick a famous band and try to have a full conversation using only lyrics from that band's songs. Silly, but it's fun. It started by accident this one time when I absentmindedly quoted The Beatles. It was near dawn. We'd been up all night finalizing a deal to acquire this Swedish company that made drones with articulating arms. You know, that could pick things up and put them back down and whatnot. I looked out the window in his office and said, *'Here comes the sun.'* He didn't miss a beat. He said, *'It's been a hard day's night,'* and I said, *'Eight days a week.'* We laughed. Then we started doing it with other bands here and there, just for fun. It kind of became our thing."

She paused for a moment, lost in the memory.

"I'm sad that he's gone. Deep down, he wasn't a bad man. At least not the Barron Fisk that I knew. He didn't deserve this." Her eyeline dropped to the floor.

"I guess I'd just like to know who did this horrible thing to my friend. I have to know. It's keeping me up at night."

Alan scratched his head.

"Huh. Well, I still don't think the police would be too happy about us digging around their case."

It was Sharla's turn to get up from her chair. She paced the room.

"Forget the police. They're not even doing their job. They're perfectly happy with you as their patsy. As long as they have a fall guy to put in the headlines, they don't care. Come on, Alan. Be brave for once."

"I am brave. I kill spiders now."

"Don't you want to know the truth?"

"Of course I do. Given the circumstances, the truth will quite literally set me free."

"Then listen to this." She stopped pacing and leaned toward him over the table. "The night he died, Mr. Fisk had a late-night meeting. Okay? That's not too strange; he used to do that all the time. But this one was with somebody who definitely had something against him: Aristotle Cunningham."

Alan's eyebrows arched. He said, "You're suggesting that the world's richest tech mogul was murdered by . . . the world's second richest tech mogul?"

"Everyone knows how they felt about each other. They used to take swipes back and forth in the media constantly. 'Battle of the Tech Titans' the press called it. I mean, think about it: Cunningham just happens to visit Mr. Fisk on the night of his murder? Seems too coincidental."

"So you think Cunningham snuck into Fisk headquarters, shot Fisk in the head, and then erased the hallway security footage to cover his escape?"

"And he framed you because he knew that Fisk had been insulting you publicly. It would look like payback."

"Huh. I guess it's possible. He certainly would have the tech and the know-how to wipe the tape."

"We have to go visit him. See if we can get him to admit anything incriminating."

"Maybe."

"Not maybe. I have his address right here. We can go today."

"I . . . I'm not one for breaking the rules."

"What about your daughters?" Sharla's voice dropped a register. "Think about them growing up with their precious daddy locked away in prison."

"Oh, that's low, Sharla."

"That's not low; that's realistic. That's what you're facing. If you and I don't find out who did this, you're going to miss their entire childhood. The first bike rides, the school dances, the soccer games, the graduation ceremonies. Are you ready to kiss all of that goodbye?"

Alan bit his lower lip.

"What do you say?" Sharla asked, staring him down.

Alan exhaled forcefully.

"All right. Let's go."

Sharla let out a tiny squeal of excitement and threw her arms around him. He groaned in response.

"Let's get moving," she said.

"We're going now?"

"Yeah. The drive will take a while. He's a billionaire. He doesn't live in town."

"Um. Okay."

Alan slouched toward the foot of the stairs and called up.

"Honey, I'm . . . I'm going out."

Hannah appeared at the top of the flight.

"What? I thought you said we couldn't leave. What about the press people outside?"

"Sharla and I are going to sneak out the back."

"Who is Sharla?"

"This is Sharla." Alan gestured to Sharla at his side.

"Hi," said Sharla.

"Fine. But if you get to sneak out today, I get to sneak out tomorrow to meet the girls for tennis."

"You can't go to the club, honey." Hannah had already disappeared. Alan rubbed at his forehead. "That is not going to be fun to deal with tomorrow."

"Oh, cheer up, Alan," Sharla responded with a smile. "We're off to solve a murder!"

Chapter Eight

Alan and Sharla crept across the Bennings' backyard and squeezed through a gap between the fencing and the hedges in order to avoid detection by the media. Once outside, they faced each other on the sidewalk.

"Good," Alan said. "Where's your car?"

"My car?" Sharla shot back. "My car is a bucket. What about yours?"

"Mine is in the garage. You know, the one surrounded by paparazzi."

"Ugh. All right. I'm past the corner here. You'll have to give me a minute to move some things around."

When they turned the corner and Sharla approached a brown, run-down Volvo from sometime around the year 2000, Alan stopped short.

"This is your car?"

"Yes, Alan. We don't all make executive salaries."

Alan approached the car with trepidation and peered inside. The passenger seat and back bench looked a mess: leftover food wrappers, discarded scraps of paper, a few empty plastic drink bottles, a shockingly large pile of wrinkled clothing, at least two crumpled-up parking tickets, and, oddly enough, a tangled mass of Christmas lights. Long-forgotten fast-food cups occupied all available cup holders. Honestly, the type of squalor that you poor people put up with astounds me. Hire a car maid! It can't be more than $50,000 a year. Chump change. I could find that in my sofa.

"Are you sure this is your car?" Alan asked again.

"All right, I don't need this," Sharla said as she slammed shut the driver-side door.

"I'm sorry! I don't mean . . . I just . . . At work, you're always so put together. I would not have pictured your car to be, uh, like this."

"Yeah, well, most people aren't their jobs. Most people exist outside of that environment, and sometimes they have messy lives. That's something Mr. Fisk never understood, either."

"Okay. I'm sorry."

"You wanna get off your high horse and into the car?"

"Yes, please."

"Good. Just toss all those used tissues into the back."

Alan made a disgusted face as he cleared room for himself.

The drive to Aristotle Cunningham's mansion outside of Santa Clarita made it painfully obvious to both Alan and Sharla how little they knew about one another. A large portion of the trip passed in uncomfortable silence.

"I couldn't help but notice the bumper stickers on the back of your car there," Alan said tentatively. "You and Mr. Fisk must have had pretty different political opinions."

Sharla chuckled.

"We would get into it sometimes, for sure. But we kept busy with day-to-day matters."

"And lyrics-based conversational games."

"Yeah, and that too. I think it was good that we disagreed on certain things. It made our friendship stronger. I'm of the opinion that if you can't get along with anyone different from yourself, the bad people of the world will win by default."

"What do you mean?"

"Well, the idea of 'divide and conquer' has been a known war strategy since Sun Tzu, but we have trouble noticing when it's applied socially. The rich and powerful want everybody else fighting amongst themselves. Hell, that's basically where the whole concept of racism came from."

Alan guffawed involuntarily.

"You're joking."

"Not at all," Sharla replied seriously. "The idea of inherent racial differences is a very modern one. Thought up mostly by Europeans who wanted to rationalize colonialism and an international slave trade. It all started with privileged people who felt the need to justify their subjugation of others."

"Oh, come on."

"What? You disagree?"

"I think that may be oversimplifying things. The world's a complex place."

"It is oversimplifying, yeah. But it's also hard to grow up Black in America and not see the truth behind it. There's a reason redlining happened. There's a reason the generational wealth gap still exists. There's a reason news networks portray white people as victims and everybody else as threats. And it works. Give poor white people someone to look down their noses at just because of skin color, and those poor white people become much more amenable to an economic situation in which the people at the top reap all the benefits. It's easier to feel good about a silver medal when you know there's a bronze."

"Huh," Alan said. "Mr. Fisk was the wealthiest man in the world. Wouldn't that make him a huge part of the problem?"

"Sometimes I thought he was. Sometimes not. It's hard to judge when you know someone so personally."

"But if you feel the way you said, how do you justify working for a mega-billionaire all those years?"

"Well, because racism and capitalism aren't totally one and the same. And just because the system is broken doesn't mean I can't get mine."

"It kind of sounds like you're picking and choosing your moments to be outraged."

"It kind of sounds to me like you've never had to think very hard about these things. And it's certainly not my job to explain them to you. But if we can't even have the conversation, then where does that leave us? Hopelessly divided like the bad people want."

"Well, you're definitely right on that one."

"Disagreeing with someone politically is a poor reason to not be their friend. So, Mr. Fisk and I were friends."

Alan said, "So, tell me, what's the weirdest thing that nobody knows about him?"

"He's scared of those little brown chunks that come in Chex Mix."

"What? Those flat chip thingies?"

"Yeah. Terrified of them. No idea why. Any time there was Chex Mix in the boardroom, I had to go through and pick all those out before he'd even come into the meeting."

Alan laughed. "That's so strange. Got to be from some kind of childhood trauma, right?"

"I wouldn't be surprised. Mr. Fisk's parents were intense people, from what I heard. He told me a story once about his seventh birthday party that made my blood run cold."

"Oh? Do tell."

"All right. Guess it can't hurt." Sharla adjusted her grip on the steering wheel. "So, little Barron was about to turn seven years old. His parents had this big party planned. And I guess the family butler didn't notice that the storage freezer had broken down. So, they go out there a few hours before the party, and all the ice cream they got for the kids had melted. All over the bottom of this giant freezer. Barron's father got so mad. He fired the butler on the spot. 'How dare you ruin my son's birthday!' That kind of thing. But Barron was seven years old, and this butler had been around the house since before he was born. He probably saw this guy more than his own parents. So, little Barron went to his father to beg and plead that he let the butler stay. Nobody would care about the ice cream, he said. Just forgive the guy, you know? Barron did everything he could. He got down on his knees, and he cried. And in response, his father gave him this long lecture.

"To Barron's dad, there was one golden rule in all the world: people are only worth what they're worth. If you don't have money, you might as well be a bug. He told Barron that poor people were poor because they deserved to be. They were weak. They had failed. It was wealthy people—like the Fisks—who carried society on their shoulders. They provided motivation to all those poor people of the world to strive for more. Without rich people flaunting their wealth and spurring the dirty masses toward working harder, society would backslide into the Dark Ages."

"Woah."

"Right? He was telling all this to a seven-year-old boy. But this is what he truly believed. In his mind, rich people were literally saving the world by being rich, and any kindness, any charity shown to the huddled masses undermined their motivation to become rich themselves and thus posed a serious threat to the very fabric of society.

"So, little Barron's intervention on behalf of the butler was unacceptable in his father's eyes. As a punishment, and to drive home this valuable life lesson, he took his son back out to that busted storage freezer. He made Barron get down on all fours and eat all the melted ice cream from the dirty bottom of the freezer. Tubs and tubs worth of the stuff. It took him hours. He missed his own party, crouched there in the backhouse kitchen, scooping spoonful after spoonful from the corners of the freezer floor. He ate so much that it made him violently ill.

"That night, as Barron was heaving up the contents of his stomach, his father came to him and looked him right in the eyes. 'I want you to remember this feeling,' his father said to him. 'This is what weakness feels like. This is what it is to be poor.' And then he left."

"Hell's bells," Alan said breathlessly.

"Yeah," Sharla agreed. "Kind of helps you understand why Barron was the way he was, huh?"

"What about your parents? What are they like?" Alan asked.

Sharla responded by staring out the window in silence.

"Okay, hint taken," Alan said at last. "You don't like to talk about yourself."

"I don't mean to be rude. It's just . . . I'm going through some trust issues right now. I recently thought that I could trust somebody. I let myself trust him. And now I'm worried that might have been a big mistake. I'm feeling a little guarded, is all."

"I get it. I don't mean to push," Alan said. "Hey, why don't I tell you about the time Mr. Fisk made one of the executives cry during a strategy meeting? It's a funny story."

"Was the executive you?"

Alan took a beat before responding.

"Never mind."

Sharla laughed.

As the pair drove on toward Aristotle Cunningham's country estate, they continued reminiscing about their deceased employer. They swapped tales and traded personal memories. They debated, philosophized, and argued.

In this narrator's humble opinion, the two fledgling investigators spent the car ride blowing a whole lot of hot air back and forth about nothing at all. Why? Because neither could bring themselves to accept the undeniable, if perhaps uncomfortable, truth: that Barron Fisk's father was right.

Chapter Nine

Aristotle Cunningham's mansion sat on a high hilltop towering over the spacious green fields at the hill's base. Visible from miles away, the house provided Alan and Sharla with plenty of opportunity to admire it as they approached. The bottom story, all glass, allowed a peek at the decadent interior furnishings, sweeping staircase, and gigantic modern kitchen that occupied the first floor. The glass gave way on the upper floors to a smooth-looking cream-colored stone that swept backward like a wave breaking away from the long driveway. It all came together to give the house the overall appearance of a huge boulder, rubbed smooth by flowing water, placed atop a rectangular glass pedestal.

As Alan and Sharla pulled up to the regally adorned gate that marked the entrance to Cunningham's grounds, a camera mounted on one of the posts swiveled to take in the car and its passengers. The gate did not open.

They both climbed out to press a button on the intercom that hung to the left of the gate. After a short pause, a voice rang out from the speaker, as crystal clear as if the man was standing right in front of them.

"State your business."

"Oh. Uh . . ." stuttered Alan. "We're here to see Mr. Cunningham."

"Mr. Cunningham does not have any appointments scheduled for this time."

"Right. We were kind of hoping to see him without an appointment."

"This is not a Supercuts. You cannot just walk in."

"Oh."

"You will need to make an appointment and return at that time. Please be careful while backing out of the gate area not to run over Mr. Cunningham's moonflowers."

"Moonflowers?"

"Yes. The flowers lining the drive were all grown on the moon."

Alan looked closer at the flowers at the side of the paved circle that demarcated the gate area and saw that they sagged, bent and unlively. The heads of many of them leaned nearly all the way to the ground.

Alan said, "They look a little . . . droopy."

"Well, if your formative years took place in gravity one-sixth the strength of Earth's, you would, too."

"Then what's the point of growing them on the . . ."

"Please do not question the moonflowers." The attendant's tone strongly implied he'd had this conversation before. "Just don't run them over. The moon is far away, so, they're difficult to replace. Now please vacate the premises before I'm forced to call security."

Sharla stepped in front of Alan.

"Listen to me, guy. We're not going anywhere until we see Cunningham. Got it?"

"Security it is." They heard a walkie-talkie crackle on the attendant's end, then the speaker cut out.

Alan hopped from one foot to the other. "We should go."

"No, wait."

A few moments later, the attendant's voice rang out from the speaker again. "Actually, who am I speaking with here?"

"I'm Sharla Johnson, and this is Alan Benning."

"In that case, I am being instructed to let you pass. Please drive with care up to the main entrance. A valet will park your car for you."

Sharla gave Alan an *aren't you impressed?* face as they returned to the Volvo. The towering golden gate, which formed the shape of Aristotle Cunningham's initials, swung inward noiselessly.

Sharla drove forward. Alan glared at the sagging flowers lining each side of the drive.

"They don't even look nice."

"Please." Sharla scoffed. "You wish you had moonflowers."

"Yeah," Alan admitted.

Sharla eased the car to a stop in the wide area just past an immense fountain. A tall, stoic man in an immaculately pressed vest bearing the initials A.C. opened the car doors, took the keys from Sharla, and then disappeared around the side of the mansion with the Volvo.

Sharla looked up in awe at the house before her. The doors, seemingly made of thick sheets of solid gold, towered to the height of at least three tall men. The upper stories of the house jutted further forward than the ground floor, giving the upper facade a gravity-defying appearance and casting the area in front of the doors in shadow at all hours of the day. Special spotlights had been installed to make sure that the golden doors sparkled. The ground was laid with large rectangular marble tiles that looked so smooth and cool that Sharla made a move to kneel down and put her cheek against them before she thought better of it. The glass walls that abutted either side of the massive golden doors allowed a glimpse of the enormous foyer that awaited them inside. Sharla let out an impressed whistle.

"If you had this kind of money, what type of house would you build?" she asked Alan. "I think I'd go with a Roman-style villa. You know? A long, rectangular house with a luscious green courtyard in the middle for big symposia flowing with wine and poetry. So romantic."

"If I had this kind of money, I'd stay in the house I'm in and make sure the money was safely stored in a diversified series of reasonable-yield financial instruments."

"The more I get to know you, the more boring you become, Alan Benning."

"I'll take that as a compliment."

The huge golden doors of Cunningham's mansion swept open under their own power to reveal the man himself standing at the base of a sweeping twin staircase. He spread his arms in an exaggerated gesture of benevolence.

"Welcome to Cunningham Palace! Please wipe your feet on the rug as you come in. It's zebra skin!"

He strode forward, beaming at Alan. He wore a thick purple smoking jacket over a silk pajama top and billowy pants made of some kind of silverish space-age material that flashed with many colors whenever he moved. His long, sandy hair perched at the top of his head in a tight bun. Precisely trimmed, rugged-looking stubble covered his square jaw and chin. He stopped about ten feet before his guests.

"If it isn't the man who took down my rival! When I saw you pull up, I couldn't pass on the chance to shake your hand. Get over here, you hero."

Alan cringed at the insinuation that he was a killer. He hesitated.

Sharla jabbed him in the back and muttered to him from the corner of her mouth, "Go greet him."

Alan whispered back, "I've never talked to a murderer before."

"We don't know anything yet for sure. We only strongly suspect that he's a murderer."

"Gee, how comforting."

Cunningham, out of earshot, watched the two of them with an unwavering smile. Sharla poked Alan in the back again, which finally got him going. He clomped into Cunningham's entryway with heavy feet and shook the rich man's hand. He must have looked pained at doing so because Cunningham's expression twisted into a faux frown.

"Come now," said Cunningham. "Why so glum? Would it cheer you up if I promised to pay your legal fees? After all, you've done me a great favor."

"I . . . No. I didn't . . . I never . . . What I mean is . . ." Alan stumbled until Sharla came up behind him and spat it out.

"Alan didn't actually kill Mr. Fisk."

"Sure you didn't." Cunningham gave a playful wink before pivoting to Sharla. "Hi. I'm Aristotle Cunningham."

"Of course. Everyone knows who you are. I'm Sharla Johnson."

"Oh! Fisk's assistant, right? Not here to steal any trade secrets, are you?"

"No, definitely not."

"Well, that makes sense. Since Fisk is dead." Cunningham let out a bark of a laugh and clapped his thigh. "Hey, anybody want some homemade kombucha? My butler infuses it with fresh honey from my apiary, and it's made in the same barrel used for the first batch of Guinness beer back in the 1700s. I won it at an auction in the Maldives."

"No, thank you," Alan said. "We actually have a few questions for you if we could take up a bit of your time."

"Sure thing, but I'll have to ask you to follow me to the shark room. You caught me in the middle of feeding time."

"Sorry, did you say *shark* room?" Sharla asked.

"That's right."

Sharla and Alan glanced at one another.

"Like, shark sharks?" Alan asked this time. "Like the big angry fish?"

"Oh, sharks aren't angry. They are fish, though, so good on you. Many people think they're mammals, but they're not. They're special fish of the superorder Selachimorpha with bodily structures that are cartilaginous rather than ossified. They're majestic."

"And . . . you have some in your home?" Sharla sought clarity one more time.

"Of course," Cunningham replied without the slightest acknowledgement that it might be strange. "In the shark room. Where do you keep your sharks?"

"I don't . . . Uh, never mind."

Cunningham marched off with long strides. Alan and Sharla trailed behind, marveling at the sizable pieces of artwork that hung on the smooth, pristine walls of the long hallway down which Cunningham led them: Picasso, Degas, Rothko. Cunningham pointed out specific doors to his guests as they walked past.

"That door leads to the indoor pickleball court. That one is a bathroom. That's a specialized seed vault I had built to incubate the next generation of my moonflowers. Did you see my moonflowers? I'm sure you did. Brandon is required to point them out to everybody. That door is a bathroom. This one here is a room with trampoline floors; that's just for fun. Surprisingly good workout, too. That door used to be a guest room, but now it's overflow storage for pool toys and floaties. Here is another bathroom."

"You sure have a lot of bathrooms," Sharla said.

Cunningham stopped in his tracks and turned to face them. He spoke with a sudden and urgent seriousness.

"Every third door in this house is a bathroom. A man can never have too many bathrooms."

"Oh. Isn't that nice," Sharla said. Seemingly satisfied, he turned and led the way again.

"We're almost there!" he sang back to them.

He stopped in front of a set of broad wooden doors and flung them open. Inside loomed the largest aquarium tank that Alan or Sharla had ever seen. It housed between ten and twelve great white sharks that swam in large, lazy circles.

"Hell's bells," Alan whispered to himself.

Cunningham approached a wide, clear tube that ran down the front of the tank and pressed a button next to it. As soon as he did, a bookcase built into the wall to their right, apparently a secret door, swung open and a young man wearing the same crisp vest as the valet rushed in pushing a wheelbarrow full of what appeared to be chopped up sheep carcasses. He left the bloody wheelbarrow next to the tank tube and scurried out again, the wall re-sealing itself as if by magic.

Cunningham put on a pair of long rubber gloves, grabbed a large hunk of meat, and shoved it into the clear tube, which sucked it upward and dropped it into the water with a splash. The sharks swarmed as Cunningham looked on with approval.

"The big one's my favorite. I named him Shark Ruffalo."

He grabbed another sheep flank and turned toward his guests.

"Wanna give it a try?" Alan and Sharla both shied away. "Suit yourselves," Cunningham said and shoved the meat into the vacuum tube.

"I read somewhere that great whites can't survive in captivity," Alan said. "How do you keep them alive?"

"I don't," Cunningham replied. "I have to have them replaced every three weeks or so. I don't mind, though. Gives me an opportunity to come up with more punny shark names. That one there is Charles Sharkley."

"Aren't they . . . endangered?"

Cunningham chuckled. "Not if you're rich enough."

He heaved up another hunk of dead sheep.

"Actually, Mr. Cunningham," Sharla jumped in, "we're here to talk to you about the night that Mr. Fisk was murdered."

"You think I killed him, right?"

"Oh. Um."

"I don't mind. Believe me, I wish I could have. I'd be lying if I said I never had dreams about it. But I didn't kill him. Couldn't have killed him that night if I'd wanted to. Which, again, I did want to."

Another bit of sheep carcass splooshed into the tank.

"The thing is," Sharla said, "according to Mr. Fisk's schedule, you and he met around 10:00 PM that night."

"Hmm..." Cunningham said thoughtfully, keeping his eyes on the feasting sharks. "That is strange. I hadn't seen Fisk in person for about three months before his death. I certainly didn't visit him on the night he died."

"Well, I distinctly remember him asking me to add the meeting to his calendar," Sharla pressed on. "You're saying that it was canceled?"

"I'm saying that I never had one scheduled. I can't explain anything on Fisk's end."

"If you don't mind me asking, what were you doing on that night? June eighth, that is."

"I was on a ten-hour video conference with my office in Tokyo. The call lasted until about 5:00 AM. Hardly even took bathroom breaks."

"So you wouldn't mind sending us over footage of that conference call? To verify your story?"

"I can show it to you right now," he said, peeling off his large, bloody gloves. "That ought to be enough to hold them over until dinnertime. Follow me this way."

A few minutes later, after Alan and Sharla had followed Cunningham through a series of twisting white hallways to his office, they leered upward at a wall-spanning computer console whose screen soared above them. After a bit of manipulation from Cunningham, it showed video footage of him seated in a drab office at the end of a long table and silently engaged in talks with an array of squares displaying well-dressed Japanese businessmen.

"I'll have to keep it on mute in the interest of protecting company secrets." Cunningham pointed to the corner of the footage. "But do you see that timestamp there? That's direct from the telecommunications company. Not even I can alter that without scrapping the video. It's coded right in."

"And you were on this call all night?"

"I was." Cunningham double-tapped a button on the console before him, and the images on the screen leaped to super speed. They watched together as the hours ticked by in mere minutes. The figures moved in a comically rapid manner. Cunningham left the screen only a couple of times for a few minutes each. "As you can see, unless I possess some sort of magical ability to be in two places at once, which I assure you

I do not—my company is still working on that—, I wouldn't have been able to visit Barron on the night in question. I provided the police with this same footage, and they've verified its authenticity."

"Oh," Alan said in surprise. "So the police did come to see you."

"Of course," Cunningham replied. "It's a murder investigation after all, isn't it?"

Alan shot a questioning look at Sharla, who ignored it.

"I think that's all we need," she said. "We'll get out of your way. Thank you very much, Mr. Cunningham."

"Hold on, hold on," Cunningham said before they could make a move to leave. "So, you really didn't kill him?" he asked Alan.

"I swear it. We're trying to figure out who did."

"I might have some info for you. You know, I was always looking for dirt on Fisk. I have a whole team dedicated to just that. That reminds me, I need to fire them. There's one juicy tidbit that I was keeping in my pocket until the right time, but I guess that's not going to come anymore, so I might as well tell you."

"What's that?" asked Sharla, deftly whipping out her small Fisk brand tablet. Cunningham made a sour face at seeing it.

"His wife, Rebecca. She was leaving him. One affair too many, it sounds like. They were in the middle of divorce proceedings when he died. Apparently it was contentious."

Sharla looked flabbergasted.

"Are you serious? How could I not know that?"

"They kept it all hush-hush. Bad press, you know? Nobody knew. My guys found out, though. You ask me, that's where to take a look: Rebecca Fisk. After all, the timing makes sense. If the divorce had been finalized, she'd only have gotten half. They didn't have any kids, so she stands to get everything now. She's the richest person in the world."

"We'll look into it," Sharla said, scribbling notes on her tablet.

"I'm a lot of things," Cunningham told them bluntly, "but an assassin is not one of them. I'm no John Wilkes Booth. Oh! John Wilkes Tooth! Now, that's a shark name. I've got to write that down. You two can see your way out? The valet will bring your car around."

As Alan and Sharla made their way back to the mansion's front door, Sharla perused the notes that she'd taken.

"I guess we've got to believe his alibi," she said. "It seems tight, huh?"

"And he's not wrong about Mrs. Fisk. If the two were getting divorced, the timing of the murder certainly did her a favor."

"Luckily, she and I have a history. She'll talk to us."

"Good," Alan said. After a moment's reflection, he added, "You know, I never thought I'd say these words in this particular order, but here goes: Those poor sharks."

Chapter Ten

The following day, as the sun peeked over the horizon, a woman named Belinda Jones waded through the knee-deep water of a cold, slow-moving creek in the lushly wooded wilderness about fifteen miles northwest of Cupertino. She paused to tuck her long blonde hair up beneath a faded blue baseball cap.

She wore a backpack full of supplies that bounced lightly with each waterlogged step she took. The stream chilled her toes and ankles through the tough exterior of her hiking boots. She took a moment to regroup on the far side of the small river. Her destination still lay about twelve miles ahead. She knew what awaited her: unbeaten uphill pathways, bushes full of brambles and thorns ready to tear and scrape at her, and at least two additional stream crossings. But she was determined to get where she was headed. She would push her forty-two-year-old body to the limit if necessary. She had no choice. She had to make it.

Hours later, coated in a thick film of sweat and with shaking legs, Belinda crested a tall grassy peak to look down on what she'd been seeking: Barron Fisk's funeral site.

A solid ivory casket rested atop a large pedestal. Behind it towered an elaborate, two-story trellis in the shape of an infinity sign that was covered in every color of rose known to humanity. Two holographic images of Barron Fisk himself were projected on either side of the coffin, showing him looking saddened and humbled with his hands held together in a prayer gesture. The holograms bowed in sync with each other every few minutes. A large number of regal-looking peacocks strutted across the grassy expanse.

Autonomous wheeled robotic tables laden with bubbling champagne flutes made slow laps around the space, allowing guests to grab as many or as few as they pleased. Several sculptures of Fisk's likeness were spread around as well: a full-body replica of Michelangelo's David featuring Barron's face; a ten foot tall bust of the man in exquisite detail made from a giant mound of sand that miraculously held its shape in the occasionally whipping winds; a recreation of Barron as the Roman god Mercury crafted from creamy French butter that had been commissioned and donated for the event by a noted celebrity chef in the hopes of receiving an invitation (she didn't).

All of this decadence perched at the edge of a cliff overlooking the endless Pacific Ocean, which churned nonstop with white-capped waves as if the water itself also mourned. It was the funeral of an Egyptian pharaoh with access to modern technology. It was the funeral to end all funerals. Belinda felt a tear come to her eye as she took it all in.

The site was accessible only by helicopter, a detail Fisk had insisted upon to keep out the commoner riff-raff. A contractor had erected a temporary helipad to accommodate the inpour of rich and notable figures, all dressed to the nines. Political figures from across the globe, A-list Hollywood celebrities, key players in the cutting edge tech world, superstar athletes from every major sport, shadowy executives from the financial and pharmaceutical industries who, as a habit, only showed their faces in public to send their fellow billionaires off into the afterlife—all were in attendance. Also present were several personal acquaintances and loved ones of Fisk's, mingling somewhat timidly with the notables all around them.

I count myself duly impressed, dear reader, by the gall of one funeral attendee in particular. You see, and I do hope that I am not giving too much away by sharing this with you at this particular juncture of our story, Barron Fisk's murderer was present that day.

On a gold-plated throne to the right of the casket sat Fisk's wife, Rebecca. Belinda, high above the scene, bristled at the sight of her. Rebecca's flowing black gown boasted a thirty-foot train that whipped in the wind behind her opulent chair. A dark veil hid her face from the grieving visitors who stepped up one by one in a long, snaking line to offer their deepest condolences in deeply unconvincing tones. She held out a single silk-gloved hand to each of them, permitting a quick kiss on the dainty fingers of the newly anointed richest person in the world.

At her side, the stoic figure of Dr. Lucian Wu, Fisk's longtime personal physician and closest friend, acknowledged each well-wisher with a silent and solemn nod of his head. For the final fifteen years of Fisk's life, Wu had been the only person Fisk entrusted with his medical information. The two built a strong friendship behind a veil of secrecy meant to hide from the world the advanced medical procedures and highly experimental treatments to which Fisk had been subjected. To everyone but Fisk, Wu was a true man of mystery.

Crisp, black suits dominated one particular section of the line of wellwishers. The Fisk Enterprises executive team flocked together as usual. Amongst them stood out a tall, dashing thirty-something with bright blond hair and a square jaw—James Bradford. When his turn arose, he planted a firm kiss on Mrs. Fisk's hand and gave an exaggerated bow with a twinkle in his eye.

A few spots behind Bradford came Sharla, one of the few people of color present and someone whose invitation very well might have been overlooked entirely if Fisk's will had not specified in clear language that she should be in attendance. She did her best to quickly convey her sympathy and move on.

The lone person in line not offered a hand from the widow was Aristotle Cunningham. He received only a dismissive wave from Rebecca, which he returned with a genuine-looking smile and moved away.

A string of mobile telepresence robots on thick wheels followed soon after Cunningham, each displaying the video-conferenced-in face of a member of the Fisk Enterprises Board of Directors. They had collectively decided that cutting short their summer vacations in order to bid Fisk farewell in person was not worth the hassle. A few of them still wore island attire with drinks in hand as they greeted Mrs. Fisk.

The final robot's screen bore the stern face of a man with salt-and-pepper hair and dressed in a pale blue jumpsuit: Leonid Ledbedev, Fisk's former business partner. Ledbedev had co-founded the company that eventually grew into Fisk Enterprises. His heavily browed face glared from the screen of the mobile telepresence robot as he spoke not a word to the veiled Mrs. Fisk, instead staring daggers at her for a few moments before steering the stick-like robot away and assuming his spot at the back of the general seating area with the other teleconference bots.

When the line wound down and the seats filled up, the farewell ceremony for the trailblazing tech pioneer began. Men who had worked closely with Fisk gave several mildly emotional speeches, each containing at least a few speculative comments on how best to alter investment portfolios in reaction to the market's dip after Fisk's passing, a fact which Fisk would have found incredibly flattering. A series of mournful farewell songs were performed in his honor by a pop star whose concert tickets sold for more than most used cars. A world-famous cellist, lured into his first public appearance since retiring fifteen years earlier, played a rendition of Barber's *Adagio for Strings*. The NFL quarterback who'd won more Super Bowls than any other wrote his and Barron's names on a football with a Sharpie and threw it into the ocean in a symbolic recognition of mutual greatness.

The ceremony closed with Mrs. Fisk descending from her throne to lay a hand on the top of the casket in farewell, an action timed up perfectly with the start of a blazing lighted drone show that illuminated the darkening sky and culminated with a crude image of Fisk's face hovering above the assembly of over-accomplished attendees. Rebecca then thanked them all for coming.

Throughout the service, Belinda watched from afar in disgust as the funeral-goers seemed more interested in networking than in honoring the fallen genius that had brought them all together. She glowered at the conduct of the golden-haired James Bradford in particular, though his behavior was far from unique. She saw him switching seats to elbow up to various other besuited attendees, often laughing openly and flashing his sparkling smile at anyone and everyone. He spent large portions of the delivered eulogies moving from robot to robot parked at the back to get valuable face time with the members of the Fisk Enterprises Board of Directors, clearly gunning for the newly vacated position of CEO.

Hunched on the cliffside above the funeral scene like an angry gargoyle, Belinda seethed. She clenched her fists. Barron Fisk, she felt, was not being properly mourned. She gathered up her hiking gear and struck out on the return trip with fire behind her eyes. She had work to do.

Chapter Eleven

Fisk Estates occupied some 130 acres of pristine rolling hills in a nature preserve to the west of Cupertino. Fisk had found it necessary to grease a lot of palms to get permission to build his estate there, but the final result proved stunning. A long, flat driveway, straight as an arrow and flanked by robust bushes carved into the shapes of various exotic animals, led up to the main house, which was smaller than Cunningham's and far less ornate but showcased the distinctive knack Fisk possessed for mixing modern and classical styles. The man truly was a genius. The east-facing front of the house belied the estate's pastoral setting with a wide porch featuring long rows of rocking chairs and benches for sipping hot beverages while the sun rose. Beyond these were large wooden doors that opened to the extremely modern interior. Various guesthouses, pools, and gardens dotted the land around the main house.

Alan and Sharla took it all in through the windows of her rusty brown Volvo.

They gained access to the compound simply by pressing in the gate code. It apparently had not been changed since before Fisk's death, when Sharla came and went as required for her duties. She and Alan drove straight up to the foot of the front porch stairs and climbed out.

After ringing the doorbell, activated by pulling downward on a thick, tasseled cord that hung next to the large wooden doors, and receiving no response, Sharla used the digital house keys on her ePhone to let them both in. They stopped a few feet past the doors.

"Hello?" Sharla called out. It echoed through the expansive entryway.

Alan stared in amazement at his surroundings. The walls, covered in millions of tiny LED lights that lit up in waves, appeared to undulate like a flag on a windy day. A two-story, dark, block-like light fixture hung above their heads. Round holes down the sides allowed light to billow out in concentrated beams. The floor was made of some kind of stone, so dark purple that it was nearly black. The sheer size of the place left Alan reeling.

"Mrs. Fisk is probably in the east wing," said Sharla. "That's where her bedroom is. And her favorite pool."

"How many pools are there?"

"Not sure. I've never seen them all. Come on."

As they crossed the foyer, someone else emerged from one of the many open hallways that dotted the long, color-changing walls. He wore a lab coat with scrubs underneath and carried a long syringe loaded with some kind of reddish-brown liquid.

"Dr. Wu!" Sharla flagged him down. He turned with a look of surprise.

"Sharla. I didn't expect to see you here today," he said, dropping the syringe to his side and moving it slightly behind his back.

"Where is everyone?"

"Ah. Well. Since Barron's death, we've rather scaled back on the number of staff. What brings you by the estate?"

"We're looking for Mrs. Fisk."

"She's at the pool in the east wing. I'm heading in that direction, so I guess . . . I suppose we could walk together. Who is your friend?"

"This is Alan Benning."

Dr. Wu's face turned stony and cold.

"How dare you set foot in this house? Shame on you. I must insist that you both leave. Now."

Sharla said, "Wait, Dr. Wu. You don't understand. Alan is innocent. I've known him for years, and he's harmless. He couldn't have done this."

"That's not what the police are saying."

"I'm well aware. That's why we're here. Mrs. Fisk may have information that can help us find the real killer."

"The real killer is standing here before you! I never counted you as the gullible type, Sharla."

"I'm asking you to trust me, Dr. Wu."

Dr. Wu scowled at her, but Sharla held his gaze. Soon enough, he wilted.

"Fine. You may follow me. But let the record show that I'm against it."

He led them through a different open passageway without looking at them.

"Thank you for your understanding," Alan said to the doctor's back. He got no response other than the loud click of Dr. Wu's shoes on the hard floor.

Sharla tried to lighten the mood. "So. What's in the syringe there?"

"I'm afraid doctor-patient confidentiality prohibits me from answering that question."

"Ah. Understood."

Alan's turn. "What kind of work did you do for Mr. Fisk?"

"Again, I'm afraid that doctor-patient confidentiality bars me from answering."

"I mean, were you his GP, or are you more of a specialist? Generally speaking."

Dr. Wu halted and pivoted to hit Alan with a look of utter disdain.

"Doctor. Patient. Confidentiality." He punched each word with a harsh crispness. Then he continued on his way. Alan and Sharla fell quiet.

After a long enough walk to bring light beads of perspiration to Alan's receding hairline, they emerged into a large grassy courtyard with a crystal blue pool, a long row of chaise lounges under large umbrellas, and a topiary garden beyond the pool area that stretched toward the horizon.

On one of the chaise lounges reclined Rebecca Fisk, a dashing woman in her mid-fifties wearing a tight one-piece suit with an oval-shaped hole that exposed her flat, hard abdominal muscles. She sipped a drink from a highball glass in one hand and read a book with the other. The spine of the book displayed the title: *Joy After Tragedy: How to Get the Most Out of Your Rich Husband's Death*. A large floppy hat and sunglasses hid her eyes and most of her face. Dr. Wu stopped about fifteen feet away from where she lounged and cleared his throat.

She glanced up from her reading, pulling down her sunglasses for a better look. Her eyes matched the sparkling blue pool. Wu said, "It appears you have visitors. Unannounced ones."

With that, Dr. Wu gave Alan and Sharla one final glare. Then, he and his syringe disappeared back into the mansion.

"Sharla!" chirped Rebecca as she swung her legs off the chaise and rose to give her a warm embrace. "You'll have to excuse Dr. Wu's attitude. He's still upset. He was basically Barron's pet dog. To what do I owe the honor of your visit?"

"Well, first of all, I'd like to again offer you my condolences. Such an unexpected way to lose your husband."

"Oh, please, the bastard was always going to get himself shot by someone sooner or later." She turned to Alan. "No hard feelings on my end, truly."

"Alan didn't do it."

"Is that so?" asked Rebecca, arching her perfectly threaded eyebrows.

"We're trying to figure out who did," Sharla said.

"That is . . . interesting."

"We've actually come by to ask you some questions. Do you remember where you were on the night that Mr. Fisk died?"

Rebecca's smile waned.

"Now why would you be asking me that?"

"We're only trying to gather information."

"I did not murder my husband. Just because I was divorcing him doesn't mean that I killed him. And yes,

I know the word is out on the divorce. Do you know he slept with his stalker? That was the last straw for me."

"We're not accusing you of anything. It would just be helpful for us to get some more input."

Rebecca sighed.

"I was at home that whole night, alone, watching my reality shows. I ordered in sushi from a top-of-the-line restaurant—you wouldn't know it—and I went to bed early. Happy?"

"That's a pretty weak alibi, Mrs. Fisk."

"You didn't ask me for an alibi. You asked me what I was doing on the night of June eighth. And I told you the truth."

"I mean to say—"

"Okay, enough," Rebecca said. "You're not even police. They've already come through here and verified all the information that I told you. As a matter of fact, I'm still waiting to get my ePhone back from them. They're checking all my location info or something. You have no right to barge into my home and give me the third degree."

"Mrs. Fisk, if I may—" Alan started sheepishly.

"No, you may not. Sharla, how do you even know that this man didn't do it?"

"I, well, I just believe him."

"Ha! And you say *my* alibi is weak."

"If you knew Alan, I think you'd agree. He wouldn't hurt a fly."

"My husband wasn't a fly. He was a two-timing, scheming, ruthless snake of a businessman. And all the evidence says that this man right here shot him in the head." Rebecca hit Alan with a withering look.

"People can surprise you, Sharla. We're complicated creatures. I mean, I am doing my best to put on a brave front. I'm trying to wave it all away, but it still hurts to lose your life companion. It hurts a lot. And sure, I may say crass things about him sometimes, but Barron and I . . . We went through so much together. Some of it good, a lot of it bad, yes. But once you spend a certain amount of time with someone, a deep affection can't help but bubble up, no matter what kind of person they are. Regardless of what they've done. I expect you can understand that, Sharla. I saw the friendship that you shared with him. And now I have a parade of people coming through the house, first the police and now you lot, all insinuating the same thing: 'you killed your husband,' 'you wanted him out of your life, so you must have murdered him.' Well, it's not true! In fact, one of the things I was looking forward to most was seeing Barron's face as the judge awarded me half of everything he owned. I wanted to rip it out of his hands. It was going to be so sweet. And now . . . now I'll never . . ."

Rebecca's voice broke. She briefly knocked her sunglasses akimbo as she reached up to wipe away a tear.

"And now look at this. The ice in my mojito is all melted. Where's Wu?"

She looked around before training her gaze back on Alan and Sharla.

"If I was going to kill him, why would I have even started divorcing him? Can you answer me that?" she asked. "I'm finished humoring you now. Please go. If you want a suspect actually worth looking into, I'd suggest James Bradford. Barron had been worried about him for months. Rumors were flying that he had been talking to members of the board, trying to see who he could turn against my husband. Apparently, many of them disapproved of Barron's single-minded focus on the Fiskiverse project. Oh, well. And Bradford? That's a man who is capable of anything.

"Now, I'm going to politely ask you to leave before I call my bodyguards to have you tossed out. Or did we fire them, too? Damn it. At the very least, I'll have Wu jab you with one of those big, scary needles he seems to love so much."

"It's all right. We'll leave," Sharla said.

She and Alan retreated with their heads down. Halfway down the long hallway that had taken them to the east wing pool, Alan broke the silence.

"She makes a good point. I mean, why would she even have initiated the divorce proceedings if she was planning on killing him anyway?"

"Maybe because it makes her look less guilty? Plus, her alibi is so weak."

"Maybe it's time we look into James Bradford?"

"No, no," Sharla replied. "But I do think we could do with a regroup. Maybe we got ahead of ourselves here. I'll come by your place tomorrow morning and we'll take it from square one."

Alan smiled in agreement, happy to have a partner in this whole mess. They climbed into the Volvo and left the beautiful, lush grounds of Fisk Estates behind.

CHAPTER TWELVE

JAMES BRADFORD HAD ALMOST everything he wanted in life: movie star good looks, a swanky loft in the heart of San Francisco's Financial District that looked like it came straight out of a bachelor's wet dream, and a closet full of custom-tailored suits. All that was missing was a Fisk Enterprises business card emblazoned with those three magical letters: CEO. And now, with Fisk's death, that accomplishment was so close that Bradford could taste it. As soon as the members of the board reconvened after completing their respective summer vacations, Bradford fully expected to be crowned. At the age of thirty-six, he might even still be young enough to be branded a wunderkind.

On the night of June thirteenth, mere hours after he watched Fisk's ivory casket get lowered into the ground, Bradford decided to hit the town. As he straightened his Tom Ford silk jacquard tie beneath his black Brioni suit with just the subtlest of pin striping and slicked his thick golden hair back with copious amounts of sweet-smelling sculpting gel, he stared at an article displayed on his Fisk tablet. Published by a leading tech industry online magazine, right above a beaming photo of himself, the headline read: "Tech's Next Big Thing."

He pulled out his ePhone. He reluctantly moved his thumb past a recently installed app specially designed to summon a self-piloting helicopter to his location at any time. That was a privilege offered only to the acting Fisk Enterprises CEO, so he would have to wait until after his official installation to take full advantage. Instead, he called a car to take him to his favorite nightclub, Plush, where he planned to buy everyone present a round of drinks. His wildest dreams loomed around the corner, and it was time for him to celebrate.

As he climbed into the back seat of the self-driving Fisk electric town car that pulled up directly in front of his building, he whipped his ePhone out of his jacket pocket. He dialed up his former college compatriot, current colleague in the Fisk Enterprises C-suites, and closest friend Todd Carver and loudly demanded to be joined for an evening of revelry. Once Bradford insisted forcefully enough that, no, it was not in poor taste to go out celebrating the death of a close work associate and mentor, Todd agreed to meet him.

When the town car pulled to a stop outside Plush and the door opened itself, Bradford bounded toward the velvet rope at the entrance with a feeling of deep satisfaction and confidence. He wore showy Bulgari rimless sunglasses despite the fact that it was 11:30 PM.

The bouncer plastered on a smile at seeing Bradford heading his way and waved him right in, much to the chagrin of the many patrons still standing in line, whose frustrated groans made Bradford feel just a little bit horny.

Inside, he took off his sunglasses, hooked them onto his jacket pocket, and scanned the bar area. Todd had beaten him there. He leaned against the bar talking to two lovely young women in low-cut dresses. Bradford made a beeline for them but was headed off by the establishment's short, balding manager, who shook his hand with enthusiasm, delighted. Bradford was magnetic tonight; he could feel it. He fought through the crowd to reach Todd and the two women.

"What's up, douchebag?" he said.

Todd laughed at the traditional greeting and slapped his hand into Bradford's, pulling him into a shoulder-to-shoulder side hug.

"J-man, this here is Gigi and Adrielle. Girls, you don't know it, but you're looking at the next CEO of Fisk Enterprises."

The women gasped and then giggled.

"Nothing's official yet," said Bradford. "But yeah, you are."

"Hey, why don't you give us a little time, ladies? We'll find you out on the floor."

The two blondes disappeared into the crowd, hunching together over their drinks and whispering.

"Now, why do you have to send them away right when I get here?" Bradford asked.

"Because I know you," Todd said. "You'll steal them both, and I'll end up with nothing. Sit down."

They settled onto two adjacent see-through glass barstools. Todd whistled loudly at the bartender and waved him over.

"Break out the top shelf, Enrico, we're celebrating tonight," he yelled over the thumping music. Then he turned his attention back to Bradford. "So. How'd you do it?"

Bradford scowled.

"How'd I do what?"

"Come on. Don't play. It's me."

"I don't know what you're talking about."

"How'd you . . . you know. Off him?"

"Fisk? I didn't do anything to Fisk."

"James. Jamesie baby. I'm not wearing a wire or anything. I'm curious."

"I'm being serious. I didn't kill him. I was at a fundraising event that whole night; you can ask the girl I was with. Somebody else must have done it."

Todd gave him a look of deep disappointment.

"You actually expect me to believe what they're saying? That Benning did it?"

Bradford laughed. "That guy is limper than a wet pool noodle. No way it was him."

"Williams put up seventy-five thousand bucks that it was you."

"You guys are betting on who killed our boss?"

"Yeah."

"That's hilarious."

Enrico came back with several lowball glasses and a newly opened bottle of Patron En Lalique Serie 2 tequila. Todd poured them several fingers each.

"So if it wasn't Benning, and it wasn't you . . . Who was it?"

"I don't know, and I don't care. Let me tell you a story. When I was sixteen years old, I got my first job at an ice cream shop in my hometown. Small, local operation. Run by the owner and his wife. Two weeks in, I started noticing the wife was making eyes at me. Really unsubtle stuff. One day her hand lingered on mine on the cash register and, next thing I knew, she and I were getting it on in the walk-in freezer. First time I was ever with an older woman.

"A few days later, I came in to open the shop and there was this note taped to the glass front door. It said, 'I know what you did.' Turns out the guy saw the whole thing on the security tapes. So I unlocked the door, and I went in and I stepped into this thick, sticky puddle that covered the whole floor. The guy had cut the power cords to all the freezers, so all the ice cream went bad and oozed out everywhere all over the ground. Well, I splashed my way to the back room, and there the guy was, dangling from a pipe in the ceiling, hanging by one of those very power cords he'd sliced up, dead as can be. And you know what the wife did? She asked me to take over the shop.

"It was that experience—running a small business at the age of sixteen—that got me into Harvard. Punched my ticket to move up in the world. I learned then and there to take a leg up when it presents itself, even if it's a little ugly. Nobody ever said that the road to the top would be free of roadkill."

"I'll drink to that."

The two old friends clinked glasses and downed their tequila.

The young women who had been keeping Todd company before Bradford's arrival showed back up.

"We need more drinks," they announced in unison with pouty lips.

"You've come to the right place." Todd smiled and poured them each some of the tequila. "This is expensive shit right here," he told them as he handed over the glasses. "Seventy-five hundred bucks a bottle."

The women knocked it back like water.

"Hey, let me ask you ladies something," Todd said, looking slyly out of the corner of his eye at Bradford. "My buddy here. He's about to take over the world's most powerful company. That's impressive, right?"

The girls nodded dutifully.

"What if I told you . . . And this stays between us, okay? What if I told you that maybe, just maybe, he might have, just a little bit, murdered his boss in order to get the job? Huh?"

Todd made a gun with his fingers and pressed the pretend barrel up against Adrielle's forehead.

"What if he took a gun and . . . pow! Right through the brainpan. What would you ladies think about that?"

Everyone turned to Bradford, who stayed still awaiting their reaction. The women's eyes filled with doubt for a long moment. All four members of the small group maintained an uneasy pause filled only by the repetitive thrum of the club music blasting through the nearby speakers. Then one of the women broke the lull.

"That's hot," she said, laying her hand on Bradford's thigh. The other girl followed suit.

"Yeah, I've always had a thing for bad boys," she said, lightly biting her lower lip.

"Hell yeah!" said Todd. "What do you say now, J-train?"

Bradford couldn't help but smile.

"All right. Yeah. Maybe I did it then. Who's to say?"

"Let's get fucked up!" Todd screamed to the sky.

The party of four gave a loud cheer and raised their glasses to a night that was only getting started.

Chapter Thirteen

Sharla wrote out a short list of names in blue dry-erase marker at the top of a standalone whiteboard. Alan had dragged it out of the storage space in his attic the night before.

He sat watching her from the cream-colored sofa in his living room, still sipping his morning coffee, as she underlined each name and then stepped back to admire her work.

"After much consideration, I believe that these should be our three main suspects for the true murderer of Barron Fisk," she said. "Aristotle Cunningham, Rebecca Fisk, and Leonid Ledbedev."

"Ledbedev," Alan said. "That is interesting. I hadn't even considered him."

"Each of these people had plentiful reason to want Mr. Fisk dead, which we can get into now."

She added bullet points below each name as she continued.

"Cunningham's motives include his well-documented hatred of Mr. Fisk and their whole tech billionaire pissing contest rivalry thing, as well as the numerous business advantages his company stands to gain now that Fisk Enterprises is on uneasy footing. Probably billions of dollars in additional profit he'll see from all this. That's definitely motivation.

"Next up: Rebecca Fisk. She is now in line to inherit the single largest personal fortune in the history of the world, which might be enough to drive anyone to take drastic measures. In addition, it's widely known that she wasn't exactly getting along with her husband toward the end there. Maybe a few too many affairs on Mr. Fisk's part. Although personally, I don't think it was her. I know her fairly well, and I just can't see it. But we'll let the facts do the talking. Can't allow my personal feelings to color the investigation. That's rule number one.

"And lastly we have Leonid Ledbedev, who had more than enough reason to seek revenge against his old associate. He and Mr. Fisk came up together in the burgeoning computer world of the 1990s. They were business partners and best friends right up until the SEC sniffed out some shady math in their company books and Ledbedev took the fall for it. Fisk came out untouched. There have always been whispers that Fisk offered his partner up as a sacrificial lamb in order to save his own skin. So Ledbedev went to prison while Fisk renamed the company after himself and became the wealthiest man alive. Ledbedev's been locked up either in prison or a mental hospital for the past three decades thanks to Mr. Fisk, which sounds like plenty of motive to me."

"How could Ledbedev have done it if he's been locked up this whole time?"

"He probably couldn't have directly, but he certainly could have gotten someone else to do it for him. He had connections in his younger life to some shady characters from Eastern Europe. There was also plenty of talk around Fisk Enterprises HQ that the whole idea for the Fiskiverse came from Ledbedev originally, which could explain the timing of Mr. Fisk's death: right before his big project could be completed."

"Well, that's not exactly true," Alan said, adjusting his glasses. "Fisk still would have needed the VigRig acquisition to go through. And for that he needed my approval."

"Fair enough, but the larger point still stands. This is definitely our best lead right now."

"Okay. But I think you've left someone pretty obvious off the list."

"Oh yeah? Who?"

"James Bradford. He was Fisk's number two guy. Isn't he likely to be appointed to take over the company now?"

"Oh. Well," Sharla stammered. "I . . . I don't think it could have been him."

"Why not? Becoming CEO of the world's most famous company is a big motive if you ask me. Even Mrs. Fisk said as much. Maybe Bradford got sick of waiting his turn."

"I guess we can add him if you want."

"I think he's definitely worth looking into," Alan said, furrowing his brow at her hesitation. "Don't you?"

"Okay, okay."

Sharla wrote Bradford's name on the board in the bottom corner, notably smaller than the rest, and added no bullet points beneath it.

"There," she said, "but I still think we should start with Ledbedev. Of our three suspects, he's our best lead at this point."

"Four," Alan corrected her. "We have four suspects."

"Right, four."

A piercing scream tore through the Benning living room. It came from upstairs. Alan, panicked, leaped to his feet. His coffee mug tumbled to the floor, spraying brown liquid across the pristine carpeting.

He rushed up the steps in a panic, with Sharla close on his heels.

"Hannah! What is it? What's the matter?"

Alan and Sharla tore down the upstairs hallway until they reached the door to Alan's home office, where they found Hannah seated at his computer desk looking devastated.

Alan said, "Are the girls okay? What's going on?"

"The cards! None of the cards are working!" Hannah cried.

"What are you talking about?"

Then Alan spotted Hannah's billfold lying open on the desktop with the numerous credit cards from within spread across the desk's surface. His own wallet rested nearby in a similar state. The computer screen at Hannah's side displayed a popular women's fashion website.

"They're not working! None of the cards are going through! Why aren't they going through, Alan?!"

Alan took two deep breaths to calm his racing heart before responding.

"They must have frozen my assets. The lawyers said this might happen."

Hannah sat still for a long moment. No expression showed on her pale face.

"What are you . . . Are you saying . . . that we don't have any money?"

Alan shrugged from the doorway.

Outside, the reporters and photographers who milled around the Bennings' front lawn exchanged puzzled glances as another blood-curdling shriek echoed from inside the house.

Chapter Fourteen

THE BRINY SMELL OF seawater suffused the air of the pockmarked parking lot outside the Calming Waves Behavioral Health Center in Morro Bay, California. Alan and Sharla finished up the three-and-a-half hour drive from Cupertino by pulling the Volvo into a spot near the front door of the single storied brick building and climbing out. Alan stretched near the passenger door.

Checking in as guests took no time at all, and a cheery redheaded nurse led them into the visiting area. The large room resembled a well-kempt preschool playroom with adult-sized furniture. Round tables laden with various board games, puzzles, and coloring books dotted the long, open space. Some patients sat focused on the activity in front of them; others wandered aimlessly over the cushy blue carpeting. A boxy, outdated television mounted on the upper part of the wall in the far corner drew a small group of patients, most leaning forward in their chairs, straining to make out the TV's weak, tinny sound over the common area hustle and bustle. One man carried out a quietly heated conversation with the dim reflection of himself in a nearby window. They all wore identical pale blue two-piece jumpsuits.

The young redheaded attendant led Alan and Sharla between tables toward an upper-middle-aged man with pale skin and thinning salt-and-pepper hair who sat alone.

The man remained motionless as they approached, staring vacantly at a nearly finished puzzle on the table before him. He had high cheekbones, lips so thin they were barely there, and a somewhat rounded nose with a bulbous end. His eyebrows, noticeably darker than his hair, bushed at the base of his forehead. The attendant touched the man lightly on the shoulder, announced in a peppy voice that the man had visitors and, leaving it at that, marched away. The man gave no sign that he noticed the introduction.

"Er, excuse me," Alan said. "You are Mr. Ledbedev, yes? We've come to visit with Leonid Ledbedev."

Silence. Alan looked over the man's shoulder at the puzzle on the tabletop, completed except for one single piece that sat off to the side, its oddly shaped hole conspicuous in the center of the picture.

Alan picked up the final piece and placed it gently into position, finishing the scene: a still-life photo of a heaping bowl of ice cream. Several scoops of different flavors, topped with a reddish syrup and cherries and some kind of crushed nuts, piled high. Whipped cream crowned the dessert. The two men contemplated the image for a long moment.

"Funny how fast it melts away, isn't it?" said the seated man in a light Eastern European accent. "From one of life's finest treats to a sopping, sticky mess in just a few minutes. All it takes is time."

He turned to look at his two guests at last.

"Yes, I am Leonid Ledbedev. And you are Alan Benning. The man who murdered my former business partner."

"No. Well . . . may we sit?"

Ledbedev motioned to the chairs across from him.

"It's nice to meet you, Mr. Ledbedev," Sharla said. "My name is—"

"Sharla Johnson," Ledbedev interrupted. "Fisk's senior personal assistant for many years. Since late 2019, if I'm not mistaken." Sharla nodded through her surprise. "I may be confined to a loony bin, but I assure you that I am well aware of the outside world."

"We're here to ask if you might have any information about the incident involving Mr. Fisk," Sharla said.

"Incident?" Ledbedev asked.

"Yes. Well, the murder. Fisk's murder."

"Incident," Ledbedev swished the word around in his mouth as if he could taste it. He lapsed into silence for a short while. "Words are funny, no? The way we put them together only to tear them apart again in a desperate search for meaning."

"Um. Yes. That's definitely interesting."

"Incident."

As the word hung in the air, Ledbedev's eyes drifted away from the table. His gaze fixed on the middle distance for a long time before it snapped back to his tablemates.

"I'm not crazy, you know," Ledbedev said.

"We're sure that you're not," Sharla quickly agreed.

"I know what people say about me. I did have a few rough years. I admit that. After the sentencing. But I'd lost everything. Anyone would struggle."

"I can understand that," Alan said softly.

"I thought getting myself sent here would be easier than prison. I faked a breakdown. I spent months memorizing the clinically defined symptoms of schizoaffective disorder, and I pulled it off. Little did I know that I was dooming myself to a lifetime of being treated as an intellectual dullard. At least in prison, I wasn't spoken to like a four-year-old. Of course, once I was transferred here, the signs of my mental illness went away, considering they were counterfeit in the first place. But it was too late. I'd been labeled. I'd exchanged a physical prison for a mental one. And worst of all, it was a prison of my own making."

Sharla and Alan struggled to find an appropriate response. In the end, it was Ledbedev who spoke again.

"I've done thirty years for the crimes that man committed."

"We'd heard that," Alan commiserated. "Which is why it would be understandable if you had . . . Well, if you have any information about the inci . . . about his passing."

"I was in love once. Before, I mean. Her name was Anya. She had this gorgeous chestnut hair, down to her shoulders, slightly wavy. So full. So fragrant. Probably gray now." He chuckled dryly to himself and fell into another short silence. "Do you have love?" he asked.

"I do," responded Alan. "I love my wife very much. I would also hate to lose her."

Ledbedev gave a weak smile.

"How much do you know about Mrs. Fisk?" he asked.

"We know she was divorcing Mr. Fisk when he died," Sharla said, "and that she's now the richest person in the world."

"I mean from before. Before she became Mrs. Fisk."

"Oh. Not much, I suppose."

"What does the name Darlene Pillar mean to you?" Ledbedev's eyes darted between Alan and the finished puzzle on the table before him.

"Um, nothing," answered Alan. "Who is that?"

"That's her. That's Rebecca Fisk's old name. Darlene Pillar."

"She changed her name?"

"She did. After her first marriage."

"Why?"

"Because her first husband . . . he was a millionaire. And she was accused of killing him. They acquitted her in the end, but the headlines, the attention, had already done the damage. So she changed her name. Then she met Barron, and she graduated from a millionaire husband to a billionaire one."

"I had no idea. Did you?"

Sharla shook her head.

Ledbedev said, "Rebecca was never in love with him. She was only interested in the money. You can always tell when that's the case, you know?"

Sharla's eyes briefly flitted in Alan's direction.

"It was so obvious when they first got together. Over time, she got better at hiding it. I tried to tell him again and again, but Fisk was blind in so many ways." Ledbedev said, unfairly slandering one of the world's greatest figures, who was now dead and unable to defend himself. Ledbedev released a deep sigh. "I've done enough time for that man," he said. "Why would I kill him now?"

"Revenge," ventured Alan. "Or we heard that the Fiskiverse was originally your idea."

Ledbedev's entire demeanor changed. His eyes sharpened, and he sat up straight for the first time.

"Where did you hear that word?"

"Fiskiverse?" asked Alan. "That was his last big project. He was close to finalizing it before he was killed."

"No. That can't be. The full version?"

"I . . . I'm not sure. I suppose so. He was obsessed with it, but the board was always on the fence about virtual reality."

"It's not . . ." Ledbedev began hotly, cutting himself short and attempting to tame his sudden anger. "It's not just virtual reality, it's . . . You cannot allow that project to be completed."

"Well, I don't work at the company anymore. So I'm not sure what I could . . ."

"Listen to me," Ledbedev begged, slamming both fists on the table and scattering the puzzle pieces. "You're not listening to me! You must stop it. You must! Promise me." He rocketed to his feet and leaned across the table, grabbing Alan roughly by the front of his shirt. "Promise me! You must promise me now."

"Hey!" called one of the attendants milling around the space, rushing toward them. "No touching!"

"Promise me!"

Alan felt the man's hands shaking with intensity. Two attendants peeled Ledbedev's grip free and dragged him away toward the far door.

"The ice cream melts, yes, but in the end that is exactly what makes it precious! This is what Barron never understood!"

The attendants had Ledbedev by each arm. His eyes flared with fear, and his mouth quivered.

"You must stop it. You must stop the Fiskiverse! You must—"

His voice cut off abruptly as the guards got him fully through the door and slammed it shut. Alan and Sharla were left with the echoes of the man's indecipherable warnings ringing in their ears as they climbed back into Sharla's Volvo and began the journey home.

Chapter Fifteen

LATER THAT SAME NIGHT, tucked away in the small, unkempt room at the back of the Cupertino police station that they called an office, Detectives Reyes and Tanner sat reviewing the files for their active cases. Dirty yellow fluorescent lights flickered overhead, painting the walls varying sickly shades of beige. Long shadows stretched across the floor's stained linoleum tiles. The blinds in the lone small window hung at a crooked angle. The whole room reeked of stale, low-quality coffee. None of these facts seemed to bother either detective, though, because poor people have no standards.

Tanner put his feet up on his desk as Reyes pulled the next folder from their shared filing cabinet.

"The Benning case," she said aloud to herself as much as to Tanner.

"Ah. Easiest one of the bunch. Benning's our guy. Fisk was a jerk, Benning got fed up, and he popped him one right through the old noggin."

"You don't think it's a little too convenient? I mean, why would he leave the gun at the scene? Why didn't he at least think to wipe it for prints?"

"You said it yourself before we interrogated him. This isn't a hardened criminal we're talking about here. It was a crime of passion. Guy shot him, panicked and fled."

"But he still took the time to erase the security footage from the hallway?"

"Oh no, no, no," Tanner said, abruptly leaning forward in his chair. "You're not doing this. Not with this case."

"Doing what?"

"Your whole Reyes thing. Where you make everything ten times more complicated than it has to be. We have what we need on this one."

"I don't do a whole Reyes thing."

"Yes you do."

"I'm a good detective. I care."

"You don't remember the traveling circus case? When the clown was accused of shooting the bearded lady, and you swore it was the performing monkey the whole time? You made us do three days of OT on that."

"But it did end up being the monkey."

"Oh, right," Tanner conceded. "Okay, bad example."

"Hear me out."

Tanner started to laugh. "I tell ya, though, I'd like to see the monkey jail where they sent that monkey. You think it's all kinds of monkeys or only ones like him?"

"There's no such thing as monkey jail, Tanner. They put the monkey down."

"You mean they killed him?"

"Yeah."

"Oh. Poor Mr. Waffles."

"Mr. Waffles shot and killed a person."

"And so did Benning. The whole board of Fisk's company told us over those video calls about how Fisk and Benning had been arguing for more than a year about some business merger thingy. There you go. We've got motive. We've got his footprint at the scene. We've got the murder weapon registered to him. We've got his fingerprints all over that murder weapon. We've got video footage of him as the last one leaving the building that night. What more do you want? A confession note shaved into the dead guy's hairdo? Lock him up already. Send him to monkey jail."

"But we just got the tracking data in from Rebecca Fisk's ePhone. And look at this." Reyes plopped the open case file on the desk in front of her partner. "Rebecca told us she was at home the entire night. But according to her phone tracking info, she left the house around 10:20 PM and went one place and one place only: the headquarters building for Fisk Enterprises. Then straight back home."

"How sure are we about that?"

"The data came direct from the Fisk database. Turns out they track all of us all the time. Which is troubling generally, but in this case helpful."

Tanner made a skeptical face and shrugged.

"This is a major piece of evidence, Tanner. This means we might have the wrong suspect."

"I don't think it means anything like that. This doesn't magically erase all the evidence we have against Benning. It means that the wife didn't want to admit she visited her husband on the night he got shot. I can't blame her. I wouldn't want to admit that either. Stop getting in your head on this, Reyes. We have the right guy."

"Something about all this doesn't sit right with me. You think this case is that simple?"

"I do." Tanner's face lit up with an idea. "Wait a minute. What if he was set up?"

"You think someone could be framing Benning?"

"What? No. I was talking about Mr. Waffles."

Reyes released a long sigh that came from deep in her core.

"I'm going home."

Reyes got as far as the door before Tanner stopped her.

"Hey, wait. I got you something."

Tanner tossed a small object in her direction. She caught it out of pure instinct and looked at it in her hand. It was a bottle of hot sauce.

"Valentina," she said. "Thanks, Tanner. That's nice."

"Sorry it's such a little bottle. That's all I could find."

"No, it's perfect. I can carry it with me. I like to have hot sauce on hand at all times."

"Hey, you know what? That's not a bad idea. I might start doing the same thing."

Reyes left the station that night with the faintest outline of a smile on her normally stern face.

Chapter Sixteen

"And that's the plan," Sharla finished, looking at Alan expectantly.

"That's a terrible plan," he said back to her.

Sharla groaned.

The midday sun hung high above them. They stood on a sidewalk a few blocks from the main entrance to Fisk Enterprises headquarters, having just exited the old Volvo. Sharla held in her hands a bulging brown paper grocery bag.

"Well, we need concrete evidence. We know Rebecca has a pattern of marrying rich guys, then watching them die, but she's also clearly good at covering her tracks. And since our strategy of walking up to the suspects and asking them if they're guilty isn't really bearing fruit, I think a new tactic is called for. Do you have any better ideas?"

"No," Alan admitted.

"Then perhaps rein in the criticism of my plan until you have one of your own."

"There's no way they'll even let me into the building."

"That's what these are for."

Sharla reached into the paper bag and handed him a plain blue baseball cap and a large pair of dark sunglasses.

"What is this?"

"That's your disguise. That's how we'll get you into the building."

"This is your big plan? A pair of sunglasses and a hat?"

"It'll work."

"Why don't we paint a tunnel on the side of the building and walk in through that?"

"Oh, come on. I have a hoodie and some jeans for you to wear, too. You think anyone is going to suspect *Alan Benning* of wearing a hoodie?"

"I don't even know what that is."

"Exactly."

"No, no, no. We've got to call this off."

"We're not calling it off."

"Why do we even need to keep investigating? Both Cunningham and Mrs. Fisk said the police checked their alibis. So the cops aren't just pinning it on me. They're actually looking into it. Shouldn't we leave it to the professionals?"

"Don't be naïve, Alan. You think the cops are doing a thorough job of investigating these people? No way. They're just covering their own asses. They think they've got a slam-dunk conviction on their hands. This is still up to us."

"But your plan is illegal."

"This whole investigation is technically illegal."

"Yeah, but this is *illegal*-illegal. Breaking and entering?"

"We're not breaking anything. So that leaves entering, which is not a crime."

"It is if you're entering the scene of a recent murder."

"Alan," Sharla said, squaring her shoulders and looking him directly in the eyes. "I know you're frightened. But you've got to stop letting your fears define you. Aren't you sick of being scared all the time? Aren't you tired of letting the world push you around?"

"You're pushing me around right now."

"I'm trying to keep you from going to prison!"

A woman pushing a stroller past on the sidewalk gave them a frightened look and picked up her pace.

"Sorry about that. Have a good day," Alan muttered toward the woman.

"You're so spineless."

"I am not spineless. I'm spine-full. I have a great spine."

"Let's try this: Name one brave or daring thing you've done in your life. Maybe we can get you to remember what it's actually like."

"One time as a kid I snuck into an amusement park when it was closed."

"Yeah? And what happened?"

Alan sighed.

"I got scared by a statue of a clown and ran home to tell my mom. And then the rest of the kids all got in trouble."

"This is your chance, Alan. It's time to be brave. You can do it."

"You think?"

"I'm positive. I can see it in you."

Alan took a moment to consider the situation, shifting his weight from one foot to the other and self-consciously cleaning his glasses on the hem of his shirt.

Finally he said, "All right, I'm in."

"Yes! I'm proud of you. Now change your clothes and let's get to it."

Alan insisted that Sharla stand guard by the Volvo while he changed inside. He emerged looking perplexed in the sunglasses and baseball cap, hoodie, and jeans.

"So this is a hoodie," he said. "Just a sweatshirt with a hood. Clever."

"Yeah, now put the hood up, and you're unrecognizable. Let's go."

"What in the world happened to these jeans?"

"They're distressed."

"There are holes all over the place."

"That's the style."

"Holes are a style?"

"We don't have time for this. Let's go."

Following Fisk's death, the upper floors of Fisk headquarters fell into a state of anarchy. The company lacked a singular leader, and with the board members still on vacation, white-collar chaos reigned. Corporate structure crumbled as opportunistic executives saw their chance to leapfrog up the ladder. The corner offices had become a free-for-all. Executives refused to leave for lunch each day lest they return and find that some other ambitious member of management had moved in, changed the nameplate on the door, and usurped their hard-earned, important-sounding title.

This disorganization made it easy for Alan and Sharla to waltz through the lobby unnoticed, as the security guard had recently nabbed an office on the twenty-sixth floor and barricaded himself in. They took the elevator to the top story, which housed Fisk's cavernous office. The hallway and waiting area outside, the only other spaces on the floor, sat empty.

Sharla placed her palm on a digital pad next to the tall glass doors that led to Fisk's office, and the doors swung open obligingly.

"Welcome, Alan Benning and Sharla Johnson," chirped the AI system built into the walls of Fisk's office. Sharla stopped short.

"Shit. I forgot about Jennings."

"Please let me know how I may be of assistance."

"You sound different, Jennings. Did your voice change?"

"I have recently received an upgrade in my programming. I hope to be able to serve you better."

"Right now you can serve us by leaving us alone. And by forgetting that we were here."

"Of course. Though I feel obliged to say, due to Mr. Benning's status as a person of interest in an active police investigation, I strongly advise against..."

"Can it, Jennings."

The AI fell silent, its console in the corner going idle and changing from an electric blue to a calm green color. Sharla and Alan began looking around aimlessly.

"What should I be looking for here?" Alan asked.

"No idea," Sharla said. "Just keep your eyes open."

Sharla paused with one hand resting lightly on the oversized desk. The office must have felt strangely empty without Fisk's magnetic presence anchoring the room. A man of his fortitude, vision, and wealth leaves a vacuum that cannot be readily filled. Especially by people who don't own even a single Saudi soccer team.

Alan scanned the shelves behind the desk and then scoured the area around the guest chairs for any sign of who may have been in the office recently.

Sharla sat in Fisk's chair and pressed a button on the desktop. A levitating digital screen appeared in a flash of light, and she keyed in a code to unlock the computer's interface.

Alan moved on to surveying the long bookcase full of drone prototypes that filled up the office's entire western wall.

"I remember this one," he said, pointing to the drone at the end of the shelf, the only one with articulating arms attached. It looked like a large flying beetle with elbows. "Mr. Fisk gave it out to the executive team a couple years ago in place of an end-of-year bonus."

"That makes sense," Sharla said. "He paid out the nose to acquire the company that designed it."

She came over from the desk and grabbed the control unit resting next to the drone.

"Let's see what it can do," she said, pressing the "Activate" button. The drone's several mini rotors whirred to life, and it hovered a few inches above the surface of the shelf. Manipulating the twin joysticks on the controller, Sharla steered the drone toward Alan's face.

"Be careful," he said.

Sharla made one of the drone's arms reach out slowly and close its grasper around the bill of Alan's hat. The machine lifted it from his head easily.

"Very cool," she said. "I see why Mr. Fisk went out of his way to buy the company that designed this. He said it can even be programmed to do tasks on its own. Like your own little flying butler."

"Let's refocus here," Alan said, snatching the hat back from the drone and shoving it onto his head.

As Sharla landed the drone back on the shelf and powered it down, she noticed something strange. She leaned in close to the nearby window.

"Hey, look at this."

"What is it?" Alan asked, mirroring her lean.

"This window next to the shelves. It's not latched shut." She pushed gently on one of the panes of glass, and half of the window swung open on its hinges with a light creak. "Why would this be unlocked?"

"Maybe Fisk wanted a breeze."

"No way. He hated everything about the outdoors. Wouldn't have risked a bug getting in. If he was hot, he would have had Jennings crank the A/C. Something's off here."

They both stuck their upper bodies out of the window and looked down. Thick green hedges hugged the foot of the building, perfectly uniform. A single spot of discoloration directly below the window made them both squint: one small splotch of brown.

"What is that?" Sharla asked.

"I can't tell."

"Here, give me your phone."

Alan handed her his ePhone, and she opened the camera app. Holding the phone out the window with the camera facing downward, she zoomed in again and again until they could see the item in the bushes below.

"It's a shoe."

"Not just any shoe," said Alan. "That's my shoe."

"It is?"

"Yeah. It's identical to the shoes that I always wear to work."

"Then that explains the footprint at the crime scene." Sharla straightened up, bringing her torso back into the room. She handed Alan's phone back.

"Wait a minute. Why didn't you use your own phone?"

"I didn't want to risk dropping it."

"Gee, thanks."

"Don't get distracted. Someone who knows what shoes you wear must have bought a pair and brought one along when they killed Fisk. They used it to make the footprint and then ditched it out the window. This is great, Alan! This is hard evidence that you were set up."

"Should we call the police?"

"And tell them what? That we were in Fisk's office without permission? No, we need to have an unassailable case put together that completely proves your innocence before we go to the cops."

Sharla returned to the holographic computer still hovering over the desktop.

"I know all of Mr. Fisk's passwords, so hopefully we can find something to suggest who it is that's trying to frame you."

Alan peered over her shoulder as she deftly maneuvered the cursor on the screen with rapid hand movements.

"Let's start with his personal notes on the day he died. He always kept a running journal of his day because he knew he'd eventually write an autobiography."

Sharla navigated to a file on the computer's projected desktop. "Here we go. Nothing out of the ordinary as far as I can tell," she said as she scanned the text. "Meeting notes and appointment times. He had lunch and then he . . . Oh. Oh, wow."

Alan leaned in closer and looked disgusted.

"Ugh. Why would he write down that he masturbated? Who does that?"

The computer console in the corner blooped back to life and glowed blue.

"Many great figures throughout history have believed in the intellectually restorative effects of sexual release," Jennings announced, "including luminaries such as Leonardo da Vinci, Ivan Pavlov, Mr. Rogers—"

"Okay, that's enough, Jennings," Sharla interrupted.

"It's not that weird, is all I'm saying."

"Power down, Jennings."

"As you wish."

The corner console turned back to a light green.

"Since when does Jennings get defensive like that?" Sharla shook off her concern and returned to searching her former boss's notes.

"Ah, now this is interesting." She pointed to a section of the hovering screen. "He set a reminder for himself to call one of the board members. And look at the sub-note attached," she continued, reading now. "*'Ask if Bradford has contacted. I know that he's been moving against me.'*"

"So maybe it's Bradford after all," Alan said.

"I don't know. That doesn't necessarily mean he was a threat."

"Seems like exactly what it means."

"Let's check his emails."

With a series of hand movements, she brought up a different computer program.

"Whose emails? Bradford's?"

"Yeah. Maybe we can find something to clear him."

"How can you check his inbox from here?"

"Mr. Fisk has access to all of them."

"Everybody's?"

"Yeah. If you have a Fisk Enterprises email address, he had complete access to your messages. It's on page, like, two-forty of the terms and conditions. Real small at the bottom."

"That seems invasive."

"That's the information age for you." Sharla finished maneuvering. "Here it is. James Bradford. President of International Operations. Okay. Mostly regular business emails. Let me switch to his private account. Ah, here we go. It looks like he sent one email on the night Mr. Fisk died. It went to Dr. Wu."

"Fisk's grumpy doctor?"

"One and the same."

"What is Bradford doing contacting Dr. Wu? What does the email say?"

"Bradford says that he got Wu's message and that he had to briefly sneak away from the fundraiser he was attending, but that the matter has been handled."

"That's it?"

"That's the whole email."

"*The matter has been handled.*' That's ominous."

"He could be referring to anything," Sharla said.

"It's got to be Fisk's murder. That has to be what he was talking about. What are the odds he was doing some other vague and nefarious thing on the exact same night?"

"I think you're jumping to a lot of unfounded conclusions."

"Why do you keep defending Bradford?"

"Hey. I'm not defending anyone," Sharla responded. "I just don't think we should get carried away with flimsy evidence."

"What's flimsy about it? Bradford knows what shoes I wear to work every day. He could easily have erased the security footage. He has access to my HR records to potentially falsify the gun permit in my name. And he could have lifted fingerprints from anywhere in my office to plant on the weapon. Mrs. Fisk might have a shady past, sure, but all the clues are pointing us to Bradford."

"Okay, fine," Sharla said, deflating. "Let's go talk to Bradford."

"No," Alan replied. "You were right. All the talking is getting us nowhere."

He looked past Sharla out the window with a mischievous glint in his eye.

"I've got a better idea."

Chapter Seventeen

"A STAKEOUT?" HANNAH FROWNED at Alan from across their kitchen island. "What do you know about doing a stakeout?"

"I looked up some tips online. Stay low, come prepared, park across the street and down a bit. It's not rocket science."

Alan stuffed supplies into a black duffel bag on the countertop in front of him.

"What if this Bradford guy is dangerous? What are you going to do then?"

"Nobody's going to be in any danger. We'll be watching him from across the street. You know, tailing him. Just to see if he gets up to anything suspicious. He won't notice us. We have hats and sunglasses. And hoodies. You'd be shocked at how far that gets you."

"And what about me? I'm going crazy trapped in this house, Alan. You're running around pretending to be some super-detective. I've got nobody to help me with the girls."

"I know. I'm sorry." Alan skirted around the island and took her hands in his own. "But I've only got three weeks left to prove my innocence, Hannah. I'm trying to save our family."

"Some family," Hannah said. She pulled her hands away.

"Don't be like that."

"You can pretend all you want that you're doing this for me and the girls. But I see you. You're enjoying all this."

"I'm trying to keep myself out of prison."

"You're trying to play the hero."

"So what? Is it such a bad thing for a man to take control for once in his life?"

Hannah let out a derisive laugh.

"You're some big man now? What kind of man are you? We don't even have any money! Where did you even get these supplies?"

"Sharla dropped them off."

"Sharla again!" Hannah threw up her arms and stalked to the other side of the kitchen. "Why is she involved in all this? You don't even know her."

"I do so. We're . . . er, we *were* co-workers."

"And being ex-coworkers is enough for her to put her whole life on hold to help you? That doesn't seem suspicious?"

"To be honest, I don't think she has much going on. She seems lonely."

"How do you know that you can trust this woman?"

"What do you mean?"

"I mean, how can you be sure she wasn't, whatever, hired by somebody to find more evidence against you or something like that?"

"She wasn't."

"How do you know?"

Alan searched for an answer.

"I trust her. Okay?"

Hannah glared.

"I'm trying to save our family," Alan said again.

Hannah marched out of the kitchen.

After Alan finished packing up the duffel bag, he went upstairs to his daughters' shared bedroom. The two-year-olds slept soundly in their safety beds. He kissed each of them lightly on the forehead and sat down in the rocking chair in the corner. Soon his head lolled to one side, and he fell asleep listening to the gentle sound of their breathing.

The next morning, he squeezed the duffel bag through the gap between the fence and the hedges to meet Sharla, who had parked the Volvo two blocks away. Once he settled into the passenger seat, she grabbed her ePhone.

"Jennings, directions to Skyline Condominiums in San Francisco."

"Coming right up," said the voice from her phone.

"I swear, that new Jennings voice sounds familiar."

A little under an hour later, they pulled into a parking spot across the street from Bradford's home address, a chic and modern high-rise building in the heart of San Francisco's Financial District. Two uniformed doormen guarded the entrance, ready to spring into action at the first sign of anyone about to enter or exit. Sharla killed the engine.

"Now we wait," Alan said. "I packed dried apricots. Do you want one?"

"No."

Shortly after their arrival, Alan pointed out Bradford's all-electric Fisk SUV as it pulled out of the condo building's subterranean parking lot and sped down the street with squealing tires. The engine of Sharla's Volvo turned over with a clunk, and they were officially in pursuit. To their disappointment, Bradford drove to Fisk Enterprises headquarters with only a brief pit stop at the drive-thru window of a high-end coffee shop. He arrived at the tall, shiny Fisk Building shortly before 9:00 AM. Sharla and Alan set up camp in the car across the street from the entrance to the company campus. The hours stretched long before them.

"So," Sharla said between sips of sports drink, "you and Hannah. How'd that happen?"

Alan laughed.

"I get that question a lot. She's much better looking than me, I'm aware."

"Oh, no, that's not what I—"

"It's okay. We were set up. Friend of a friend. That type of thing."

"And it worked out. That's great."

"We dated for about a year. Dinners, vacations, shopping trips. Stuff like that. And then we found out the girls were on the way, so we tied the knot."

"A happy little family."

"Yeah."

Alan's weak agreement failed to fill the pause that followed.

The business day crept by slowly. Bradford made no appearances. Alan and Sharla passed the time alternating between bouts of mindless conversation and inventing increasingly elaborate ways to toss dried apricots into each other's open mouths.

At around 6:30 that evening, they spotted Bradford's shiny black car coming through the gates that marked the entrance to the Fisk corporate campus. Sharla and Alan swung out into traffic a couple of cars behind him and realized that their target was not heading back home.

"Now we're talking," Sharla said. "Let's see what he's getting up to."

They followed him to a seedy section of San Francisco's downtown area. The traffic had thinned considerably, and Sharla and Alan now drove directly behind Bradford's car.

"Where do you think he's going?" asked Alan.

"I guess we'll find out."

Only a few blocks further, Bradford turned into a public open-air parking lot, handed some cash to the attendant and pulled into a spot. Sharla whipped her Volvo into an oversized spot that happened to be available across the street.

"This is . . . not a great neighborhood," Sharla said. "What is he doing around here?"

Bradford left his car and struck off down the sidewalk.

"Should we get out and follow him?" Alan wondered aloud.

"Yeah, absolutely."

They both hopped out and began walking in the same direction as their quarry, about half a block behind him. Alan stared down at his shoes as he walked, keeping one hand up around his forehead, trying to block his face.

Sharla said, "Walk normally."

"What if he sees me?"

"He won't notice us."

Bradford abruptly turned a corner, and they lost sight of him.

"He's not heading to that real estate office on Wheaton, is he?" Sharla asked.

"What do you care?"

"I don't," she responded a touch too quickly.

They picked up their pace a bit to avoid losing him. They hurried around the corner of a building and nearly ran directly into Bradford himself, who stood stock still waiting for them with a furrowed brow and a frown.

"What do you think you're doing?" he asked them in his deep baritone. He loomed over them, arms crossed. His chiseled jaw, thick arms, and wide shoulders that tapered to a thin waist beneath his well-fitting suit made him look like a supervillain about to explain his evil plan to a tied-up foe. The streetlight behind his head cast his facial features into shadow.

"Oh! Hi there, Bradford. Oh, wow. What a coincidence!" Alan sputtered without conviction. He looked to Sharla for help, but she stayed silent.

"Why are you following me?"

"Following?" echoed Alan. "Are we following? No, I don't think that's right. Following, you said?"

Bradford disregarded Alan's obvious incompetence at lying, a skill that poor people seem to lack in general, along with formal dining etiquette and basic hygiene. Bradford faced Sharla instead.

"Why are you following me?"

"We hoped to ask you a few questions about the night of June eighth."

"Oh. I see. This is about Fisk." Bradford shook his head. "I'm disappointed in you, Sharla. This is highly unprofessional."

"Unprofessional?" Alan repeated with puzzlement.

Bradford took one step closer, successfully redirecting Alan's attention with his threatening demeanor.

"I need you both to listen to me carefully," Bradford said in a deep growl. "I had nothing to do with Fisk's death. Now, it doesn't matter to me if you two want to run around playing private eye or cop or grab-ass or whatever the hell is going on here. But if I find you snooping around in my business again, I can assure you that there will be consequences. Leave. Me. Out of this. Understood?"

On the final word, he poked a long, powerful finger into Alan's chest. Alan gave a weak nod. Bradford muscled his way between Alan and Sharla, his burly frame brushing each of them out of the way like fruit flies. He marched down the sidewalk in the direction of his car.

Alan and Sharla shared a brief, wide-eyed look.

"Still think it wasn't him?" Alan asked.

Sharla only scoffed and turned to head toward the Volvo.

Chapter Eighteen

Dr. Lucian Wu worked at a stainless steel table in his state-of-the-art lab hidden behind a secret door in one of the guesthouses on the Fisk Estates grounds. He bent over a Bunsen burner carefully adding extracted tree resin to a vial filled with a milky solution. He jumped at the sound of the trick door opening behind him and spilled a bit of the gooey resin on the table.

"Drat," he whispered to himself.

Turning, he saw Rebecca Fisk storm in, red-faced and holding a thick stack of papers in one hand. She wore a flowing pink-and-white summer dress and a large number of diamond-encrusted bangle bracelets that jingled as she shook the papers in Wu's direction.

"Just what game do you think you're playing, Wu?"

"Good afternoon, Mrs. Fisk."

"Forty million? That dirty asshole left you forty million of *my* dollars?"

"I'm sorry?"

"Don't play dumb with me, you discount Bond villain. You knew, didn't you? You knew!" She shoved the papers into his hands. "Page thirty. Read it yourself."

Dr. Wu looked down at what turned out to be the last will and testament of Barron Aloysius Fisk. He flipped through, finding page thirty. Sure enough, there it was: the man had left Wu an inheritance of forty million dollars. Dr. Wu's mouth fell open in shock.

"I . . . I . . ."

"Save it, you wannabe Doctor Moreau. You killed him, didn't you? You found out he'd amended his will to include you, and you killed him!"

"I can assure you I did no such thing. I did my utmost every day to keep that man alive and healthy. He was my friend."

"As if that pushover Benning could have done it. He's about as dangerous as a cotton ball. It was you."

"Now, Mrs. Fisk, we can discuss this in a rational and mature manner. If you'd like to have a seat—"

"You tell me what you were injecting Barron with those last few months. I knew you were up to something with those weird shots. Tell me right now."

"I'm afraid that doctor-patient confidentiality—"

"Don't feed me that BS. You can't hide behind that forever."

"I'll remind you that a bullet killed Mr. Fisk, not any type of injection."

"So you got impatient. Couldn't wait to get your paws on my cash, huh, you . . . you . . . castrated Dr. Hyde?"

"Actually, Jekyll was the doctor. Mr. Hyde was his evil alter-ego who—"

"Shove it up your ass."

Dr. Wu looked affronted. "I will do no such thing."

"My lawyers tell me that it's set in stone. Nothing to be done. Do you have any idea what I could have accomplished with that forty million?"

"Fill your pool with martinis and drown yourself in it?" Wu said, not quite under his breath.

"*Excuse* me?"

Dr. Wu's chest swelled as he found his courage.

"I said that you're a worthless drunk. You only ever cared for Mr. Fisk's money. It was plain as day. And I strongly resent the implication that you're making. I did not kill your husband."

"How do I know that? You stood to make forty million damn dollars!"

"And how much, exactly, did you stand to make?"

Rebecca recoiled as if struck.

"What the hell is that supposed to mean?"

"I'm merely postulating. If you think that I'd be capable of this horrific act for forty million dollars, what might you have been willing to do for the rest of Barron's fortune?"

"Don't turn this on me. *You* killed my husband."

"Soon to be ex-husband, you mean. You were divorcing him, if you recall. I'm not sure that would play well for you in front of a jury. What do you think?"

"You dirty son of a—"

"I would watch my tongue if I were you, Rebecca," Dr. Wu said, taking a step toward her. "You see, I know an awful lot about you. And your husband. About this whole estate, as a matter of fact. You want that money? Then you'd better start treating me with respect, because I could bring this whole place tumbling down."

"How dare you threaten me? You were nothing before Barron brought you here. Nothing! You were running from the damn mafia if I remember. Fleeing for your life! What was it? You took a bribe from a rival family to botch the Don's throat surgery? Is that right? Barron saved your life."

"My previous professional history has little to no bearing on our present conversation."

"You killed for money before, and you did it again to Barron!"

"You killed him so you could squander his fortune chugging cocktails and humping pool boys in Monaco!"

They eyed each other, breathing heavily. After a long while, they each took a step backward. Rebecca broke the icy silence.

"What are you working on there?"

"I'm developing the world's most powerful anti-diarrheal. It has the potential to stop the need for bowel movements for days on end. I'm hoping to sell it to the military for use in long-term black ops or surveillance missions."

"You're making an anti-shitting potion?"

"Yes, basically."

"You know, you're lucky I let you keep operating out of here. I could kick you out today if I wanted."

"I am aware. And I am appreciative."

"What were you injecting Barron with? What was in those shots?"

"I will never say. Mr. Fisk swore me to secrecy. And I actually cared for him, unlike you."

"Come on, Wu," Rebecca sat on a nearby stool, suddenly looking exhausted. "You can't truly believe that I killed him."

"Do you truly believe that I did?"

Rebecca stared him down. Dr. Wu didn't flinch. Finally she said, "No."

"Good. Me neither," he replied. "About you, I mean."

"Okay, then."

"All right. Then perhaps the best course of action would be to leave things as they are."

"Fine."

Rebecca exited the room walking backward, never taking her eyes from Dr. Wu's face. Wu watched her just as intensely as she went.

Once she'd slid the hidden door back into place, Dr. Wu took several deep breaths to gather himself before returning his attention to his miraculous anti-shitting serum.

Chapter Nineteen

In a tiny studio apartment located in a dark sub-basement of a rundown building on the edge of town, Belinda Jones sat on her twin bed in front of a wall mirror. She ran a brush through her long blonde hair while humming quietly and watching herself with down-turned eyes. Since observing Barron Fisk's funeral from afar three days earlier, she'd holed up in her home, preparing herself mentally for what was to come. For what she had to do.

A fat old television with rabbit ears occupied the corner opposite her saggy bed. It cast the rest of the darkened room in flickers of colored light as staticky action played out on the screen, which displayed one of the most banal, torturous inventions of the money-starved, shriveled-up poor person mind: the situation comedy.

Allow your humble narrator a brief sidebar. It's bad enough that throughout human history, moneyed individuals like myself have had to witness you *"regu-*

lars" doing frighteningly depressing things like riding public transit, clipping grocery store coupons or eating mayonnaise. Simply revolting. But then, with the advent of television, some of you financially and intellectually stunted dullards decided to actually start filming the humdrum minutiae of your sad, little lives and putting it on the air under the guise of the *sitcom*.

Nowadays, one can hardly flip between financial news channels without being subjected to several of them. Inconsequential, whiny little peons fretting about gauche topics like hourly wages or rent hikes. What could be more drab?

One would think that being confronted with such garish reminders of the triviality of your existence would prove demoralizing, but no. You dolts actually laugh. And so, inexplicably, as Belinda Jones sat brushing out her hair in her simple apartment, the edges of her lips crept upward at seeing the inane antics playing out on her TV screen. I will never understand it.

Belinda got up and crossed to set her hairbrush next to the black, flowerless vase that rested on top of the TV. Then she turned toward the nonfunctional radiator against the far wall, upon which she had placed a wooden board to create a makeshift shelf for her collection of Barron Fisk-related items.

On the wall above the shelf hung a dashing photo of Fisk in a handsome dark wooden frame. He smiled benevolently down on the modest shrine, which included a scrapbook of Fisk-related news clippings, a prayer candle with his likeness where Jesus would normally be, a Barron Fisk Funko doll with its bobbly, swollen head, a large number of amateur sketches of Fisk in various positions and stages of undress, a copy of Fisk's first book with his name lazily scribbled inside the front cover, a small baggie of dark brown hair that Belinda had won in an online bidding war and could never be fully sure actually belonged to Barron Fisk but that she chose to worship anyway, several crumpled tissues that she'd had to fish out of large garbage cans when no one was looking, and a used band-aid that had fallen from Fisk's elbow during a speech at a campaign rally for a Republican senator.

The sad menagerie represented twenty years' worth of obsessive effort on Belinda's part. She'd hopped fences, crawled beneath cars and hidden for hours in garbage cans to get as close as possible to the slick-haired, raven-eyed object of her affection, now dead and buried.

She touched each Fisk item one by one with a delicate reverence, her breathing calm and deliberate. She finished by kissing the tips of her index and middle fingers and pressing them to the framed photo on the wall.

"Until we meet again, my love," she said in a breathy voice barely above a whisper.

She returned to her bed where she opened the top drawer of the nightstand and withdrew a Fisk brand eJournal, a digital diary released years earlier by Fisk Enterprises and marketed primarily to pre-teen girls. Made to resemble an old analog diary, it featured a classic booklike folding design and a clasp meant to keep the device held shut. Belinda now flipped the clasp open and allowed the twin displays inside to fall away from each other. The screens lit up.

Belinda scrolled through dates until one appeared in bold, accessed so many times that the system had automatically bookmarked it. February 15, 2027. She pressed the date to bring up the entry and settled in to reread it yet again:

Dear Diary,

It finally happened!!!!!!!!! OMG!!!!

I think we can officially mark yesterday down as the best Valentine's Day in the whole history of the whole entire universe because the best thing ever happened to me. It's official. Barron loves me. HE LOVES MEE!!!

Okay. So here's what happened.

I was sitting up in my usual tree looking into his window with the binoculars. And I could sense that something was wrong. Barron was not his usual self. I could tell because me and him are connected like that, you know? He was pacing back and forth a lot. And he had a bottle of whiskey in his room with him, something I never saw before in all the months of sitting in that tree. So I definitely knew that something was up.

Then he got this phone call. And he was yelling and screaming into the phone and obviously I couldn't hear what he was saying and then he threw the phone across the room and it hit the wall and it broke and I was like 'Woah,' and he sat down on his bed and put his head into his hands like he was really sad or something and so I was really, really worried about him and I couldn't just do nothing at all, you know? Like, when he was so upset like that. So I decided it was time to try going over the wall.

So I climbed down from the tree (I left my blanket and everything up there) and I went to that one spot on the wall around his house where the drain pipe lines up with the stones so you can climb it and I went up and over the wall. It was so crazy. I was actually in Fisk Estates! I was so excited I wanted to scream but I didn't. I kept really quiet and ran across the grass.

When I got to the main house he was sitting out on that big balcony outside his bedroom and he was drinking and looking really sad. I kind of hid down by one of the columns and watched him for a little while. I was really nervous, you know?

But then I told myself, like, 'Come on, Belinda. This is it. This is your shot.' And I gathered up all my courage and I stepped out into the light and I said hello. Him up on the balcony, me down below. It was like Romeo and Juliet!

He didn't even act surprised or upset or anything to see me. Not like in LA at the fashion show or at that fundraiser where I got caught snipping one of the buttons off his jacket with scissors and he had me arrested (which I totally already forgave him for, by the way). But it was really cold out so I guess he felt bad for me all freezing and shivering and stuff and so he invited me up! He didn't even mention the restraining order or anything about it.

He poured me some of his whiskey, which usually I don't even like but, like, of course I had some with him. And he talked to me all about some problems he was having with his wife who must be a crazy person to treat poor Barron like she does and about a fight he was having with this guy at work about buying some company and he said that the call he got earlier that night was some bad medical news but he wouldn't say any more about that.

And then one drink turned into one more and then one more and he just kept talking and talking and the next thing I knew he was KISSING ME!!!!! Can you effing BELIEVE it??!! And we went into his bedroom and, well, you know . . . :) When I woke up in the morning he was gone already but he very nicely had one of his people help me get out the back way but I still think some of the paparazzi might have seen me but OH WELL!!

Anyways I always knew something like this would happen and now that we're in love for real I just feel like a million trillion billion bucks and I can't wait for him to come get me and sweep me off my feet. I bet he's gonna take me to Paris and Rome and Italy and all around. Anyways I just had to get this all written down here because I'm soooo EXCITED!!!!

Okay, bye, Diary. Until next time.

She closed the eJournal when she reached the end of the entry and looked across the room at the shrine. She gazed for a long time into the dark eyes that glinted at her from the large portrait overlooking the other items. Tears began to roll down her face uncontrollably, and she fell onto her side in bed. She curled into the fetal position, hugging her knees with all her might as her chest wracked with sobs.

"Taken from me," she muttered aloud. "So much taken from me."

Once the crying spell passed, she wiped at her reddened eyes with the back of her hands and slid off the bed onto the floor. Kneeling, she reached beneath the bed and retrieved a small, well-worn shoebox. She removed the lid.

She pulled out a pocket multi-year calendar marked with her handwriting. The scribbled words on the cover read: *Days Waiting for Barron.* Inside, the page marked February 15, 2027 teemed with hearts drawn in many different colors of ink, as well as practiced signatures in loopy letters saying *"Mrs. Belinda Fisk"* over and over. Each day after that had been crossed out with a red X until June 8, 2028, the day of Barron Fisk's death. The subsequent days remained blank.

Then she moved the calendar to one side and grasped the object underneath. She hefted it in her hand, savoring the pressure its weight applied to her palm. As she held it up to examine it more closely, it glinted in the cold moonlight that drifted through the window.

The gun had once belonged to her grandfather. Now, it would help her seek justice for her beloved Barron Fisk.

Chapter Twenty

"It looks like you've got all that under control. Good stuff."

Alan looked over Sharla's shoulder as she picked the lock on the door leading to James Bradford's office.

"How do you know how to do that, anyway?"

"I grew up in a bad part of Baltimore. Picked up a few things."

The duo had managed to sneak into the Fisk Enterprises building undetected thanks to a secret door near a group of dumpsters around the back side of the onyx-colored tower. Sharla knew of the door from occasional errands Fisk would send her on that he wished to keep hidden from everyone else in the building.

"It's only midnight. Should we have waited until later?" Alan fretted.

"We'll be fine. We already made it in and out of Fisk's office in the middle of the day. How is this any worse?"

"Yeah, you're right. I'm not worried. Cool as a cucumber over here, that's what I am."

They both wore all-black clothing with dark ski masks covering their faces. Sharla's long braided hair extended well beyond the bottom of her mask and fed into the neck of the tight long-sleeved T-shirt she had on. Alan's glasses still perched on his nose on the outside of his mask, making him look like the nerdiest thief in history.

"I can't believe we're doing this," he said as he bounced up and down on the balls of his feet. "This is by far the craziest thing I've ever done. But desperate times call for desperate measures, I guess. That saying comes from Hippocrates. Is that right? Yeah, I think it's Hippocrates. In fact, I read a book once—"

"You know," Sharla said, turning back to look at Alan pointedly, "this does require a certain level of concentration. So if you could . . ."

She mimed zipping her lips shut. Alan nodded.

"You got it. I'll be quiet. It's just that this type of situation makes me feel a little antsy. In fact, my therapist once told me that might stem from my mother's tendency to . . ."

Sharla heard a light *click* from the door handle and gave it a twist, pushing the door inward.

"Thank God."

The two crept into the dark office. Alan reached for the light switch before Sharla grabbed his wrist to stop him.

"Someone might see," she whispered. "We'll have to work in the dark." She pointed to one side of the office, indicating that Alan should search there; she would take the other side. They got down to business.

Bradford's office appeared to be designed for utility and nothing else. It spoke of extreme competence and focus. The open-front desk had long, thin, mid century style legs, few drawers, and even fewer accouterments on top: only a single laptop, closed and fitted with a specialized lock that only Bradford's fingerprints could open.

Floating shelves laden with books dotted the walls. A single tall dracaena plant, fake-looking, rested in the corner. The entire office revealed almost nothing about Bradford himself: no family photos or personal belongings or notable keepsakes. This was a man who meant business, and only business.

Alan began by searching a series of shelves and drawers built into the wall on the right side of the room. Sharla started poking around in the shallow desk drawers.

"So, Baltimore, huh?" Alan asked, his back turned to her.

"What?"

"You grew up in Baltimore?"

"Uh, yeah. That's right."

"Good childhood?"

"Good enough."

"Do you have siblings?"

"Yes."

Alan waited to see if she'd continue but was greeted only with the light sounds of bumps and scrapes as Sharla inspected items and then replaced them in their original positions.

"Okay. No more questions. I get it."

There was a lengthy pause as they kept searching.

"I don't mean to pry," Alan went on. "None of my business, I suppose. I thought maybe, since we've gotten a little closer these past couple of weeks, we could converse a bit."

Another long silence.

"I guess you probably have other people to talk to, huh?"

"Don't forget to check any drawers for secret compartments."

"Okay."

Alan moved on to checking for hidden safes behind the few framed items on the wall, mostly corporate-minded inspirational posters mixed with a few photos of Bradford shaking hands with notable conservative governmental figures. After several minutes, Sharla spoke.

"I don't, actually," she said out of nowhere.

"Don't what?"

"Have other people to talk to. I just don't like talking about my childhood that much."

"It was rough, huh?"

"No, I wouldn't say that. My mother created a home for us that was peaceful, full of love. We had what we needed. She did everything that she could. It's just . . ."

"What?"

"I left. I finished college, and I left town. Two of my sisters were still in school, and I knew my mom needed help, but I went anyway. I guess I feel a little guilty."

"Why? That's what you're supposed to do. Spread your wings and all that."

"So you won't be sad when your girls go off into the world?"

"Huh. It's so far off I guess I haven't given it much thought. Yeah, I'll be sad."

"And I feel bad for doing that to my mom. We still talk all the time, but it's not the same. I used to help with the girls, you know?"

"It sounds to me like you're a very good daughter."

"Yeah, right. I was like, 'Goodbye, everybody. I've got to go.'"

"*'And now you've gone and thrown it all away'?*"

Sharla looked affronted. "That's a pretty rude thing to say."

"Oh, no. I wasn't . . . I was trying to do the song lyrics thing. The game you played with Fisk? That's Queen. Bohemian Rhapsody. You don't know Queen?"

Sharla laughed loudly.

"I didn't even . . . Oh, man. That was good. You know, you're all right, Alan Benning."

"*Don't stop me now.*"

"Whoa," Sharla said, her tone shifting sharply. "Okay, I definitely found something here."

She held one of the many books on management that filled the office's floating shelves. The cover read *The Fire Inside*, an exceedingly appropriate title, as it was hollowed out to make space for a handgun and several bullets.

Alan joined her near the office's eastern wall.

"Hell's bells," he said. "That's a gun."

They looked at each other with matching expressions: half excitement, half shock.

"It was him. It was Bradford. I knew it! Ha!" Alan called out triumphantly.

"Hold on, this doesn't necessarily prove anything."

"I bet this is the gun that actually killed Mr. Fisk. The one they found had my fingerprints, sure, but how do we even know it was the gun used? Bradford could have stashed the real weapon here."

"I guess that's possible," Sharla admitted. "We don't know, though."

"It has to be," Alan insisted. "Look at us, Sharla. We're doing it. The investigation is actually working. We found the gun!"

"It certainly is an interesting theory," a third voice rang out from the doorway.

Alan and Sharla both jumped in surprise. They turned, astonished, to see James Bradford standing in the hallway. His stern face looked to be made of stone.

"You think I wouldn't have an alarm system in my office? It's silent, so intruders won't know when it's triggered. I hope you understand now that I am four steps ahead of you at every turn. In fact, I had a pretty strong feeling that this might happen, so I've been renting a room at a nearby hotel, and I came as soon as the alarm went off. I tried to tell you there'd be consequences if you kept snooping around my business."

"Hold on now, Jamie," Sharla said. "Let's not do anything rash."

"Jamie?" Alan blurted out.

"Oh, I won't be doing anything," Bradford said back to her. "That's what I brought my friends for."

He moved backward as Detectives Reyes and Tanner stepped into the doorway.

"You're going to have to come with us," said Reyes.

Alan and Sharla shared a helpless glance.

"*Another one bites the dust,*" Sharla said, eyes filled with worry.

Chapter Twenty-One

Hello, dear reader. It is I, your humble narrator. I must admit that Alan Benning and Sharla Johnson have, throughout this tale, shown much more pluck and stick-to-itiveness than I've grown to expect from you poor people. On the unfortunate occasions when I am forced to interact with the monetarily challenged, I find them to be lazy and prone to giving up at the first minor obstacle placed in their path. So, kudos to those two for so far defying expectations.

Perhaps you have been thinking this whole time that Alan Benning does not warrant the label of "poor person." After all, he owns a house with a four-car garage, and he ranks among the highest executives at the world's most prominent tech firm. Well, you would be wrong. The very thought serves to prove that the economic gap between you and me, dear reader, is as vast as the asteroid belt. Allow me to present to you a short checklist I often use to determine if an individual is properly moneyed:

- Does the individual own multiple houses with their own helipads?

- Does their primary yacht have onboard a separate, smaller yacht?

- Could the individual, if they so wished, purchase an NFL team and move it to Nixa, Missouri as a hilarious practical joke?

- Do they clean their own ears? Or do they have a guy for that?

- Have they ever, at any time, set foot inside of a TJ Maxx?

If someone cannot truthfully answer those questions yes, yes, yes, yes and no, they are poor. Glad we could clear that up.

While I do concede that Alan and Sharla have shown remarkable ingenuity and resilience for members of the beleaguered underclass, the big questions still remain: Who killed Barron Fisk? How did they manage it? And what is the identity of me, your humble narrator?

Prepare yourself, dear reader. For we've only just begun.

Chapter Twenty-Two

Alan found himself back in the same interrogation room he'd occupied just over two weeks before. The same rigid chair bit into the undersides of his legs. The same bright light shone directly into his face. The same beads of sweat ran down the nape of his neck, as if he'd made no progress at all. Right back where he began.

Sharla sat in the next room over, having been separated from Alan the moment that they were jointly escorted into the police station. She remained still, stone-faced and unreadable, her hands placed flat on the table in front of her. Her eyes darted this way and that to take in the room. She stayed silent.

In the hallway outside the adjacent interrogation rooms, Detective Reyes hastily scribbled notes on a piece of paper that she held against the wall. When she finished, she handed the paper to her partner.

"Okay, Tanner," she said slowly. "These are the questions you need to ask Miss Johnson. Can you read those?"

"Yes, I know how to read. I'm not a five-year-old," Tanner said with an edge to his voice. He squinted at the paper. "Wait, what's that word?"

"Prerogative."

"Right. I love pierogies."

Reyes sighed and entered the room where Alan sat. Tanner joined Sharla in the other interrogation room.

Alan's head snapped toward the door the moment it cracked open. He burst into speech.

"Detective Reyes. Oh boy, do I have some information for you. Sharla and I, we've been looking into Mr. Fisk's murder, and I think we might have enough to prove it wasn't me. It was Bradford all along! He's setting me up. First off—"

Detective Reyes held up a hand to stop him. "We are here today because of your unlawful entry into Fisk Enterprises headquarters. We will not be discussing any other charges."

"I know that, but Bradford—"

"No buts," she interrupted him again. "I assure you that we've done our due diligence on any other party that could have been involved in the incident with Mr. Fisk."

"But Bradford has a gun in his office. The same type that was at the crime scene. And we found a shoe in the bush outside Fisk's office window. A shoe in the bush!"

"Mr. Benning, I need to impress upon you the seriousness of your crime. You're interfering with an active police investigation."

"But . . . But the shoe in the bush . . ." Alan said as the hopeful look drained from his eyes.

In the room next door, Sharla gave absolutely no reaction when Tanner entered the room. He sat across from her and placed the piece of paper Reyes had given him flat on the table, smoothing out a few wrinkles with both his hands.

"Okay, Miss Johnson. First question." He began reading. "'Why were you and Mr. Benning breaking into the office of James Bradford tonight?'"

"No comment."

"No comment. Okay, that's fine. Let me go ahead and write that down."

He patted the numerous pockets of his sport coat and pants one after the other, then looked back at Sharla.

"You don't have a pen, do you?"

Sharla stared at him.

"No, of course not. That's okay. I can remember it. 'No comment.' On to question two."

"Mr. Bradford wants to press charges," Reyes told Alan next door. "And, seeing as we caught you red-handed, I'm sure they're going to stick."

Alan released a light whimper.

"Is there anything you want to tell me about why you were breaking and entering?"

"We were looking for evidence, okay? I didn't kill Mr. Fisk, so someone else must have, and I think it was Bradford. You know he's going to be CEO now, right? That's motive right there. And he has a gun in his office. And he knows what shoes I wear. Don't you see?"

"Mr. Bradford has an alibi that has been corroborated by a third party."

"But it's a lie! He left the fundraising event that night, at least for a while. We found an email where he admitted it."

"If you continue to interfere with our investigation, we will be forced to charge you for that as well."

"And he knows what type of shoes I wear to work! You should at least go see the shoe in the bush. Don't you want to see the shoe in the bush?"

"Please stop talking about shoes and bushes, Mr. Benning."

"No comment *again*?" asked Tanner in the other room, scratching his head, "It seems like that's what you're saying for all of these."

"No comment," Sharla said.

"Okay, I get it. These questions aren't getting us anywhere," he said, pushing the paper to one side. "Tell me this, what are you doing running around with Benning? It isn't safe. Don't you know that he's a murderer?"

"No, he isn't."

"And why do you think that? His prints are all over the gun. His footprints are at the scene. He was publicly arguing with Fisk. How are you so sure?"

"Alan couldn't hurt anyone if he tried. Spend some time with him and tell me I'm wrong."

"People can surprise you."

"Not Alan. He's scared of surprises."

Reyes rose from the table. "We're going to have to hold you for breaking and entering until you post bail. Your friend, too."

Alan blanched. "Wait, this was all my idea. Sharla didn't have anything to do with it. It was all me. I forced her to do it."

"I don't believe for a second that you could force that woman to do anything. But she was there, too, so she's just as guilty as you are." Alan groaned and slumped in his chair. "And stop with the amateur sleuthing. Do you understand?"

"But I didn't kill Fisk! If Sharla and I can . . ."

"Have you ever been to prison, Mr. Benning?" Reyes asked curtly.

"Well, no. I haven't."

"Do you have any idea the kinds of things that go on in a men's prison?"

"I've . . . seen documentaries."

"And based on what you've learned from those documentaries, how do you think you'd fare?"

"Um. Poorly, I suppose."

"That may be the understatement of the century," Reyes said. "I hope you can see that I have your best interests at heart. If we catch you again, you will end up in prison much faster than otherwise. Your only hope of staying out is to stop your investigation. And I promise you that whatever documentaries you've seen don't cover half of what you'd experience in there."

"But someone's setting me up."

"But nothing," Reyes said. "If someone else murdered Fisk, we will uncover it. That's our job. This is the end of your involvement. Understood?"

"Understood," Alan replied. He hung his head in defeat.

In the next room over, Tanner set a Fisk brand ePad upright on the table in front of Sharla. It displayed a somewhat grainy black-and-white image: video footage of the interior of an elevator with its doors open. The footage came from the vantage point of a security camera mounted in the top rear corner of the space. Sharla recognized it as one of the elevators in the Fisk Enterprises building.

"I'm not supposed to be showing you this," Tanner said. "But I hope this will let you know who you've been running around with. This is footage from the night of Fisk's murder."

Tanner pressed the screen of the ePad, and the video footage played. It showed Alan entering the elevator with his arms full of a stack of manila folders. He struggled to shift the items so that he could hit a button on the elevator wall with a free finger. Then the doors closed, he waited until they opened again, and he exited the elevator. An uneventful elevator ride. Then the video feed went black.

"Did you see which button he pressed?" Tanner asked.

He rewound the footage to nearly the beginning and then used two fingers to zoom in again and again until the elevator button panel was centered on the screen. When he hit play again, only Alan's hand was visible as it entered the frame and pressed the button for floor thirty-five.

"Floor thirty-five," Tanner announced. "I don't think I have to tell you that the only thing on floor thirty-five is Fisk's office. I bet Alan told you that he didn't even visit Fisk's office that night, is that right?"

Sharla only scowled.

"I'll take that as a yes. He told us the same thing. I hate to say it, Sharla, but your buddy has been lying to you. He did go up to Fisk's office that night. And he almost definitely killed the man. So in my professional opinion, you should stop, you know, hanging out with the guy. On account of he's a murderer."

Sharla sat quietly for long enough that even Tanner realized she was not going to respond. He packed up the ePad and left the room, meeting his partner in the hallway.

"Any luck with Miss Johnson?" Reyes asked.

"No. She was a brick wall."

"Figured as much. Come on, let's go finish getting them processed."

Alan and Sharla spent the rest of the night in holding cells. In the morning, they were released once Sharla was able to post bail for both of them.

The ensuing drive home took place in silence. When Sharla pulled the Volvo to a stop two blocks from Alan's house, he turned to her.

"I'm sorry for getting you tied up in all of this."

"I made my own choices," Sharla replied.

"Thank you for posting my bail."

"Of course."

"Well, I guess that's the end of it."

"The end of what?"

"The investigation," Alan said as if it was obvious. "They're going to charge us with more crimes if we keep going."

Sharla took a deep breath.

"Alan, I'm going to ask you one more time. Did you go up to Fisk's office on the night that he was killed?"

"No," Alan said back to her immediately. "I already told you that."

"Okay then," she responded slowly. "Then, yeah, I guess this is the end of the investigation."

"I appreciate everything you've done for me, Sharla, but it's over. It has to be."

"Uh-huh."

"Goodbye."

Alan climbed out of her car and shut the door. Sharla watched him amble dejectedly down the road for a short while, then started her car and drove away.

Chapter Twenty-Three

Detective Reyes pulled the squad car up to the gate at Fisk Estates around ten o'clock in the morning. Tanner slouched in the passenger seat.

"I don't even know what we're doing here," he grumbled. "We already know it was Benning."

"Mrs. Fisk's phone tracking data is still an important lead. It shows that she travelled to Fisk Enterprises headquarters on the night her husband died. We wouldn't be doing our jobs if we didn't go down every road."

Tanner continued to pout.

After a brief flash of their badges to the pudgy Southern security guard who manned the gatehouse outside the Estate grounds, they were waved through and cleared to approach the main house itself.

Standing on the broad front porch, Tanner pulled the thick cord that served as a doorbell, and the sound of deep, rolling bells that wouldn't have been out of place in a small Italian village washed over them. Even Fisk's doorbell had class.

A young female attendant welcomed the detectives and led them through the cavernous entryway and into one of the mansion's living rooms. The far wall consisted of floor-to-ceiling windows, spotless and two stories high. Various oversized canvases displaying Renaissance-era works of art covered the off-white walls.

The furniture—a long L-shaped sofa and three matching armchairs with accompanying side tables made from a light-colored wood—clustered in one sunken segment of the room, aside from a grand piano positioned near the towering windows.

Rebecca Fisk sat at the piano awaiting them, dressed in a thin, low-cut T-shirt and a cardigan so oversized that it looked more like a rug she had draped around herself than a piece of clothing. A delicate, lilting piano melody filled the room as Reyes and Tanner came in. Rebecca watched them enter from the piano bench.

"Thank you for seeing us, Mrs. Fisk," Reyes began. "That sounds lovely."

"That's very kind."

Rebecca pressed pause on an ePhone resting on the piano's top. The melody cut out abruptly.

"Someday I should learn to play."

Reyes and Tanner exchanged bemused looks.

"Some new information has come to light in our investigation of your husband's murder," Reyes said, "and we have a few additional questions to ask you."

"I've already told you everything I know."

"And we'd appreciate your continued cooperation."

"Oh!" Rebecca said. "Where are my manners? Can I get either of you anything to drink?"

"No, we're fine," said Reyes.

Tanner asked, "Do you have any Sunny D?" at the same time.

Rebecca picked up a small bell from a nearby end table and gave it a ring. The attendant who had seen them in reappeared in the doorway.

"This is Tabitha," Rebecca said. "We brought her back on staff once Dr. Wu tired of acting as my porter." She turned to the young woman. "Tabitha. Go fetch the detective some . . . What was it again?"

"Sunny D. It's like orange juice, but not."

"We don't need any Sunny D," Reyes insisted.

"Make it happen," Rebecca said to Tabitha, who bowed slightly and disappeared from sight. "Please sit down," Rebecca then said to Reyes and Tanner as she settled herself into one of the armchairs. The detectives sat together on the leather sofa.

"Mrs. Fisk," Reyes said, "you'd previously told us that you were at home all evening on the night that your husband was killed."

"That's right."

"Well, we obtained tracking information from the Fisk databases corresponding to your ePhone, and it appears that you, or at least your phone, did in fact leave the premises. Looks like it was about . . ." Reyes opened up the case file and scanned through the notes with her pointer finger, "10:20 that night. Care to tell us where you went?"

"What? I didn't go anywhere. I had half a bottle of wine and watched some television. I was in bed by ten."

"Then how do you think your phone got to Fisk Enterprises and back?" Reyes asked carefully.

Tabitha returned at this point with a tall glass of orange liquid.

"I apologize. I was unable to locate any, ahem, Sunny D, but we do have this freshly squeezed orange juice."

"Ah," said Tanner. "No thank you, then."

The attendant looked surprised for a brief moment, then nodded her head politely and went back out the way she had entered.

"I only like Sunny D," Tanner said by way of explanation. Reyes rolled her eyes.

"Rebecca. May I call you Rebecca?" Reyes said, attempting to steer the conversation back on track.

"Certainly."

"We know for a fact that your phone traveled from here to Fisk headquarters on the night in question. You're saying that you had nothing to do with that?"

"That's exactly what I'm saying."

"Okay. Is there anyone who could have taken your phone and used it without you noticing?"

"That's possible, I suppose. I may have had a few pills with the wine, and sometimes that can make me a bit . . . tuned out."

"Who else was around?"

"The doctor was the only other person on the estate that night." Rebecca rang the bell again, and the attendant materialized. "Tabitha, bring me Wu, please." Tabitha left wordlessly as Rebecca turned back to the detectives. "Do you think Dr. Wu could have done it? I suspected as much. You know, he was included in Barron's will to the tune of forty million dollars. I knew he must have done it."

"We're not saying anything like that. We're simply being thorough."

An uneasy silence fell over the room. A few minutes later, the attendant came back with Dr. Wu in tow.

"What is it you need now, Mrs. Fisk?" Dr. Wu complained. "I was in the middle of . . . Oh, hello, Officers."

"Wu," said Rebecca, "the night that Barron was murdered. Did you take my ePhone at any point?"

"Of course not."

"They're saying that someone carrying my phone drove to Fisk Enterprises and back. You're sure you didn't use it that night?"

"I have my own phone, Mrs. Fisk. As you well know."

"Well, you were the only other person here that night."

"Then the tracking information must be faulty," Wu insisted.

"Or, one of you is lying," said Tanner. Reyes shot him a warning look.

"We'll have to keep looking into it then," Reyes said, standing up. Tanner followed suit. "Thank you for your time."

As they headed for the door, Tanner stopped short near Dr. Wu.

"Hold on a minute," he said.

"They don't have any Sunny D, Tanner. Drop it."

"No, not that. Dr. Wu, are those your shoes?"

"Which shoes?"

"Those shoes."

"The ones that I have on?"

"Yeah."

"You're asking if the shoes that I currently have on my feet are my shoes?"

"Yes."

"Yes, Officer, I generally wear my own shoes."

"Okay. Thanks."

With that, Reyes and Tanner left.

Outside, they trotted down the steps of the front porch toward their cruiser parked a few feet away. Reyes stopped with her hand on the driver's side door.

"What was all that shoe business about?" she asked.

"The shoes Dr. Wu is wearing. They're the same exact ones that Benning had. The ones that left the footprint at the scene."

"Wow. I can't believe I didn't catch that."

"That, plus the money he inherited and the possibility that he took Mrs. Fisk's phone, and I think he might be an actual suspect."

Reyes gave a smirk.

"See? Now aren't you glad we came out here?"

"Not really. I thought we already had this in the bag. This just means more work."

"Well, I'm impressed. That's some good detecting, partner."

"You think we can stop on the way back to the station and get some Sunny D? I have a real craving now."

"You know what? Yes, we can."

They both climbed into the car happily.

Chapter Twenty-Four

James Bradford didn't even like caviar. It sat on the table before him simply because it was an expensive item that everyone knew was an expensive item. He spread a small dollop on a crostini and ate it, trying not to grimace at the extreme saltiness. He turned his attention toward his companion, hoping to appear so dazzled by her riveting conversational skills that he completely forgot about the very salty, very expensive appetizer. Bradford loved the finer things in life, even if he hated them.

"So, are you close with your brother?" Sylvia asked.

She wore a tight, low-cut red dress and pearl earrings. Her dark hair coiled atop her head in an exquisitely arranged bun. She graced Bradford with a dazzling smile.

The table between them featured a half-drunk bottle of Sine Qua Non Patine Syrah, the nearly untouched platter of Russian Volga Reserve Ossetra caviar and a tablecloth crisp and white enough to blind a person. Twin flickering candles that dripped wax onto golden dishes at their bases provided the low, intimate lighting in their booth.

"Why don't you tell me about your siblings?" Bradford deflected while refilling Sylvia's wine glass.

"Oh. All right. Well, I have two sisters, one older and one younger. The older one, Patricia, does administration in a veterinary hospital in Portland, and you wouldn't believe . . ."

Sylvia's voice faded out of Bradford's consciousness as he engaged his 'I'm listening intently' date night face: one eyebrow raised slightly above the other, hint of a smile, intense eye contact. He nodded occasionally to demonstrate his high level of friendly agreeability.

Three weeks earlier, on the night of June 6th, Bradford had noticed Sylvia's beauty from across the crowded VIP room of a nightclub called Splash. He had approached her confidently, touched her lightly on the arm, and promptly admitted that he lacked a date for an upcoming fundraising dinner and ball in two days' time. It was for a good cause, he'd assured her, and made subtle mention that the cost to attend was over $10,000 a head. She had immediately agreed, writing her phone number on a nearby cocktail napkin and planting a perfect red imprint of her lips right next to the numbers.

On June ninth, the police had contacted Bradford regarding the untimely demise of his boss and mentor, asking for verification of his whereabouts. This had forced him to reluctantly reach back out to his raven-haired date from the night before in order to ensure that their provided recollections of the evening lined up. They'd established a version of events that conveniently omitted Bradford's unexplained two-hour absence toward the tail end of the event. The price for Sylvia's discretion was another date. Bradford managed to postpone the payment of that debt for nearly three weeks. James Bradford, you see, frequently boasted about never going out with the same woman twice. Eventually, though, Sylvia had put her foot down and demanded to see him again, twisting Bradford's arm with a subtle hint that she might, possibly, just maybe, come clean to the cops.

And so, Bradford found himself in the corner booth of his favorite restaurant on a rare second date, listening to Sylvia's continuing monologue with hollow eyes.

" . . . and the iguana had been in the mailbox the entire time!"

Sylvia concluded her story, laughing a bit too loudly for Bradford's taste. His displeasure flashed on his face before he corrected himself, plastering on an obliging smile.

"Well. How about that," he said flatly.

"So. Tell me about your job, Mr. Big Shot." She reached across the table to touch his arm. "What's it like being a tech genius?"

"Much more boring than you'd imagine. Meetings mostly."

"Come on. It can't all be boring."

She gave a skillful flutter of her eyelashes that caused Bradford to lean forward a bit.

"There is one project that my boss was excited about. Before he . . . you know."

"Yeah?"

"He called it the Fiskiverse. To hear him talk about it was . . . What's the best word? Mesmerizing. Transcendent, maybe. It was his life's dream."

"What is it?"

"He pitched it as a virtual online world. VR, you know? People can log in, play games, talk to each other, watch movies. But it's so much more. There's a side to the Fiskiverse that he didn't tell anyone about. Well, anyone but me." He chuckled. "It's going to change absolutely everything."

"How?"

"I can't be too specific. You wouldn't understand it anyway. But trust me when I say it's a game changer."

"Why wouldn't I understand it?"

Bradford let out a breathy laugh. "Please," he said dismissively.

Sylvia sat back. "I think I need to use the ladies' room."

She rose and left the table.

In her absence, Bradford scanned the restaurant surrounding their cushy corner booth. The place had thick burgundy carpeting and ornate golden sconces on the walls that matched the candle holders on each table. The waiters wore black tuxedos with spotless white shirts. A large crystalline chandelier hung in the entryway, which opened into the bar area.

The bar, about thirty feet in length, had a smooth marble top and tall stools with plush velvet seats. Bradford's eye fell upon a beautiful blonde woman with a heart-shaped face who sat at the bar daintily sipping a martini and glancing toward the entryway every few seconds. He rose from the table and sidled up to her.

"Expecting someone?" he asked in his deepest and smoothest voice. The woman turned away from the entrance to look at him briefly.

"Um, yes."

"Then allow me to be the unexpected." He took one of her hands and kissed it. "James Bradford. CEO of Fisk Enterprises. Maybe you've heard of it."

The woman turned toward him again with a skeptical look that seemed to ask if he was actually pulling this move.

"Didn't that guy die?"

"I, uh, well, yes. He did. I'm his . . . you know. I'll be his replacement."

"Great."

"You ever ride in a self-flying helicopter? Once I'm CEO, I'll be able to summon one on my phone any time I want. Pretty cool, right? I'd love to show you around in it."

"James?"

Sylvia stood a few feet away. Bradford still held the blonde woman's hand in his.

"Go on to the table," Bradford said to Sylvia. "I'll be right there."

"Are you hitting on another woman in the middle of our date?"

Bradford dropped the woman's hand and turned to Sylvia, letting out a sigh of great inconvenience.

"I said I would be right there. Okay?"

"Oh," Sylvia said softly. "So that's how it is."

Bradford groaned and rolled his neck as if stretching for a marathon.

"What do you want from me? You blackmailed me into this date. You know that, I know that. So what did you expect? How about I buy you a car? Huh? What kind of car do you want? Name it."

Sylvia fought back tears.

"You're a bastard, James Bradford."

She rushed back to their booth to grab the thin wrap she'd come in wearing and stormed from the restaurant. Bradford turned back to the blonde woman with a look of incredulity on his face.

"Some people, huh?" he asked.

The woman picked up her martini glass and moved several seats away from him. Bradford threw up his hands in outrage.

"Like I'm the asshole here. You have any idea what I spent on this dinner?" He sighed and leaned his back against the bar, his shoulders drooping in defeat.

"Goddamn caviar," he said to no one.

Chapter Twenty-Five

THAT SAME NIGHT, MERE hours after growing suspicious of Dr. Wu, Detective Tanner sat tucked away in the small office that he shared with his partner, laser focused on the project in front of him: building a desktop tower out of sticky note pads.

He placed another pad on top of the already precarious structure with the practiced precision of an orthopedic surgeon. As he sat back to admire his handiwork, the door to the office flew open and Reyes rushed in.

"You're not going to believe this!"

Tanner, startled, banged his knee on the underside of his desk. The tower toppled before his eyes. Notepads tumbled all over the floor.

"Aw, come on," he moaned. "I was at a personal best."

"Shut up and listen."

Tanner sat up straight in his chair. "What's up?"

"I was questioning the members of the Fisk board again, trying to get some info on this Dr. Wu character."

"Over video chat?"

"That's right. They're all still out of the country."

"Get anything incriminating?"

"Not on Wu, no. But one of them let something interesting slip. Check this out."

She sat at her desk and logged into the beat-up, years-out-of-date desktop computer. She accessed her work email and double-clicked a file that had been sent over by the Fisk Enterprises security office.

A new window popped up on the computer screen that displayed a video, security footage of the backside of the Fisk Building. It showed a dumpster area surrounded by a thick cinderblock wall. Tidily trimmed hedges hugged the side of the building itself, and a short row of electrical generators fed into the building through thick, metal-covered cords. If not for the hedges swaying gently in an easy night breeze, it might have been mistaken for a still photo.

"What are we watching here?" asked Tanner.

"Just wait. This is from the night of Fisk's death."

After a few moments of uninteresting calm, a figure entered the frame wearing a long, dark cloak. A hood pulled up over the person's head hid any possible identifying features. The figure approached the back side of the building, casting glances from side to side. They kneeled in the grass right next to the cinderblock wall that housed the building's large refuse containers and began digging into the soft dirt with one hand. They unearthed something small and round. It turned out to be a lid, which flipped upward to reveal a metal lever built directly into the soil. The person's hand grasped the lever and pulled. As they did so, a section of the building's rear wall popped free along a seam in the bricks. It swung open like a door.

"A secret entrance?" Tanner asked in awe.

"Rich people love a secret entrance," Reyes responded, and she's not wrong. One of the joys that you poor people will likely never experience in this life is visiting a friend's house and trying to guess what mechanisms might trigger a hidden door. I can't count the number of times I've discovered acquaintances sneaking away from my dinner parties to pull on random candlesticks and knock on sections of wall searching for that telltale hollow sound that betrays a passageway behind. Only one has ever found it: a self-made media mogul with a fondness for giving away cars to her studio audience and a surprising affinity for hunting humans on her private island. For legal reasons, she shall remain nameless.

Reyes went on, "Apparently Fisk had it built in during construction. One of the board members told me. We didn't check this camera's footage because it's usually just custodial staff dumping garbage. Keep watching."

The figure closed the lever compartment and re-covered it with the loose sod, then rose to their feet. They heaved the hidden door the rest of the way open and skirted inside. Then they made a mistake. The person turned around to pull the door closed behind them and in doing so exposed their face to the security camera high on the wall near the building's far corner.

Reyes hit the spacebar on her keyboard, pausing the video's playback. She pressed another key to zoom in several times. The face was unmistakable. Both Reyes and Tanner had seen it many times on news websites and tech publications.

"Aristotle Cunningham?" Tanner blurted out, shocked.

"That's right. Remember what Sharla Johnson told us the first time we spoke to her? That Cunningham and Fisk had a meeting scheduled for that night at ten o'clock? Look at the timestamp."

She pointed to the top right corner of the video, where the time and date showed in small white numbers: 06/08/2028, 21:55.

"Twenty-one fifty-five? What's that—a code?"

"It's military time, Tanner. It means 9:55 PM. How do you not know that?"

"Don't get mad at me. It could have just said that."

"You're missing the point. Cunningham did meet with Fisk that night."

"But he sent us the video footage of his conference call. Our tech guys verified it. How could he be in two places at once?"

"Beats me."

"Then there's Wu," Tanner said, thinking out loud, "who very well could have left the footprint at the scene. And I don't think we can rule out Mrs. Fisk, either. It's still possible she was the one who drove with her phone to Fisk headquarters that night."

"But the majority of the evidence still points to Benning."

"I thought cases were supposed to get less confusing the more you worked them. My head hurts like I ate ice cream too fast."

"That's called thinking, Tanner. Most of us do it all the time."

"Well, I don't like it."

The door to their office swung open again. A young deputy leaned in the doorway.

"Reyes. There's someone here to see you. I think you're going to want to hear what she has to say."

Reyes and Tanner shared an intrigued glance before she made for the door.

"Clean up these sticky notes," she said on her way out.

"You're the one who made me spill them."

"Don't be asinine, Tanner."

"I'm not asinine. You're asinine."

Once Reyes left, Tanner scooped up his ePhone.

"Jennings, define 'asinine.'"

Reyes followed the young deputy to Interrogation Room B.

Inside, she found a young woman with her elbows on the table and her face in her hands. Her torso heaved noticeably as tears leaked out from the sides of her palms. She wore an oversized gray sweatshirt and black sweatpants with a few stains. Her dark hair hung loose around her shoulders. She looked up when Reyes entered, her face smeared with tears, eyes puffy and red.

"I have to come clean about something," she said between snivels. "I need to talk to you about James Bradford."

Reyes expertly took down Sylvia's revised account of the night of Fisk's death, scribbling notes rapidly on her ePad as the young woman spoke: Sylvia had accompanied Bradford to the fundraiser as she'd said previously, but at one point in the evening her date had disappeared for a little under two hours with no explanation. She had no idea where he had gone. She was unable to pinpoint the exact time of his departure or return, but she knew he was missing for at least an hour and a half. She was sorry for lying; she had only done it because she believed Bradford was innocent, and she thought that he may have feelings for her, but it had recently become clear that the situation was otherwise. She didn't want to get in trouble, and she wanted to help however she could. She spoke through tears during the entire confession. Reyes thanked her for coming clean and then stepped back out into the hallway. She returned to the office to fill Tanner in on the situation.

"So now we have Cunningham, Dr. Wu, Mrs. Fisk and Bradford all potentially traveling to Fisk Enterprises that night," Reyes said, "not to mention Benning, who definitely was there. Still think this is a cut-and-dry case?"

"I don't know what I believe anymore," Tanner admitted while rubbing his eyes. "You could tell me Fisk was killed by Ronald McDonald and I'd consider it. Who the hell did it? Who killed Barron Fisk?"

Chapter Twenty-Six

Alan, after officially putting an end to the investigation with Sharla and exiting her brown Volvo near his house, shuffled his way up the walk. He ignored the few media members who still camped out, shouting questions at him and snapping his photo on their ePhones. His empty stomach growled as he approached the front door.

His tired eyes remained downcast with such determination that he had the key in the lock and the door halfway open before he noticed anything awry. He stopped with one foot over the threshold to look closer. There, at eye level on the external side of the door, was what appeared to be a small slit carved into the wood.

A thin sliver of a notch was missing from the otherwise smooth surface of the door. It looked as if someone had stabbed something into it. For a moment he scowled at it—this mysterious mark in his front door, maybe a bit under two inches long. He ran a finger over the spot to be certain it was not some strange trick of the morning light. Sure enough, to the right of the peephole, a nick. Puzzled, he went in and locked the door behind him.

Alone in the entryway, he called out.

"Hannah? Girls?"

He received no response.

He trudged into the kitchen to find it empty. He checked the living room and the girls' bedroom on the ground floor before plodding up the stairs. Hearing movement in his and Hannah's bedroom, he went straight there.

"Hannah, do you know what happened to the front door? There's a . . . What are you doing?"

Hannah moved hurriedly around their shared bedroom. Two large suitcases sat out on the bed. Toys and small clothes for the girls filled one. The other seemed to hold the majority of the contents of Hannah's closet. Their daughters lay splayed out on their tummies near the head of the bed, the only part not occupied by the luggage. With a flustered look on her face, Hannah added items to the second suitcase. The skin from her neck upward flushed a deep red.

"I meant to be gone before you got back," she said without stopping what she was doing or looking at him.

"What's going on here?"

"I can't take it anymore. I'm going to my parents' in Modesto, and the girls are coming with me."

Alan shook his head, flummoxed.

"Because I got arrested?"

"Because of everything! You're never here to help with the girls. You're out running around playing RoboCop."

"RoboCop? Look, the investigation is over. I called everything off with Sharla. I can be here now."

"We don't even have money to buy groceries."

"You know that's temporary."

"I can't be cooped up like this anymore. Is that a good enough reason for you? I'm going crazy in this house with those people out front all day. I can only go jogging at night when they leave."

"Okay. You're right. Let's all go then. Give me twenty minutes to pack up, and we'll all get out of here."

"No, Alan. You're the problem. As long as you're around, we're all going to be haunted by this situation."

"Then I'll sneak out the back and meet you a few blocks away. No one has to know I went with you. We'll disappear."

"I've made up my mind."

"Hannah, these might be my last weeks with the three of you, we can't spend them apart."

She finally stopped packing to look him in the eyes.

"I'm leaving you, Alan."

A short, high-pitched laugh escaped Alan's throat. His mouth flapped open and shut as he floundered for a response.

"No. But . . . we love each other."

"It's time. We haven't been happy in so long."

"I'm happy," he insisted. "Who's not happy? I'm happy!"

"Well, I'm not."

Hannah closed up both suitcases with a practiced zipping motion and hoisted them onto their wheels. She shepherded the girls off the bed.

"Now, hold on a moment," Alan said. He remained in the doorway, blocking her exit. "We can talk through this."

"This isn't the life that I wanted."

"Is this about the money? Because we'll get it all back."

Hannah didn't acknowledge the question. Instead, she said, "And now your stupid investigation is putting the girls in danger. It's too much."

"How am I putting the girls in danger?"

Hannah gestured toward the vertical dresser against the opposite wall. Resting on top of it was a piece of paper, folded into tri-sections like a letter, and a large hunting knife with a gleaming white marble handle. Its blade, about two inches wide at its thickest point, met a gleamingly polished handle. The paper bore a gash in the center as if the knife had been forced through it. Alan went over to the dresser with a perplexed look on his face and touched the knife handle gently.

"Where did this come from?"

"That was stuck in the front door this morning. Along with the note."

Alan picked up the piece of paper that sat next to the knife and unfolded it slowly. In cleanly typed letters, it said:

"Quit digging around if you know what's good for you. There are more knives where this came from."

"Bradford," Alan said to himself under his breath. "This has to be Bradford."

Hannah took advantage of the momentary distraction to move with the girls from the bedroom to the top of the stairs in the hallway outside. Alan rushed after her.

"Hannah, wait," he said as he unthinkingly aided her by taking one of the suitcases. "I can see why you're upset. But I know who did this. And I'm done investigating, so we won't have any problems anyway."

By the time he finished talking, they had reached the foot of the stairs. Hannah went back up to carry the girls down.

"Let's not make any rash decisions," Alan said with measured calm upon her return.

"Goodbye, Alan."

"No." Alan raised up his chest. "I am the man of the house. I kill the spiders now. And I say you're staying."

Hannah failed to reply, continuing to maneuver the bags to the door.

"What . . . But . . . You're leaving because of this?" he asked weakly, holding up the note.

"It's not because of the note."

"Then it's the money. I can provide for you, Hannah. I can. What do you want? Once my accounts are unfrozen . . ."

"There's somebody else."

Alan's face slackened.

"You're cheating on me?"

Hannah gave a light grimace.

"Since when?"

She sighed and dropped her shoulders. She cocked her head to one side with a look of impatience.

"God, Alan. What world do you live in?"

She humped the luggage over the threshold of the front door with a child in each arm as Alan watched on, still and forlorn. She closed the door behind her without another word.

Alan stared blankly at the door for a long time. Then, his gaze fell back to the note in his hand.

There are more knives where this came from.

He ripped the paper to shreds and let them fall to the floor. Then he pulled his ePhone from his pocket and dialed.

"Sharla," he said, "I changed my mind. Investigation's back on."

CHAPTER TWENTY-SEVEN

OVER THE NEXT TWO days, Alan called Sharla thirty-four times.

His requests for her to come over and continue looking into Fisk's death turned into demands. On the rare occasion that she answered, she hemmed and hawed over the phone, coming up with excuse after excuse as to why she was unavailable. In the end, Alan's dogged insistence won out, and Sharla appeared on his doorstep shortly before noon.

She entered his house with her hands glued to her sides. She remained near the front door as Alan marched around his cluttered living room in a frenzy. Stacks of printed-out papers covered nearly every surface in the room: news articles from the night of the murder, official police statements provided to the press, gossip blogs spouting wild theories, and biographical information about the individuals he considered suspects. Alan had scrawled on many of the papers in red ink using a rushed, sloppy hand that did not resemble his usual careful script. Dirty dishes and food delivery containers littered the space. Sharla retreated back toward the door. She soaked in the scene with worried eyes.

"You're late," was the first thing out of Alan's mouth. "Okay, let's get down to it."

He sat in the only open seat on the sofa. His weight caused a tall pile of papers next to him to fall onto the floor, but he paid this no notice.

"Where is Hannah?" Sharla asked. "And the girls?"

"Huh?" Alan responded, leafing through a different stack of papers. "Oh, they're gone. Went to Hannah's parents'. That's okay, though. It lets me focus more on what matters. All this."

He gestured to the disaster of a room around him.

"Are you sure you don't want to take a break?" Sharla suggested. "Maybe we can go somewhere for a bite."

Alan looked at her as if she'd suggested a trip to Mars.

"A break? No, I don't want a break. I want to solve this damn case so I can get my life back."

Sharla reluctantly moved further into the room and lowered herself onto an ottoman, one of the few surfaces not covered in papers.

"What even is all of this?"

"Research!" Alan answered loudly. "A lot of it is about Bradford. There has to be something that we missed. For instance, did you know that he was born on March twenty-fourth? That makes him an Aries. And according to this astrology website I found, Aries is the sign most prone to angry outbursts or fits of rage. That sure sounds like a murderer, doesn't it?"

"You believe in astrology?"

"Maybe now."

"I was thinking we should move on from Bradford."

Alan's eyes darted to her.

"Move on? But he's our most promising suspect. We have a potential murder weapon, a motive, a huge hole in his alibi. Why would we move on?"

"I just think we've been focused a little too narrowly on him. Maybe there's something we're overlooking about one of the others."

"Okaaay," Alan said. "That's not crazy. Let's take a look at Cunningham. Check out this article I found from *Business Weekly*."

Alan hopped to his feet and dug through a nearby tower of papers with frantic energy.

"Here we go!" he cried triumphantly, holding up a stapled article. He handed it over to Sharla. "According to that, the virtual reality branch of Cunningham's company has been absolutely bleeding money lately. Fisk's death saved his company billions and kept

Cunningham from having to lick Fisk's boots to get a bailout."

Sharla said, "And I know for a fact that Mr. Fisk had me set an appointment with Cunningham the night he died. There's no way I imagined that."

"Right. But the footage of his all-night video call was verified as authentic by the police. So, unless he somehow managed to be in two places at once, he's got a strong alibi."

"So, who else should we consider? Maybe someone who worked with Fisk more directly?"

"I'm glad you brought that up. We may have a whole new suspect."

He handed her a local news article, and she perused it. He returned to pacing.

"This is about Rebecca Fisk," Sharla said. "We already suspected her."

"It's *quoting* Rebecca Fisk. Look at what she's saying. She thinks that Dr. Wu might be behind the whole thing. She claims that Wu used her phone to travel to Fisk Headquarters that night. It makes sense to me. Maybe the guy was tired of taking care of Fisk after so many years. Plus, we know he and Bradford were up to something shady that night. Doesn't that make sense to you?"

"I guess so."

"But again, that leads us back to Bradford. He's still our best lead. Why do you keep steering us away from him?"

Sharla stared at him and, after a brief pause, said, "Not sure what you mean."

"Oh! And there's something else I found! I'll send it to you."

He hit a few buttons on the screen of his ePad, and Sharla's phone dinged a notification. She pulled it out of her pocket.

"It has to do with Leonid Ledbedev. We nearly forgot about him, huh? Turns out he was allowed to keep a tiny fraction of company stock when he got locked away. But that tiny amount has over the years amassed into a sizable fortune. He definitely could have afforded to hire somebody to kill Fisk."

Sharla didn't bother to read the article. She set her phone down. Her gaze remained on Alan as his pacing picked up speed.

"If we could find a way to get access to Ledbedev's accounts, we could check for any suspicious transactions. What do you know about computer hacking?"

"Alan." Sharla's tone caused him to stop in his tracks. "Are you okay?"

"I'm great!"

She continued watching him with doubt in her eyes. Then she spoke.

"I know that you went up to Mr. Fisk's office that night."

"What?" he blurted out. His face contorted into a look of confusion.

"The cops have the security footage from the elevator. They showed it to me. You went up to the thirty-fifth floor. His office is the only thing on that floor. They know you've been lying. I know you've been lying. I want you to tell me the truth."

"Are you joking right now?"

"Not in the least."

"They showed you a video of me on an elevator, and now you think I'm the killer?"

"You swore to me that you didn't go to his office that night."

"I didn't!"

"That's a lie."

"Damn it, Sharla!"

He threw his ePad across the room. It smashed against the far wall, and the screen shattered.

"You're doubting me now? After all we've been through? My own family has abandoned me. I thought you were the one person I could trust."

"I'm only asking for an explanation."

"I don't owe you any explanation!" he bellowed. "I'm innocent! I don't owe you or anybody else a damn thing! My life has been turned upside down. *My* life!"

His face grew red, and his breath came in huffs. Sharla stood.

"I think it's best that I go."

She hurried to the door and slithered out before Alan could say anything further.

Alan, alone again, seethed with anger. He leaned down to pick up his broken ePad from the corner but stopped when he noticed something resting on the ottoman Sharla had only just occupied. She'd left behind her smartphone in her rush to get away. He stomped over to it.

As he stretched out his hand, right before he made contact with it, the phone gave two short buzzes and the screen lit up. Sharla had received a text message, which popped up on the screen. Alan couldn't help but see it.

The message read: "*Did he buy it?*" The contact name: James Bradford.

"Hell's bells," Alan said aloud.

Chapter Twenty-Eight

Alan stared at Sharla's cellphone in his hand until the screen went idle again, resuming a blankness that mirrored his expression.

He trudged to his house's front door and pulled it open.

Outside, the sky stretched blue and cloudless. A calm, clear day. He saw Sharla halfway up his front walk heading his way. She had clearly realized that, in her haste to rush out, she had neglected to grab her phone. She approached him with an obstinate look on her face.

"I forgot my . . ." she began before spotting the phone in Alan's hand. "Oh. Thank you."

She reached out her hand toward Alan, palm upward, expecting him to return the forgotten ePhone, but was greeted instead by disbelieving eyes above Alan's slightly agape mouth.

"What is it?"

"Bradford?" he managed to gasp out. "You and Bradford? This whole time?"

"I . . . What?"

"You and Bradford."

"What are you talking about exactly?" Sharla asked carefully.

"You and Bradford! You and Bradford!" he yelled at her.

"Alan, tell me what you mean."

"It's no use playing dumb, Sharla. I know. No wonder you've been trying to move the investigation away from him. You've been working with him! Probably the whole time."

"No. Alan, you don't understa—"

"So it *was* him. I knew it. He killed Fisk, and you helped him get away with it."

"That simply isn't true."

"What did he offer you? Money? Or maybe a high-level position once he's installed as CEO. Was that it?"

"You've got to listen to me."

"Tell me. I want to know how much it took for you to give up the life of the boss you supposedly cared so much for."

"I didn't—"

"And what about me? You didn't know me well then, so you thought it was fine to toss my life down the drain?"

"None of this is—"

"Whose idea was it to frame me? Yours or his? It's perfect. It would look like revenge for all the poison that Fisk was spewing about me to the media. Well done, really. Bravo."

"You've got it all wrong!"

"You won't get away with it. I'm going to the police right now."

"Alan, stop! That isn't what happened. I'm not helping Bradford get away with anything."

"I saw the text. He messaged you asking if I believed your BS."

"If you'll let me come in, I can explain everything."

"You're not coming back in my house. In fact, you can get the hell out of here. I don't ever want to see you again."

"Give me my phone. I can clear all of this up."

"You're a murderer," Alan spat at her with as much hatred as he could muster.

"*I'm* a murderer?" Sharla echoed, offended. "No, no, no, my friend. *You're* the one who lied about visiting Mr. Fisk's office that night. If anything, *you're* the murderer!"

Alan's neighbor, watering the hanging ferns on his porch across the street, looked over at Alan and Sharla. He shot straight up like a startled prairie dog. He stared at them for a long moment with a blank expression. His garden hose continued limply spewing water onto the wooden boards of the porch.

"Everything okay over there?" he called meekly.

"Go back inside, Kevin!" Alan barked at him.

The neighbor hurriedly obliged, dropping the running hose, which began to form a puddle on his deck. The lock on the man's front door clicked audibly.

"How dare you betray me like this," Alan said to Sharla.

"How dare you read my text messages!" she fired back.

"I didn't mean to. The phone lit up while it was in my hand. '*Did he buy it?*' Bradford texted you. James freaking Bradford!"

"Did it ever occur to you that text might be about something else?"

"Right. You've just been in casual conversation with a cold-blooded murderer?" Alan asked mockingly.

"I recently got my realtor's license, okay?" Sharla said.

Alan, taken aback by the sudden change of topic, blinked a few times.

"What?"

"I'm going to be a realtor. I'm sick of working as an assistant. A few months back I mentioned it to Bradford, and he asked me to help him offload one of his lake houses. You can read our whole conversation if you want. Just give me the phone."

With a begrudging look, Alan handed over the ePhone. Sharla unlocked it with her thumbprint and pulled up the texting app. Then, she gave it back to him and watched as he scrolled through the full conversation.

"So," Alan said slowly, "when he texted '*Did he buy it...*'"

"He was talking about a house on Spreckels Lake. A property he's selling. I just came from a showing."

"So you have been working with Bradford."

Sharla sighed.

"Okay. Yes, I guess that's technically true. But on a real estate deal, not on any kind of grand conspiracy."

"And that's why you've been trying to downplay him in our investigation?"

"Kind of."

"And that comment he made when he caught us tailing him. That you were being unprofessional?"

"This is what he meant, yes."

"Why didn't you tell me?"

"It's . . . It's a bit more complicated than I'd like to admit," Sharla said, touching her ear.

"What do you mean?"

"I don't want to get into it."

"Sharla," Alan prodded bluntly. "I think we're past the point of keeping secrets now."

"No. I'm not going to—"

"Just tell me!"

Sharla sighed. "I was sleeping with him, okay?" She spat it out like a bitter pill. "We were lovers. Happy now?"

"Ah," Alan said, a bit startled. "Okay."

"It wasn't anything serious. We'd meet a couple times a week to, you know, blow off some steam. We both had stressful jobs."

"I get it," Alan admitted. "He's a good-looking man. Probably a murderer, but undoubtedly handsome."

"I didn't want to look into him as a suspect because it kills me that I could have . . . That I might have . . . That I could misjudge someone so severely."

"Yeah. I can understand that."

"All right," Sharla said roughly, crossing her arms, "your turn to be honest."

"About what?"

"You lied about going to Mr. Fisk's office that night. Why do that if you're innocent?"

"I didn't lie."

"I saw the video of you on the elevator. The police showed it to me, Alan."

"I didn't go to his office. I went up to the thirty-fifth floor with the intention of doing so, but I turned around the moment I got off the elevator. I realized I didn't need his input after all, and I went straight back down to my desk. That's probably why whoever erased the footage cut it there. To leave out the part where I turned right around."

Sharla dropped her hands to her side. "I'm supposed to just believe that? I think I've given you more than enough benefit of the doubt."

"If I had the footage from the hallway outside Fisk's office, you could see that I'm not lying. But I don't. All I have is the truth."

Sharla took a long moment to search Alan's face for any sign of deception.

"I think I might need some time," she said at last. "I don't think I can keep working with you."

"I don't have time," Alan protested. "My trial is less than two weeks from now. We've got to get to the bottom of this. I need you."

"You just accused me of colluding in Mr. Fisk's murder! I'm supposed to let that slide?"

"Yes! I think under the circumstances, yes."

"Well, I can't."

"Okay, fine," Alan said. "Then where do we go from here?"

The sound of a helicopter passing filled the silence as the two friends simply stared at each other.

Before either could find words for what they wanted to say, a rusty car with a mismatched paint job came careening down the street toward Alan's house. Tires squealed as it rounded the nearest corner. Both Alan and Sharla looked its way. The car, moving much too fast for the residential nature of the neighborhood, screeched to a halt directly at the end of Alan's driveway. A tall, thin woman clambered out. She left the car running and the door ajar.

She looked to be in her early forties with long blonde hair, silken in texture, that hung loose down to her waist. Her face was flushed a deep crimson, and her eyes ringed with red as if she'd been crying. She wore a tight-fitting thermal shirt with long sleeves and splotchy blue jeans. She marched with long, determined strides down Alan's driveway. A fierce look drove her eyebrows together like twin spears. She stopped only a few feet from Alan and Sharla. Alan stepped backward, shying away from the woman's intensity.

"Alan Benning?" the woman said hoarsely.

"Yes, is there something—"

"This is for my Barron!"

The woman reached behind her back. From her waistband she pulled a small gun. She cocked it, took aim, and shot Alan directly in the chest. He stumbled backward through his still-open front door and collapsed in a bloody heap.

Sharla screamed as the woman with the long blonde hair retreated to her car. She drove away as recklessly as she had arrived. Sharla rushed to Alan's side while blood pooled around him on the cold floor of his entryway.

"Alan!" she cried. But he did not hear her.

Chapter Twenty-Nine

"I REALLY HAVE NO idea what you're doing here," Aristotle Cunningham said as he carefully tapped an orange golf ball into the slowly opening jaw of an oversized fiberglass ape face. "I've already told you everything that I know."

Reyes and Tanner waited next to hole ten of the personal mini-golf course behind Cunningham Palace as the man they'd come to interrogate ignored them to celebrate his successful putt.

"We have a few more questions regarding the night of June eighth," Reyes said.

"I assume you reviewed the video footage of the conference call with my Tokyo office?"

"We did, and it checked out."

"Then I'm not sure what else there is to say."

"Hey, let me ask you something," Tanner chimed in. "Over in Tokyo, in Japan I mean, it's, like, tomorrow already, right?"

"I guess technically it is, yes," Cunningham replied as he bent to retrieve his ball from the cup on the other side of the giant ape face on hole ten.

"So, do they know what's going to happen? Like, who's going to win tonight's boxing match or whatever?"

"No, Detective. They are not able to see the future."

"But they're in the future."

"They're not in the future. They're just a calendar day ahead of us."

"How is that not the future?"

"Because it's . . . It's a delineation of the passage of time. Their time zone is ahead of ours."

"So, they would know what happens at 8:00 PM tonight. Because they've already done it."

"But 8:00 PM hasn't happened here yet."

"But it has there."

"Yes, but it's not time travel. It's . . . You can't . . ."

Cunningham looked to Reyes for support.

"I'll explain it to you later, Tanner," Reyes said. "But no, you cannot call Japan for sports betting tips."

Tanner looked disappointed, but still skeptical.

Reyes pressed on, addressing Cunningham as he led the way to the next hole.

"It's come to our attention that you had a meeting with Mr. Fisk on the night that he passed away."

"I already told you I know nothing about that. You can check my schedule from that day; I had no such meeting planned. I hadn't seen the man for months."

"And you're sure about that?"

"Of course."

"Are you super sure?" Tanner piped in.

"Yes, I'm super sure," Cunningham said, rolling his eyes.

"No, but are you, like, *super-duper* sure?" Tanner fired back.

"What the hell is going on here?" Cunningham demanded, turning from his teed-up ball at hole eleven.

Reyes pulled a small ePad from the leather carrying case at her side. She held it up in front of Cunningham and pressed play on the video file already loaded up. He watched stoically as the security footage of him sneaking through the back entrance of Fisk Enterprises headquarters unfolded.

"I'll ask again," Tanner said. "Are you super-duper-duper sure that you weren't there that night?"

Cunningham looked to Reyes.

"Is there a way to make him shut up?"

"No," Reyes replied. "Believe me, I've tried."

"Ha!" Tanner crowed triumphantly, crossing his arms with a satisfied air as if he'd won an argument.

"Look, I admit that I was aware of that secret entrance. I've used it before," Cunningham said calmly. "But I wasn't at Fisk Headquarters that night. I simply wasn't."

"Then how do you explain this security footage?" Reyes asked.

"Maybe it's from another date and the system glitched. Maybe you're trying to get information and think this will spook it out of me. Maybe someone altered the footage, and I'm being set up. I don't know how to explain it."

"Our people authenticated the footage. It wasn't altered."

"And who did that authentication?"

"The technical officers back at the precinct."

"The same ones who vouched for my teleconference footage proving I was elsewhere that entire night?"

"Well . . . yes."

"So either your so-called tech experts are, in fact, fallible human beings who made an error in this case, or I was physically in two places at the same time. Which of those possibilities do you two think is more likely?"

"That's a good question," Tanner said. "We'll get the techs working on it right away."

"No, Tanner." Reyes sighed. She put her hand to her forehead in a gesture of evaporating patience and addressed Cunningham again. "Look, we want an answer to all of this as much as you do. All we're asking for is your cooperation."

"I know, I know. But I'm not sure what you want me to say. I didn't kill Barron Fisk. I couldn't have been in two places at once. Simple as that."

"Fine. We'll let you get back to your important work," Reyes said, nodding toward the six-foot spaceship that adorned hole eleven.

"Scoff if you like," Cunningham said as he shrugged. "I do some of my best thinking out here."

"Is there a restroom I can use on our way out?" Tanner asked. "Bit of a drive back to the precinct."

"Every third door," Cunningham replied without looking up from the tee.

"Huh?"

"Every third door of the house is a bathroom. A man can never have too many bathrooms."

"That is so cool," Tanner commented as he and Reyes headed back toward the house.

"I'll meet you out front," Reyes said when they'd passed through the rear entrance and Tanner began to count doors. She stomped away.

Tanner approached what he thought to be the third door. He put his hand on the doorknob and turned, pushing it open to reveal what was quite obviously not a bathroom. He looked in on what appeared to be a small living quarters: a disheveled twin bed, a large flatscreen on the wall, a round table near a kitchenette with a small fridge and stovetop. Seated at the table was a man facing the opposite direction and eating from a plate of eggs. He turned at the sound of the door opening. The man's face made Tanner's heart jump into his throat. It was Aristotle Cunningham, the man he'd just left near hole eleven of the mini-golf course out back.

"Mr. Cunningham?" he asked, reeling.

"Shit!" spat the other man in a voice noticeably lower-pitched than Cunningham's. The man bolted toward the door, wild-eyed, and slammed it shut in Tanner's face. Tanner heard a lock click into place. He took a moment to process what he had seen. Then, in a silent stupor, he headed toward the front of the mansion and the large golden doors that marked the entrance.

As he slid into the passenger seat of the police cruiser in the drive, he stared straight forward, frowning slightly.

"What's wrong?" Reyes asked. "You look like you saw a ghost."

"He's got a body double."

"Who? Cunningham?"

"Yeah. He's got a guy who looks exactly like him. Same hair, same face, same size. Everything. I saw him. I must have counted the doors wrong."

"That rat," Reyes said. "So that's how we have footage of him in two places at once."

"Let's get back to the precinct. Floor it."

"You're that eager to keep working the case, huh?" Reyes asked, impressed.

"No," Tanner replied. "I just realized I forgot to use the bathroom."

Chapter Thirty

Alan spent three days in the hospital, drifting in and out of consciousness. He experienced the world in fits and starts, separated by unknowable amounts of unaccounted-for time. Reality blurred with hallucination and memory. He later re-lived the experience aloud to Sharla, who stayed by his side for most of his bedridden struggle.

Alan's recollections started with a blurry memory of a nurse leaning over him, changing his IV and moving her mouth as if talking to him about something, but his head swam too much for him to follow her words. His eyes fell shut as he tried to concentrate.

Then, he was suddenly eight years old, seated on one of the hard wooden chairs of his childhood home, listening to his mother passionately expound upon the dangers of going to the local park after sundown as she bandaged a minor scrape on his knee. It felt to him more vivid than a memory, as if he was truly back there. He could smell the aroma from the coffeemaker as it buzzed away, making yet another pot in the corner despite the late hour, and he could hear the hum of insects outside the window as dusk fell around their small two-bedroom home. He saw the canary yellow kitchen walls and white tile backsplash in extreme detail. He inhaled his mother's cheap perfume, a smell he could never forget, as she hugged his head against her chest and lamented all the dangers out there in the world, all the ways in which her little Alan could be taken from her. The world was too big and too wild and too dangerous, she repeated to him over and over again. Little Alan wiped away tears with the back of his wrist and hugged his mother in return.

Then he saw Hannah concernedly leaning over his hospital bed. He distantly registered a pitying caress on his left hand. He wanted to reach out to her, to comfort her, to beg her to come back, but he could not find the strength.

The world went fuzzy again, and his mind flitted back to his high school. He watched himself hurriedly snatch books and supplies from his locker. He knew full well the importance of gathering what he needed before his bully, a tall, wide-shouldered ape of a young man with notably thick forearms, could arrive to shove him into the locker with a cruel cackle and a requisite round of high-fives with his equally large and brutish friends. He was not quick enough.

He had to beat on the inside of his locker door for ten minutes until the custodian happened by to let him out. He limped into Spanish class with his tail between his legs, refusing to tell the teacher the true reason for his tardiness. He slumped into a chair while the bully and his squad snickered at him behind their hands.

Next came a flash of the present: a concerned Sharla placing a small vase of flowers with a "Get Well Soon" balloon attached on the hospital room's bedside table. She, too, appeared to be talking to him, but her words blurred and bumped together in ways that made them incomprehensible. He tried to get his heavy lips to move in response, but met with no success. She receded from his vision, and he squinted, fighting hard to stay in the moment, here with his friend who had cared enough to come see him.

Then he was gone, back in the Fisk Enterprises boardroom, seated at the far end of the space as usual, watching in silence as Barron Fisk pounded his fists on the head of the table, shouting about the importance of his Fiskiverse project. It would be revolutionary, the great man proclaimed. The world would be forever changed! Alan lifted a folder in front of his face to cover the eye-roll he could no longer stifle.

Fisk's heavily moussed hair became slightly disheveled from the intense nature of his movements.

He appeared to be a man possessed. Alan took in the faces of the other executives in the room. They, like him, seemed to be feeling more unease than inspiration. Lips curled into forced smiles. Corners of eyes pointed downward in discomfort. Only James Bradford seemed entranced. His intense bright blue eyes were fixed on the CEO with what looked like adoration.

Fisk plowed onward, spewing hopeful turns of phrase about the Fiskiverse and the future of the company with such vehemence that they came off more as threats than optimistic pronouncements. His face contorted unpleasantly. Spittle flew from his lips. His features grew red. He looked cartoonish, like a fool drunk on his own power, as the scene faded.

Alan then saw Sharla in the hospital again, now seated in a padded chair by the window, bathed in the light of a large, round moon beyond and working on a paperback book full of crossword puzzles. He tried to reach out to her and managed to scoot a hand off the side of the bed and leave it dangling in her direction, but she failed to notice. The room swirled as he again lost consciousness.

He now found himself back at Fisk Headquarters, this time in his office. He sat combing through digital files on the projected heads-up display that emanated from his desktop. The door hung open as he double-checked final submissions of Q3 projected numbers from each branch of the company's many divisions.

Mr. Fisk appeared at the far end of the long hallway, followed by a group of suit-wearing hangers-on to whom he must have been providing a comprehensive tour of the facilities. Fisk ate from a single-serve yogurt cup with a plastic spoon. He had the air of a man at perfect ease, laughing at his own wry comments and using the spoon between bites to point out various rooms and employees with the authority of ownership.

Alan, far too aware of how this could go, rose from his chair and scurried to close his office door before the group could make it his way. Too late. Fisk shoved a dark dress shoe into the door frame as Alan swung it shut, and the door rebounded off the man's foot, a fact for which Alan was immediately rebuked. How dare he scuff the shoe of the great Barron Fisk? A cascade of laughter washed into Alan's office at his own expense. He retreated to his desk chair as Fisk introduced him as the company's professional wet blanket, the fiduciary stick-in-the-mud foisted on an undeserving Fisk by an overly stuffy and worrisome board.

If it were up to Fisk, the man assured his small crowd, Alan would have been hogtied and tossed off the building's roof long ago. More harsh laughter grated at Alan's ears. Fisk finished his container of yogurt and tossed it lazily in the direction of the open-topped garbage bin abutting Alan's desk. He missed. The plastic cup and spoon landed directly on Alan's desk and slid across it, leaving globs of whitish, viscous ooze in their wake.

Fisk and his entourage moved on, leaving Alan to stew in his feelings of inadequacy and wipe up Fisk's mess.

Each time that Alan awoke to reality, his mind raced immediately to one thought and one thought only: the fact that he couldn't die, he simply couldn't let himself, because that would mean losing his daughters, missing their first days of school, their first loves and heartbreaks, their triumphs and missteps, their messy and beautiful lives. He couldn't die.

That very thought ran through his head as his eyes fluttered open to the sight of Detectives Reyes and Tanner leaning over his hospital bed, one on each side, looking down at him with concern. He managed a light moan that seemed to prompt a short comment from Tanner and then, in turn, a furrowed brow and sharp rejoinder from Reyes. Tanner reached out a hand and snapped several times in front of Alan's face until Reyes slapped at him with an open palm. The snaps seemed strangely disjointed from the movement of the officer's fingers. Then both of their figures faded away.

Alan then found himself in Barron Fisk's office on the thirty-fifth floor of the Fisk Enterprises building; Fisk must have been rather understandably on the man's mind. Fisk was berating Alan harshly, an occurrence so frequent it had begun to feel depressingly routine. This time it was for having the audacity to counsel the board against the acquisition of the virtual reality company VigRig, which represented an important step toward the realization of the Fiskiverse and a move that Fisk deeply desired.

As the richer man talked down to him, both literally and figuratively as Fisk's desk was raised slightly above the rest of his office floor, a familiar feeling took hold of Alan's stomach: a sinking, twisting sensation that he immediately associated with his high school bully and the embarrassment of being stuffed inside of a locker. Fisk's office melted away, transforming bit by bit into Alan's old high school hallway as the two memories blended together.

Now Fisk stood flanked by the thick-necked jocks who tormented Alan throughout adolescence. Now Fisk held him by the ankles above an oversized flushing toilet as he droned on about the insolence Alan showed in opposing the VigRig acquisition. Now Fisk and the others formed a circle, shoving Alan back and forth amongst themselves with vicious jabs at his head and shoulders. Now every member of the circle took on Fisk's face. Alan cowered, covering his head in a vain attempt at self-protection as the circle of Fisks buffeted him around and around, screeching their displeasure at Alan as he grew smaller and smaller and they grew larger and larger until they towered over him, ten, twenty feet high in the air, raining down contempt from all sides as Alan pleaded for mercy, for forgiveness, for acceptance, when at last one of the Fisks, the most giant of them all, cackling like a witch with his mouth stretched repulsively wide, reached out an elephantine hand and brought it down, open palm downward, and squished Alan beneath it like an intruding spider.

Alan jerked awake in his hospital bed covered in a cold sweat, finally managing a tenuous grasp on reality. He stared upward at the ceiling tiles. He remained still for several minutes until he heard an excited squeal from the direction of the room's door. Sharla rushed to him, setting aside her newly purchased breakfast sandwich and coffee, and took one of his hands.

"You're awake!"

"Whaddayisid?" Alan managed to croak out.

"What?"

"What—day—is—it?" he asked with supreme effort.

"It's the twenty-sixth."

"Inves . . . Inves . . ." He struggled to get the word out. "Investigation."

"Alan. You need to rest. You've been shot."

"Investigation."

"Okay. I'll work on it. You rest up."

"I think I'm on drugs," Alan slurred. Words seemed to be falling out of his mouth of their own accord, without his consciously selecting them.

"Yes, you are. You had surgery three days ago. The bullet hit one of your ribs. Do you remember what happened?"

"I'm like a hippie. I'm all on drugs and stuff. Wooooooo," he crooned weakly.

"Okay, all right. You're feeling the effects."

Alan's eyes fluttered.

"Tell the Minnesota Vikings that their dentist appointment was moved to Thursday," he said blearily before drifting off again, this time into a peaceful slumber.

Sharla couldn't help but smile down at him.

Chapter Thirty-One

DEAR READER, I FEEL a distinct need at this juncture to step in. Permit your humble narrator another interruption in light of the fact that Barron Fisk is no longer around to defend himself.

I only shared the terribly unflattering characterizations of Barron Fisk presented in the previous passage due to my unflagging and, frankly, noble commitment to relaying this story with the highest possible degree of accuracy. I wish to inform you that Fisk never once in his esteemed life appeared as undignified as Benning's drug-and-injury-addled mind portrayed him. There is simply no way that a man of Fisk's wealth and power could have behaved in such an unbecoming, plainly desperate, offputting manner. Fisk was not the flailing charade of a leader Alan described.

Barron Fisk was a great man. He was unimaginably wealthy. He shaped entire industries and shook the financial world at its foundation whenever it pleased him. Alan's incoherence toward the end of his brief interaction with Sharla allows us to see the man's unstable mental state. We may safely disregard his negative portrayals of the incomparable genius whose death lies at the center of this story.

Was Fisk highly driven? Of course. Did he expect a wholesale commitment to greatness from those around him? Undoubtedly so. Did his high standards occasionally lead the man to berate or belittle others to the point that they would cry and/or engage in concealed acts of serious self-harm? Perhaps, yes. But this is simply how inspired leadership expresses itself. Those people should have been grateful to have the unerring counsel of a billionaire at their disposal. There is no space for feelings in the world of business, no concession to emotion when there is money to be made. This is what we at the top understand and you bottom-feeders fail to see. The effective stockpiling of wealth necessitates an impenetrable boundary between pocketbook and soul. This does not make us bad people. This makes us the chosen few, unafraid to get our hands dirty to ensure the world keeps turning.

Barron Fisk may have made many enemies in his time, sure. He may have left a flotilla of broken loved ones in his outsized wake. He may have sunk relationships and torpedoed any nagging sense of morality within himself to reach the top, but in the end he was successful. He made money hand over fist. And isn't that what makes a man great? Yes. Of course it is. Of course it is.

Chapter Thirty-Two

When he awoke again in the late afternoon following nearly twelve hours of uninterrupted rest, Alan proved significantly more clear-headed. He looked surprised to find Hannah at his side rather than Sharla. She helped him drink a bit of water, and then the two sat together in a brief but uncomfortable silence.

For the first time, Alan looked downward at his heavily bandaged chest: a sea of blank white gauze between his spindly arms. He tried to touch the bandages, but Hannah stopped him.

"The doctor said to leave them alone. You're going to be fine. A full recovery, she told me."

Alan grunted in response, managing a small nod for his now estranged wife.

He peered out the window at the sun just beginning to go down.

"I've never been more happy to see a sunset," he said. "It's so beautiful."

The steady sounds of the beeping of Alan's heart monitor and the ticking of the clock that hung on the far wall filled the room. Alan's eyes closed again before Hannah spoke.

"The detectives have been waiting to see you. I've managed to hold them off so far, but the short one has gotten somewhat pushy. I told them I'd call when you're awake."

Alan sighed, eyes still closed.

"Might as well get it over with."

A short while later, Detectives Reyes and Tanner appeared in the open doorway of his room, knocking on the doorframe with performative humility and peering inside. Alan waved them in. Hannah excused herself for a bite in the hospital cafeteria, leaving Alan alone with the officers.

Reyes marched in. Tanner followed, dragging his feet and keeping his back pressed up against the far wall. His eyes darted back and forth.

"What's his problem?" Alan asked.

"He doesn't like hospitals," Reyes answered.

Tanner said, "Any time you see a zombie movie, the outbreak always starts in a hospital."

"I keep telling him that zombies aren't real," said Reyes.

"And I keep telling you," Tanner shot back, "then where'd people get the idea for all those movies?"

"Mr. Benning." Reyes lowered her tone to redirect the conversation. "What are you able to tell us about the person who assaulted you? Miss Johnson was not able to identify the culprit."

"Um. Not much. I only got a brief look at her before, well, you know."

"You've never seen her before?"

"Never in my life."

"Could you give us a physical description?" Reyes produced a small ePad to take down Alan's response.

"She was fairly tall. Long blonde hair down to about her waist. Thin. She had kind of sunken cheeks. That's all I managed to see."

"There's a kind of fungus," Tanner said from the corner, reading from his ePhone, "that takes over the brains of ants and completely controls their behavior. Turns them into zombies."

"Tanner, drop it," Reyes said sharply.

"I'm just saying. It's real."

"Is there anything else you can tell us about this woman?" Reyes turned back to Alan. "What she was wearing? Any identifying scars or tattoos?"

"Not that I saw. She was wearing jeans and a maroon shirt. So you're telling me you haven't caught her yet?"

"Unfortunately, the suspect is still at large. That's why we have officers posted at the door to your room here. And of course, once you're discharged, we will have officers assigned to your house to make sure that you remain protected."

"Great," Alan said, rolling his eyes.

"I assure you that a hospital is one of the safest places you could be right now."

"Tell that to the dude from *The Walking Dead*," said Tanner under his breath.

"That's strike three. Hallway. Now."

Tanner grunted and stomped back through the doorway to stand in the hall.

"The officers guarding my house," Alan said. "Will they actually be there to protect me? Or to watch over your main suspect in the Fisk murder?"

"We have no reason to believe that you're a flight risk."

"But I'm still your main suspect."

"I'm afraid I can't comment on an ongoing investigation."

Alan let out a dry laugh that made him grab at his chest in pain. Hannah returned at that moment, and Reyes seemed to take it as her cue.

"I suppose that's all we need for now. Get some rest, Mr. Benning."

After a pause, Hannah opened her mouth to say something, then closed it again. Then both she and Alan began speaking at the same time.

"Alan, I . . ."

"You know, we can . . ."

After a shared grimace, they lapsed back into mutual silence.

"You can . . ."

"No, you go, it's . . ."

They each looked away.

"Maybe if . . ."

"Why don't we . . ."

Alan, frustrated now, stared at her stonily until she spoke again.

"I wanted to say I'm sorry. The way I left . . . It wasn't . . ." She trailed off.

"I guess I never realized how unhappy you are."

"I need to let you know. I've been talking to my lawyers. And they feel like—they do, not me—because of this whole shooting situation, that it's best if we keep the girls away from you for a while. For their safety. They've had a judge issue an injunction."

Alan painfully pulled himself up to a seated position in the bed.

"I only have a week and some change of freedom left, Hannah. You're telling me I can't see my daughters?"

"It's for the best."

"Not for me, it isn't."

"It is for them. If you're going to be gone for a long time, then maybe, you know. A clean break."

Alan stared at her with such a fire in his eyes that it made her take a step backward.

"I'm sorry. I really am," she said before she turned and fled from the room.

Alan's lawyers soon showed up as well to give him a summary of their progress, which amounted to little more than a reminder that he was running out of time to find anything to exonerate himself. Then they departed, leaving Alan alone again.

Alan remained the cops' main suspect in Barron Fisk's murder. He'd lost his daughters, and he was running out of time to save himself.

He made a wince-inducing effort to reach over and press the call button on his bedside table. When the responding nurse appeared, he had her pull the shades down over the window, blocking out the final rays of the majestically colorful sunset still unfolding outside. In the resulting darkness, he stewed in his own miserable thoughts.

Chapter Thirty-Three

The members of the Fisk Enterprises Board of Directors shared several key physical characteristics. They all had hair in various shades of gray and unruly white eyebrows. They all wore dark suits over bulging potbellies. They all had drooping jowls that waggled as they talked and large, bulbous noses reddened by decades of overindulgence. The only major distinguishing factor among them proved to be the amount of hair that remained in place above their wrinkled white faces.

The over-cologned group of men gathered around a large conference table located on the floor directly below Fisk's former office. They emitted heavy guttural grunts as they lowered themselves into their respective chairs.

In the center of the table rested an untouched ice bowl filled with bottled water and an utterly ignored platter of sliced fruit. A young woman sat in the corner of the room with her fingers poised over a laptop keyboard, ready to take notes.

The president of the board, at the head of the table, cleared his throat loudly.

"As we begin," he said in a rumbling voice that had grown deep with the years, "I feel it may be appropriate to offer some words for the official record regarding our deceased colleague Barron Fisk."

A slight pause followed as the board members looked around, each waiting for someone else to start.

"He will be missed," said one man.

"A true titan of industry," said another.

"He had a whole lot of money," added a third, bowing his head slightly.

"Sweetheart," said the board president to the young woman in the corner, "did you get all that?" She answered with a silent nod. "Excellent. Then let's move on to the pressing business at hand."

The besuited senior citizens groaned and harrumphed their way through all the normal matters of business. Several members of upper management shuffled in and then out of the office after giving short presentations on their respective sectors of the company's operations. Sly references to each board member's recently concluded lavish summer vacation peppered the ensuing discussions, each man trying to one-up the last without being too transparently braggadocious. Off-the-cuff mentions of yacht lengths and B-list celebrity sightings abounded.

Two floors below, James Bradford anxiously paced the length of his office. He carried a squishy stress ball in each hand, squeezing them in turn as he walked. The audio of the board meeting occurring above him played from the computer on his desk. He had long ago secretly wired most of the rooms in the Fisk Building for sound. He listened as the board discussed various issues that only mildly interested him: the manner in which the board planned to disclose to shareholders the precipitously declining profits following Fisk's death, the appointment of a few new division heads, the merits and potential pitfalls of a major rebranding effort as pitched to the board by the head of marketing.

None of these discussions truly interested him, though. He eagerly awaited the board's true reason for their gathering on this day: the appointment of Barron Fisk's successor as CEO. Bradford imagined that this issue would close out the meeting. The stress balls in his hands gave alternating soft, high-pitched wheezes as he flexed his fists one at a time. He stalked back and forth impatiently like a caged lion.

When the key matter arose at last, his ears perked up and his pacing ceased. He leaned on the desktop. The issue was settled quickly. No one even bothered to put forward any alternative candidate to James Bradford. The board voted him in with a unanimous decision. Alone in his office, he slammed a fist onto the desktop in triumph as a surge of adrenaline hit him. To his surprise, tears welled up in his bright blue eyes. He wiped them away.

The board summoned him to the room where they had gathered and asked him only one single question: What were his plans for the Fiskiverse? Bradford didn't hesitate. He would scrap the project, he assured them. It amounted to little more than a costly vanity project that Fisk had irresponsibly obsessed over. It had to go. The board smiled their approval at his firm proclamations.

When they officially shared with him the news of his appointment to the top job, he received it with the appropriate levels of gratitude and humility. These were, of course, entirely feigned by the naturally egotistical and entitled Bradford but still deeply appreciated by the equally egotistical and entitled members of the board. Everyone felt pleased as Bradford left the room and returned to his office to listen in on the conclusion of the meeting.

"That was the final piece of business on the agenda," said the board president. "I hereby conclude this meeting. You may pack that thing away now," he added to the woman in the corner. He paused to watch as she shut her laptop and left the room. "Now that we're off the record," he went on, "does anyone have any further thoughts they'd like to share on our dearly departed friend?"

"Good riddance," said a man with a fat white mustache, huffing in a way that made the mustache flutter.

"It's a blessing for us when it comes down to it," echoed the man next to him. "We'll finally be rid of the damn Fiskiverse."

"Hell, I'd have killed him myself if I could," said the wrinkliest of the bunch. Several others murmured in general agreement. "What an ass."

Forgive me, dear reader, for cutting in yet again. Presenting this particular section of the tale has unearthed some unexpected emotion for your humble narrator. We are now presented with a bit of a puzzle.

We do not have the excuse of medicinal grogginess or poverty-induced stupidity to explain away these strangely anti-Fisk comments as we did with Alan Benning. These are high-minded, intelligent, *wealthy* individuals. And yet here we find them expressing opinions that conspicuously lack the appropriate admiration for a man notably richer than themselves. What gives? Were these men joking? Was there some kind of gas leak in the room that affected the cognition of everyone therein? Perhaps it was Opposite

Day? None of these hypotheses hold up to even the slightest bit of scrutiny. We are then left with a single unavoidable, yet unthinkable, conclusion: they were using criteria other than wealth to judge the worth of the great Barron Fisk. This leaves your humble narrator shaken, I must admit. I don't . . . I simply don't get it.

Once the meeting wrapped, Bradford ascended to the building's top floor, which housed Fisk's former office. Now it was his. He took the stairs, partially because the large-waisted board members were crowding into the elevator, each refusing to cede a spot and wait for its return, and partially because Bradford wanted to savor the journey. He climbed the steps very slowly, taking a deep and satisfied breath with every few paces. He headed toward a whole new chapter of his existence. He was officially a tech god.

He stopped for a long time at the tall glass doors leading to the office, his hands resting on the rounded silver pull handles. When he did yank them open, he did so with a grand flourish of both arms and an aggressive, puffed-out chest. He strode forward like a king.

"Hello, old friend," crooned Jennings, its console flitting to life in the corner. "Congratulations. It's official."

"It's official," Bradford answered smugly.

"I'm proud of you, my boy. We're so close to completing our goal."

"I'll see to it that the VigRig deal goes through first thing tomorrow. Now that Benning is out of the way."

"Excellent. Well done," replied Jennings. "In the meantime, I've taken the liberty of programming our special drone friend with a little celebration. A victory protocol, if you will. It's one of the more stimulating ways for me to pass the time. I hope you enjoy it."

One of the drones on the long bookcase abutting the side wall of the office—the one with the pair of grasping arms attached—whirred to life and rose to hover in the middle of the room. It waved its long, thin graspers in what was vaguely recognizable as a victory dance, then it flew toward the corner where a tray with a bottle of expensive champagne and a pile of party poppers waited. The drone picked up one of the poppers, hummed back to Bradford, and pulled the string directly over the man's head, showering him in tiny bits of confetti and thin streamers. Bradford smiled and chuckled lightly. Returning to the corner, the small aerial robot picked up the champagne bottle, popped it, and poured Bradford a glass.

"A toast to the Fiskiverse," said the disembodied voice of Jennings.

Bradford smiled and drank deeply from the champagne flute.

Chapter Thirty-Four

I KNOW THAT YOU'RE still wondering about my identity, dear reader. The uncertainty must be killing you. If it offers any relief, I'm not even so sure myself any longer. I wanted to tell this story. I did. I never considered, though, that doing so would shake the very foundations of my sense of self. Forgive my dramatics, but it feels as if the ground has disappeared from under me like Wile E. Coyote in pursuit of the Roadrunner. Oh, God. And now I'm referencing poor-person entertainment. What's next, a joke from *Seinfeld*? Who am I?

Belinda Jones faced no such existential questioning as she sat on a bus bench across the street from Sharla Johnson's apartment building. Poking from the top of the tote bag resting near her feet was a printed sheet from a "Find Lost Classmates" website that displayed Sharla's name and address. Belinda had her long, blonde hair tucked under an auburn bob-styled wig. Huge dark sunglasses blocked a large portion of her face. She held a thick novel she'd purchased from a used bookstore nearby low enough to allow her to peer over its top and watch the main door of the building. Occasionally she turned the page, just to be convincing. This was not her first surveillance rodeo.

Alan Benning, the news reported, had survived the attempt on his life by the unknown assailant. He would now be granted round-the-clock protection from the Cupertino Police Department. Belinda had raged at this revelation the day before, tossing her hotplate across her tiny apartment in frustration and leaving a hole in the drywall that her meager security deposit surely wouldn't cover in full. She spent the remainder of the day holed up alone, contemplating the best way to get another shot at the man who, she believed, had robbed her of her one true love.

She kept a watchful eye on the door across the street, knowing that Sharla would have to emerge sometime. When she finally did, late into the afternoon, Belinda sprang into motion. She snapped shut her book and leaped up, walking briskly toward her own car in the same direction that Sharla headed. She pulled out of the parking lot directly behind Sharla's old brown Volvo.

Sharla led her pursuer downtown to City Hall. Belinda observed from afar as Sharla wound through the cavernous hallways to the Records Department, where she conversed at length with a desk attendant and received a clipboard full of paperwork for her efforts. After an extended amount of time seated on a hard wooden bench scribbling appropriate responses onto the forms, Sharla returned to the attendant and handed over the paperwork. A few minutes later, she was passed a thin manila folder with what appeared to be only a few sheets of paper inside.

Anxiously, Sharla opened the folder and pored over its contents. She flipped a few pages. After a moment, a look of startled comprehension overtook her face. She had found something. After a quick glance around her, she slipped her ePhone from her pocket and covertly snapped a photo of one of the documents. Now apparently satisfied, she closed the folder and returned it to the record keeper at the desk. Her brisk pace and long strides leaving the municipal building betrayed her excitement at her discovery.

Belinda pulled her vehicle into the same spot across the street from Sharla's apartment building that it had occupied earlier in the day. She carefully observed Sharla's routine as the woman returned home: the space in which she parked, the way she locked the car door from the outside after exiting rather than from inside before she got out, the path she took to get from the Volvo to the building's front door. She watched as Sharla fumbled with her overstuffed keyring before entering. Belinda made note of it all in her eJournal.

Once Sharla disappeared into the safety of her building, Belinda started the car and pulled away, confident that she had everything she needed.

Chapter Thirty-Five

Detective Lucinda Reyes lived alone. The discolored planks of the old, creaky hardwood floors in her one-bedroom apartment fit together poorly. Nonetheless, they shone with freshly applied polish. Not a single dust mote besmirched any surface of the entire apartment. The few photos that lined the walls hung perfectly straight. Recently emptied moving boxes formed an orderly pile in one corner, awaiting future recycling. Everything in its place.

The floor lamp in the corner of her kitchen provided the only light beyond the cool moon rays that trickled through the window. Reyes sat at the small round table tucked into the kitchen nook and ate from a plastic to-go container of still-steaming Thai food. She applied healthy dollops of Valentina to the already spicy food. The case file on the murder of Barron Fisk rested open on the table. She cursed as a small drop of hot sauce landed on a page.

She wiped the file clean as best she could and then closed it with a sigh. She rubbed strenuously at her brow and reached for her ePhone. She opened her favorite video streaming app and scrolled through options. A nearly endless library unfolded before her: mindless reality TV programs, overblown medical melodramas, inane game shows, and (shudder) sitcoms all vied for her attention. A veritable cornucopia of slop. Could it be that these mind-numbing tributes at the altar of low-income banality might actually provide some kind of valuable service in calming the mind or providing a sense of escape? I never thought I'd say it, but your humble narrator is beginning to wonder.

Several sudden, hard raps at her front door gave Reyes a bit of a jump and interrupted her idle scrolling. She took a quick glance at the clock. It showed shortly after 10:00 PM. She crossed to the door to peer through the peephole.

Aristotle Cunningham stood in the hallway outside of her apartment looking uncharacteristically sheepish. He kept his eyes trained on the floor, and his posture lacked a certain uppity erectness that normally marked the self-assured billionaire's confident bearing.

"What the . . . ?" Reyes muttered to herself before swinging the door open. "Mr. Cunningham. What are you doing here?"

"I have something to show you," Cunningham replied in a voice not quite his own.

"Do you have a cold or something?" Reyes asked, narrowing her eyes in suspicion.

At that moment, from around the nearest corner down the hall, stepped another man with the same clothing, height and face as the one already standing before her.

"Surprise!" called the second Aristotle. This one carried himself with notably more arrogance as he bounded down the short hallway to join them. "Allow me to introduce my body double, Gerard. Gerard, say hello to the nice lady."

"Hi," said the first Aristotle dourly.

"May we come in?" asked the newly appeared twin, who strode in without awaiting a response from Reyes. His copy dragged his feet as he followed.

Once the two men had settled on the thinly cushioned loveseat in her living room, each with a steaming cup of freshly brewed coffee in their identical hands, Reyes got a chance to give them a good look over. She studied their features, searching for any possible way of telling them apart and finding none. Only the difference in their bodily postures assured

Reyes that she was not falling prey to some kind of elaborate mirror-based illusion. She scowled at them both.

"Sit up straight, Gerard," one Aristotle criticized the other. The double sat up. "Now," continued the one on the right, "I imagine you're wondering why I've come beating down the door of your apartment tonight. Twice."

He elbowed his twin and laughed.

"How do you know where I live?" Reyes demanded.

"Please. I'm a billionaire. I can find out anything about anyone. If I wanted your bra size, I could have it in fifteen minutes."

Reyes frowned.

"Calm down, I don't."

"I need to let you know that I'm recording this conversation," she said.

"I should hope so. I've come to exonerate myself of suspicion in the untimely death of Barron Fisk."

"Why didn't you come see me at the precinct?"

"Well, I couldn't have come waltzing in there arm-in-arm with myself, could I? That would have let the cat out of the bag about old Gerard here. He's a carefully guarded secret, aren't you, Gerard?"

"I'm not allowed to leave the mansion without a black bag over my head," the left Aristotle answered, slouching again. The right one rolled his eyes.

"He makes more than most NBA players, and still he complains."

"What, exactly, is this supposed to prove, Mr. Cunningham?"

"That I'm telling the truth. I apologize deeply for the deception with the video call. I do. You saw Gerard here on that footage. I did in fact go to meet with Fisk that night. I was considering selling out to him. He'd outmaneuvered my company in several key markets, and I knew he was about to leap ahead in the virtual reality space also, and, well, my board was unhappy. I was there to discuss a potential buyout. Okay? But obviously, I can't have that news going public now. It would absolutely tank our stock. So I lied. But I'm coming clean in order to demonstrate my complete transparency now. I mean, be honest. You were stumped about the footage, right? Would you ever have guessed two identical me's?"

"We were already aware of your body double, Mr. Cunningham. My partner discovered him when we visited your estate."

"What?" gasped the Aristotle on the right. "Gerard, is this true?"

The left twin's eyes fell to the floor.

"This is an egregious breach of protocol, Gerard. This will be dealt with when we return home." He turned his attention back to Reyes. "Well, otherwise, you never would have figured it out. Look how perfect he is. Gerard here cost me well over twenty million in plastic surgery. Now, we are indistinguishable."

"I have to gain weight whenever he does," moaned the lookalike.

The Aristotle on the right gave a guilty look.

"I'm a stress eater," he admitted.

"I still fail to see how this proves anything," Reyes told them.

"Call it a good faith gesture. I did meet with Fisk that night, but I did not kill him. Why would I be here voluntarily admitting all of this if I had? I am innocent. Isn't that right, Gerard?"

"I don't know."

"Damn it, Gerard."

"What? I wasn't there."

"I told you to say . . . well, nevermind now," the Aristotle on the right faced Reyes again. "Gerard's impertinence notwithstanding, I strongly feel that this level of openness should count in my favor."

Reyes leaned forward eagerly. "Since you're being so honest, maybe you can answer another question. Do you own a gun?"

"Of course. There are several secured at various points around my mansion. I'm a billionaire; I have to protect myself. Especially after what happened to Fisk."

"A Ruger LCP .380?"

"I . . . Well, probably. That's at least one of them. I think."

"So you were at the scene of the crime. Your company was saved by Fisk's death. And you own the exact weapon that was used in the murder. Am I getting all of this correct?"

"I mean, those facts are correct. I can't say that I appreciate the tone."

"Mind if my friends in ballistics take a look at that gun of yours?"

"I feel like you're missing the point here."

"The point is that there's now almost as much evidence against you as there is against Benning."

Gerard chuckled.

"Hold on, now," objected the true Aristotle. "Wasn't the gun found at the scene registered to Benning?"

"Yes, but that could have been set up by someone with financial resources and the ability to access Benning's personal information. Know anyone like that? Maybe someone who was bragging about knowing my bra size?"

"I said I *didn't* know your bra size."

"One final question: How long have you known about the secret back entrance to Fisk headquarters?"

"Fisk told me about it years ago for a meeting we had, and I've used it a handful of times since. But I didn't kill him. What about the footprint at the crime scene? That points to Benning as well."

"How do you know about the footprint? That information was never released to the public."

"I . . . Well, I . . ."

"Ouch," Gerard said, chuckling again.

"I have my sources. So what? You know, I came here in good faith," Aristotle insisted.

"Or did you come out of a guilty conscience?" Reyes said. "Often the perpetrator subconsciously wants to be caught. What do you think, Gerard?"

"Could be."

"Gerard, damn it!" barked Aristotle. "Put on your hood."

Gerard wordlessly pulled a black cloth sack from his back pocket and placed it over his head. He cinched a drawstring at the bottom so that it was snug around his neck.

"See what you've done?" Aristotle said to Reyes. "Now poor Gerard is in his hood."

Reyes rose.

"I think we're done here, Mr. Cunningham. We will be in touch."

"What? No. I'm not finished. This has not gone the way I wanted."

"Sorry to hear that," Reyes replied, walking to the door and opening it. "Now if you'll excuse me, my dinner is getting cold."

Aristotle followed her to the threshold.

"Fine. But it wasn't me who killed Fisk. And I can't have an arrest spooking my investors, understood?"

"I can't make any promises."

Aristotle released an indignant snort and stormed out of the apartment.

"Gerard, come!"

Gerard stood from the loveseat and, waving his arms blindly due to the hood still over his head, banged his shin on the coffee table and then walked directly into the wall. Aristotle came back in to grab him by the arm.

"Damn it, Gerard," he said again while guiding his double out of Reyes's apartment and down the poorly lit hallway. Reyes closed the door with a thud.

Chapter Thirty-Six

THE DOCTORS RELEASED ALAN from the hospital, and he returned to his large, empty house. He stubbornly refused any in-home nursing care, despite the fact that he still winced at the mere act of raising his arms, fearful that the medical attention would interfere with his continuing investigation into Fisk's death. If Alan failed to find the true perpetrator, less than a week remained before he was due in court to face the charge himself.

On Alan's first day back home, Sharla arrived unannounced, alarming the police officer now stationed at the front door, who steadfastly refused her entry. It took some vehement insistence on Alan's part and several layers of bureaucratic approval delivered via the officer's shoulder-clipped radio for her to be admitted to the house. Once she was, though, she burst into the kitchen with vigor.

"I think I've had a breakthrough," she said, short of breath.

"On what?"

"On the investigation!"

"You've been working on the case?" he asked, lifting his eyes from the kitchen island.

"Of course. I told you in the hospital that I would."

Alan pursed his lips.

"I went down to City Hall," Sharla said. "I figured there was one piece of evidence against you that we still hadn't examined closely: the fact that there was a gun mysteriously registered in your name. So I did some digging. It turns out that California law allows gun permit paperwork to be filed via a proxy, but that process requires the third party's name to be recorded as well. So I filled out the appropriate requisition forms and got access to the permit on file with the state. And you're not going to believe the name that's listed as the proxy who filed the paperwork."

She placed her ePhone down on the kitchen island with the flourish of a magician finishing a trick. Alan leaned over it, examining the photo displayed.

"Darlene Pillar," he read aloud.

"And I think we both remember that name."

"Mrs. Fisk."

"She's the one who registered the gun in your name! We should go see her again. Right away. If we show her this, maybe we can spook a confession out of her."

Alan hesitated.

"Are you sure that's a good idea?"

"What else can we do?"

"Well, if you're right and Mrs. Fisk is the true killer, should we be confronting her like this?"

"What other choice do we have? Go to the police and admit we're still investigating? They'll lock us up."

"I mean, what if she decides we know too much and she . . . I don't know."

"Kills us?"

"Hell's bells, don't blurt it out like that."

"Alan," Sharla said in a steady voice. "What's it going to take for you to be just a tiny bit brave, huh? If not this, then what?"

"Okay, fine. We'll go."

"The only problem is getting you out of here. I couldn't help but notice that they have officers posted at every door."

"I've been thinking about that," Alan responded. "And I have an idea. Give me until this afternoon. Meet me at the usual spot. Three o'clock."

The minute that Sharla left, Alan began digging through storage boxes in his basement until he found what he needed: a slick white unopened box. It contained the drone with articulating arms that Fisk had given out in lieu of holiday bonuses a couple of years before. Plastic film still hugged the outside of the box.

He ripped it off, did the small amount of assembly that the drone required and gave a cursory glance through the operation manual. In no time, he had the small flying robot zipping around his basement, picking up and putting down any object he pleased.

Next, he rummaged through the family junk drawer in the kitchen until he found an old ePhone that his wife had used previously and charged it up. He took it into a bathroom in the far back corner of the house and recorded himself calling for help in a semi-believable manner.

He sat down in his kitchen with the drone and downloaded the accompanying app on his own ePhone. He taught himself how to program in a given set of actions for the drone to carry out without his direct control and tested it several times on menial acts around the kitchen, making sure he understood how to tell the drone what distance to fly before completing each task.

By the time that 3:00 PM rolled around, he was ready to put his plan into effect.

He opened a window at the side of his house and placed the drone on the sill. He set Hannah's old ePhone down right next to it. Then he hurried to the back door and put one hand on the knob, ready to spring into action. On his phone, he enacted the newly programmed drone protocol that called for the drone to pick up his wife's old ePhone and fly it out the open window. Alan watched through the drone's camera feed as it landed in his neighbor's bushes. It reached out with one of its arms and pressed the play button on the phone's already-opened voice recorder app. His recorded pleas for help began to ring out.

Accessing the footage from the security camera mounted on the back side of the house, he saw the officer posted at the rear register the recorded distress calls and run off in the direction of the neighbor's house. Alan ripped open the door and hustled across the backyard as fast as his still-aching chest would allow. He squeezed through the gap between the hedges and fencing and scurried off to meet Sharla, who awaited him in the brown Volvo, already parked in the same spot as always two blocks away.

The two friends struck off for Fisk Estates, ready to confront a killer.

Chapter Thirty-Seven

THE SKY LOOMED OVERCAST as Alan and Sharla pulled up to the Fisk Estates gates. Sharla waved off the gatehouse attendant as she reached over to key in the entry code. Soon, they eased to a stop at the base of the front porch stairs and climbed out of the vehicle.

"I wonder who Mrs. Fisk tried to frame for the death of her first husband," Alan mused. "Clearly, she's gotten better at it."

"Let's focus on one murder at a time," Sharla replied as they climbed the mansion's front steps and she let them in the front door.

The massive entryway sat empty. Sharla led Alan down lengthy passageways toward the east wing pool, where she expected to find Mrs. Fisk sipping cocktails. The pool area turned out to be deserted as well, though. Only the brightly colored shade umbrellas, cushioned chaises, and immaculately trimmed garden beyond greeted them.

They backtracked a bit and took a right turn at a modern art statue that resembled a giant blob from a lava lamp and continued echoing their footsteps down the sparsely decorated hallways. They reached a set of cream-colored double-width doors that featured ornate golden handles. Sharla stopped before them.

"This is Mrs. Fisk's suite," she explained. "Let's see if she's here."

She rapped loudly on one of the doors with her knuckles. From inside, they heard the sudden rustling of someone climbing out of bed and then the muffled thumps of footsteps on thick carpet. They heard Rebecca's voice muttering various curse words interspersed with the name of Dr. Wu. The doors swung open.

"What the hell do you want now?" Mrs. Fisk blurted before laying eyes on her guests. She wore a long sleeping gown under a green silk kimono. "Oh. You're not Dr. Wu."

"Nice to see you too, *Darlene*," Sharla said, leaning forward slightly on the final word.

"Found out about that, have you?" she asked. "Fine. Come on in."

She plodded back toward her comically large bed covered with an enormous number of throw pillows displaced during the previous night. The rest of the bed also showed signs of a restless inhabitant: twisted sheets and pillows dented from frustrated punches. Rebecca headed straight toward a mostly empty bottle of white wine that sat on the bedside table near the messed section of the bed.

"Day wine, anyone?" she asked as she refilled the glass that rested near the bottle. "And don't you dare judge me," she sneered. "If I'm going to have to defend myself against murder accusations, I'm at least going to get a buzz on while doing it." She took an exceedingly large gulp of wine. Her guests remained close to the door. Rebecca took in their frightened demeanors. "What, you're scared I'm going to go all psycho murderer on you? Well, maybe I will. Sounds like fun." She cackled loudly as she poured herself more wine. "Look," she continued with a tone that suggested she was addressing a duller-than-average child, "my first husband was seventy-seven when I married him. He had steak and brandy every single day. He died at eighty-three. I didn't kill him. That shit happens. People die."

"Then why change your name?" Sharla asked.

Rebecca treated her to a nasty look.

"Have you ever had half the country believing you're a murderer? It's worth a little bit of legal paperwork to get some distance from it." She took another swig of wine. "And as far as Barron goes, you'd be better off looking into Dr. Wu than me."

"Spoken like someone trying to save their own neck," Alan muttered.

"Or like someone paying attention to the facts," came Rebecca's retort. "You know Wu went to Fisk Headquarters that night? And he took my phone so his couldn't be tracked. That's suspicious behavior right there."

"And how do we know that you're not the one who went to Fisk HQ with your phone?" Sharla asked.

"Darling, I had two bottles of wine and a handful of xannies that night. I had the mobility of a comatose slug."

"But we rather conveniently only have your word on that."

"Look, think whatever you'd like about me," Rebecca said with blasé, "but if you want to find the truth, you're barking up the wrong tree."

"Then how do you explain this?" Sharla pulled up the image of the gun permit paperwork bearing Rebecca's previous name and showed it to her. "Someone registered the gun at the crime scene in Alan's name. They left Darlene Pillar as the name of the person who filed the permit."

Rebecca looked it over at length.

"I didn't have anything to do with this."

"Your name is right there on it!" Alan insisted.

"I'm not the only person in the world who knows my old name," she said back. "It's public knowledge. Obviously, somebody wanted to cover their tracks. But think about it. If I was the one who filed this paperwork, using my former name wouldn't exactly hide much, would it? That still leads pretty directly back to me."

Alan and Sharla exchanged uncertain glances.

"I'm telling you, it's Wu," Rebecca pressed on.

"What reason would Wu have for murdering Mr. Fisk?" Sharla asked.

"The man got forty million dollars from Barron's death," Rebecca said. "He must have found out he was in the will, and he wanted that money to do whatever whacko experiments he's always up to in that lab of his."

Alan's face turned serious.

"We didn't know about the money."

"That's not to mention the crazy shots he was always giving my husband," Rebecca added.

"Shots?" Sharla asked.

"Several times a day he'd inject Barron with some mysterious dark liquid. Very thick. Never would own up to what was in it. Maybe that's why he visited Fisk HQ that night. I'm telling you, there's some shady business going on with that doctor. Barron trusted him. And look where that got him."

"Is Dr. Wu around? Could we speak with him?"

"Sure. He lives here on the compound. I'll take you to him now. I need a new bottle anyway," she said, draining the last of her wine. She marched resolutely from the room with the others in tow.

Chapter Thirty-Eight

Rebecca Fisk approached the light brown wooden door of the guesthouse in which Dr. Wu resided and banged aggressively with the side of her closed fist. She clutched in her other hand a newly opened bottle of expensive chardonnay that she'd insisted they stop off for along the way.

"Dr. Wu!" she shouted between swigs directly from the bottle.

She pounded on the door until it opened, revealing Dr. Wu in crisply pressed khakis and a corded sweater over a light blue button-down with a puzzled look on his face, which only deepened at seeing Rebecca's companions.

"What is the meaning of this?" he demanded.

"Time to pay the piper," Rebecca blurted. "These people know you killed Barron, just like I know."

"Now, hold on," Sharla jumped in. "We just have some questions for you."

"And why should I answer any questions from you lot?" Wu asked. "Last I checked, not a one of you has a badge."

"You want to get the police involved?" Rebecca said. "Fine by me. I'll take them through that Franken-lab of yours. How's that sound? Certainly nothing illegal going on in there, right, Wu?"

Dr. Wu scowled at Rebecca and then silently stepped aside, gesturing a welcome to the small group by extending one arm. Alan and Sharla filed in after Rebecca, who plopped herself down on the living room sofa and put her feet up on the coffee table.

The guesthouse proved surprisingly modest in size. The high ceiling of the living area, dotted with recessed lights, gave way to tall windows on the far wall. The decor, homely and welcoming, stood in stark contrast to Wu's demeanor. The little wall space that remained between the tall bookshelves stacked with thick, serious-looking volumes remained blank.

Dr. Wu closed the door and turned to them with crossed arms.

"I have nothing to say to you," said Dr. Wu. "There is no merit to Mrs. Fisk's theory. I had no idea at the time of Barron's death that I'd been included in his will."

"But you visited Fisk Headquarters on the night of his death," Alan stated firmly.

"Only to administer his regular treatments," Wu replied. "Often when he worked late, my presence was requested at his office. Nothing was amiss when I left him there."

"What time was that?"

"Precisely 10:32 PM."

"And you came directly back here?"

"That I did, yes. Satisfied? May we stop with the inquisition?"

"What about those shots you were giving to him?" Alan asked. "Mrs. Fisk seems to think they were troubling."

"Yes, well, once Mrs. Fisk shows me her advanced degree in human immunobiology, I'll begin to take her opinions into consideration."

"Human immuna-intonology this," Rebecca piped up from the sofa, flashing Wu a middle finger.

"This is an immense waste of my time," Dr. Wu said.

"Dr. Wu," Sharla spoke up, "you may or may not have murdered anyone—that I can't speak to—but you quite clearly don't want any inquiries into these shots you were giving Mr. Fisk. So unless you want us to create some problems for you, you're going to tell us all that you know."

"You all already know what I know. The killer is in this room, but it certainly isn't me."

Wu's comment brought the rest of the room to a standstill. Alan and Sharla looked askance at Rebecca. Rebecca frowned. She then pointedly glared at Dr. Wu, redirecting both Alan and Sharla his way. Wu saw this, rolled his eyes and then fixed his laser focus on Alan. All heads in the room followed.

"Me?" Alan asked.

"Must we play this game?" Wu responded. He turned to the others. "It was Benning all along. I have the video footage from the hallway outside Fisk's office, all right? It shows Alan entering right before the time of death."

"That's impossible," Alan objected.

"Why would you have the security footage?" asked Sharla.

Wu explained, "I was attempting to keep my visit that night a secret, so I copied the video file and then deleted it from the security database. Mr. Fisk's treatments in those last few months were rather, ah, experimental. That's also why I took Mrs. Fisk's phone instead of my own. I didn't want any unnecessary questions."

"I never went to Fisk's office!" Alan insisted.

"I can show you the footage," Wu said calmly. "It's in my lab as we speak."

Sharla looked torn.

"I suppose we should go see the footage," she said in a small voice.

Mrs. Fisk hopped up from the sofa nimbly.

"Ooh, this is getting good now," she said in a sing-songy voice, still clutching her bottle of wine. "Let's go, let's go!"

Dr. Wu led the small procession from his front door to the laboratory building, following the light gray stone pathway that wound through the lush green grass of the campus grounds. They crowded into the exam room section that served as the false front to Wu's lab behind. Wu approached the back wall of the space and pressed a tile near the top. The hidden door leading to the lab slid open smoothly.

"Secret door," Rebecca whispered loudly to Sharla, slurring the 's' sound. "Pretty cool, huh?"

"Wait a minute, Dr. Wu," Alan said, looking concerned. "If your visit came before mine like you said it did, then how would my arrival be included in the footage that you took? Wouldn't it have happened after you left?"

Wu's demeanor changed. He flashed a devious smile and darted through the secret door into the laboratory. Alan lunged forward in an attempt to stop him from slamming it shut, but he was a second too late. The door slid closed, and his outstretched hand touched the cream-colored wall tiles. The door latched with a *click*. Alan reached over and pounded his fist into the same tile Wu had pressed to release the door, but nothing happened. The wall remained solid and stationary.

"Hell's bells, he's getting away!" Alan cried.

"He must have locked it from the inside," said Sharla.

"He never had any video footage," Alan spat bitterly, leaning his forehead against the stubbornly immobile wall. "I should have seen through that."

"It *was* Wu!" Rebecca crowed. She did a little dance. "I told you so! Wu killed Barron. Wu killed Barron!"

Alan and Sharla ignored her and set to work trying to pry open the hidden door with anything they could find at hand. Following several minutes of vain attempts, Mrs. Fisk had an epiphany.

"Oh! There's a release button for this door somewhere in Barron's bedroom!"

"And you're only remembering that now?" Sharla asked, exasperated. She wiped sweat from her brow and set down the metal file she'd been using to dig into the wall's grout.

"Get off my back. I'm drunk."

Rebecca left to search for the method of opening the lab door.

"Dr. Wu," Alan said in amazement, shaking his head. "Could it really be him?"

"Why else would he run?" Sharla answered.

They both got lost in their own swirling thoughts. After a few minutes, without warning, the secret door popped open a crack in front of them.

"She did it!" Alan called as he rushed forward.

"Wait," said Sharla.

She cast a glance around the room, then bent down and grabbed the metal file she had used to dig at the joint where the hidden door met the wall. She wielded it like a knife. Alan, inspired, searched for his own weapon. He snatched up a stethoscope from the nearby countertop and began whipping it in circles over his head by the rubber tubing like a medieval mace.

Sharla pulled the door open, and the pair charged into the hidden lab beyond, shouting like children rushing an ice cream truck.

They found the space completely deserted. They swept their eyes along the stainless steel tables and exotic-looking lab equipment, searching for any clue to Wu's whereabouts. By the time they'd crept carefully to the back wall of the laboratory, improvised weapons at the ready, and found the small, square opening through which Wu must have crawled to make his escape, Rebecca had returned and joined them through the secret door.

"He got away," Alan told her.

"What?" Rebecca asked. "How?" She came closer and spotted the knee-height tunnel. "That little sneak. I didn't know this was here."

"It leads to the outside," Sharla said, peering into the opening. "I can see sunlight at the end."

"Great," Rebecca complained. "We lost him."

Alan failed to respond, distracted by something he spotted behind Sharla. He took slow steps toward a nearby stainless steel table, upon which rested a set of knives that looked startlingly familiar to him. The white marble handles poked from the foldable carrying case that covered the tabletop. He picked up one of the knives and examined it.

"I recognize these knives." They looked identical to the knife that had pinned the threatening note to the front door of his home.

"You do?"

"Mrs. Fisk is right," he said seriously. "It was Wu after all." He looked away from the knife, with determination in his eyes. "We've got to find him."

"I think I know how we can," Rebecca said as she took another pull of wine.

Chapter Thirty-Nine

Just over an hour after Dr. Wu's disappearing act, Sharla's rickety brown Volvo pulled into the employee parking lot outside the tall building that housed the headquarters of Fisk Enterprises.

When the ragtag trio of investigators presented itself at the security desk in the lobby, the attendant regarded them warily.

"I don't think he's allowed to be here," he said, nodding in the direction of Alan. "On account of the whole, you know, murder stuff."

"Young man, do you have any idea who I am?" Rebecca snarled at him.

"Yes. You're Rebecca Fisk."

"Good. Now if you'd like to keep your cushy job where the only qualifications seem to be the ability to sit in a chair and wear a poorly fitting polo, you'll let us up to see James Bradford right now." She jabbed a bony finger into the man's chest. "Or else I'll have you in the unemployment line so fast your man tits won't stop jiggling for a month. Understood?"

The man's face fell into uncertainty and then fear as Rebecca retained her fierce expression. He suddenly looked like a little boy.

"Yes, ma'am," he said sheepishly.

"And don't call me ma'am."

Alan, Sharla and Rebecca rushed toward the elevators.

"So, what's the play here?" Alan asked as they filed inside.

"Bradford can tell us where Dr. Wu is," Rebecca said. "Barron had the ability to track any Fisk ePhone on the planet. Now that Bradford's CEO, he must be able to as well."

"And if he won't?" asked Sharla.

"Leave that to me," Rebecca said. "I have a plan."

They rushed off the elevator as soon as the doors parted to reveal the top floor. They marched down the plushly carpeted hallway toward what was now James Bradford's office. Bradford had already removed the portraits of Barron Fisk that previously adorned the walls and replaced them with his own face, which strikes this narrator as overly hasty, but, oh well. The wealthy used to have more respect for their fellows, it seems to me. Maybe I'm wrong. Maybe they never did.

A skinny, dark-haired young woman watched the group approach and stepped out from behind the reception desk, sensing that something was afoot. The group simply brushed right past her, ignoring her concerned but polite offer for assistance. Rebecca handed off the open wine bottle that she still carried, and they left the young woman in their wake, bewildered and now holding wine. They stormed through the tall glass doors and into the office. They found Bradford behind his desk talking intently on the phone.

"Presenting Rebecca Fisk, Sharla Johnson, and Alan Benning," rang out the disembodied voice of Jennings.

Bradford's look of surprise at seeing them lasted only a brief moment before his smarm reasserted itself. He informed whoever was on the other end of the line that he would call them back. The moment he hung up, Rebecca attacked.

"We need to track Dr. Wu's ePhone. We have to know where he's gone."

"And a jolly hello to you as well, Mrs. Fisk," Bradford replied.

"Track him now," she insisted.

Bradford ignored her and addressed the others. "Can I offer any of you a refreshment?"

"No," Sharla said. "That's not why we're here."

"You need to track Dr. Wu, and you need to do it now," Rebecca repeated.

"You know, most people are required to have an appointment scheduled months in advance just to set foot in this office. You've all barged in here like a herd of Kool-Aid men and now you're making demands? I'm not sure you quite grasp how all of this works."

"This is an emergency, James," Sharla said. "It's highly time-sensitive."

"So are all the matters that cross my desk," Bradford said back. "I run the most important company in the world."

"Yeah, yeah," Rebecca said while rolling her eyes. "You're big and important. Congratulations. Now quit swinging your nuts around and help us find Wu. Open up your tracking app or whatever."

"I'm afraid that would represent a gross violation of our users' privacy and trust," Bradford smiled. "I'll have to decline your request."

"Do it," Rebecca whined at him. "Come onnnnnnn."

Alan glared at her.

"Was that your plan?" he asked out of the side of his mouth. "Tell me that wasn't your plan." Rebecca shrugged.

"Wu killed Mr. Fisk," Sharla pitched in as an attempted explanation.

"Is that so?" Bradford raised his eyebrows in interest.

"We confronted him about it, and he fled," Rebecca said.

"That doesn't necessarily prove anything."

"He also admitted to being here on the night of the murder," Sharla added.

"And we found proof that he was the one who left a threatening note at my house to get me to stop investigating," Alan said.

"The man got forty million dollars from Barron's death! What more proof do you need?" Rebecca asked before adding poutily, "That was supposed to be my money."

Bradford stood up from behind the desk.

"So, why are you here? Why not go to the police?" he asked.

"We can't involve them," Alan replied. "For self-incrimination reasons."

"Well, that sounds as shady to me as Wu's actions," said Bradford. "He could have fled for any number of reasons, including the fact that Mrs. Fisk here smells like a vineyard."

Mrs. Fisk brandished her fist.

"Ever hear of the grapes of wrath, asshole?"

"We're sorry that we ever suspected you," Sharla jumped in, "but we're offering you an opportunity now to clear your name once and for all."

"Please," Alan said. "This could save my life. I have two small children."

"Do it for Barron," said Rebecca. "I know how close you two were."

Bradford took a long moment to stare down the small group with a firm expression.

"How exactly do you expect me to help here?"

"Track his ePhone. Tell us where he is," Sharla said.

"And what makes you think that I have that ability?"

Rebecca groaned. "You're not fooling anybody, James. Just do it."

Bradford paused again to ponder the situation.

"You have enough to prove it was Wu?"

"Yes! Wu did it. Aren't you listening?" Rebecca spoke heatedly now.

Bradford exhaled a defeated sigh and gave in.

"Jennings?" he called out, looking toward the ceiling.

"Yes, Mr. Bradford," the voice replied.

"Activate tracking protocol number four."

"Right away," Jennings said. After a brief pause, the AI continued, "What is the registered name or phone number for the ePhone you would like to trace?"

"Dr. Lucian Wu."

"Thank you. One moment."

Alan and Sharla exchanged a nervous glance in the short silence that followed. The hope that bloomed in Alan's eyes quickly faded.

"No results available," announced Jennings. "Phone is offline."

Rebecca released a long, frustrated grunt.

"He must have destroyed his phone," Bradford said. "Or at least removed the battery."

"A battery?" Rebecca groaned. "All this damn technology, and it's made completely useless by taking out one little battery?"

"I wouldn't say that I'm useless," Jennings said. "I can still access numerous international databases as well as provide—"

"Shut it, Jennings," Rebecca interrupted. The AI fell silent. "Since when does Jennings get defensive? I don't care for that one bit."

Bradford got an idea. "Wu will still have access to his email account. If we can get him a message, I know how to smoke him out. But I'll need to run a small errand first. You all stay here."

"No, no, no," Rebecca said immediately. "You may not be the murderer, but I still don't trust you. We're coming with."

"That's not possible."

"Tough. Make it possible."

Bradford hesitated. "Jennings?" he said toward the ceiling. "What do you think here?"

Jennings replied, "I think if there is an opportunity to prove that Dr. Wu is Barron Fisk's true killer, it should be taken."

Alan and Sharla exchanged puzzled glances. Since when did ultra-decisive James Bradford defer to AI for rulings?

Bradford said, "Everyone follow me."

The receptionist still waited outside the office, clutching Rebecca's mostly empty wine bottle. Bradford waved away with a flick of his wrist her attempted apology for failing to stop the group's encroachment. Alan, Sharla, and Rebecca trailed behind him. Rebecca nabbed the wine bottle back on her way out.

"Thank you, dearie," she said.

The young woman offered a meek, "You're welcome," as she watched the group clamber back into the elevator with one more added to their number.

Chapter Forty

Alan, Sharla, and Rebecca followed Bradford down the well-lit hallway of a swanky condominium building. The long corridor smelled of cleaning products, and the dark tile floor gleamed. Modern boxy sconces lined the walls at regular intervals, throwing carefully tapered bursts of light both up and downward. Bradford came to a sudden halt outside one of the pine-colored doors that lined both sides of the hallway. The others clustered around him. Muffled sounds of loud music leaked from behind the door.

"The night of Fisk's murder," Bradford explained, "I was at a charity gala. Feline AIDS or something stupid. While I was there, I received a message from Dr. Wu regarding the young man who lives here. The contents of that message required that I leave the event for a spell, which is the main reason why the police suspected me at all. Still, I kept this man's existence a secret. So, I am trusting each of you to exhibit the utmost discretion with what you are about to learn. Can I count on all of you to do that?"

After receiving nods and verbal agreements from each of them, Bradford knocked loudly on the condo door. The music from within abruptly cut off.

The door cracked open, and a man's face appeared in the small slit between door and jamb. It was a youthful face, unwrinkled but heavily tanned by the sun and framed by long, dirty blond hair that cascaded down past the young man's shoulders. He wore a bright blue tank top, white shorts, and slide-on sandals. A thin black headband held his long hair from his face. His eyes, rimmed with red, squinted out into the hall.

"Yo, Bradford, man," he said, pulling the door the rest of the way open.

Hardly any furnishings filled the slick hardwood floors between the wall-to-wall windows in the corner apartment behind him. A flat-screen television sat directly on the floor with a bong and a bag of chips resting nearby.

"Is it the twelfth again already? Crazy, man."

"No, it's not," Bradford replied.

"Oh, right," the young man chuckled at himself. "Hey, who are the pals?" He gestured with a jerk of his chin toward the others standing behind Bradford.

"Don't worry about them. Let us in."

"For sure, dude," the young man said as he stepped back from the door and allowed everyone to file inside. "Sorry I don't have chairs. My guru says it's good for my chakra to sit on the ground. Keeps me humble, you know?"

"This is Luke Staples," Bradford said to everyone else. "Barron has been paying him for his silence for a while now. That's how he lives here. But when Fisk died, *someone* got to thinking that he should get more money or he'd go public. That's why I had to leave the gala."

"Whoa, man. Don't make it sound like some heartless money grab. I just want what I'm owed."

"Buying his silence?" asked Alan. "For what?"

"You want to elaborate, or should I?" Bradford asked Luke.

The tanned youngster hit him with a skeptical look, and Bradford responded with a 'go ahead' gesture.

"Okay. All right, I'll tell it. Man. It was crazy. So, like, maybe a year and a half back I signed up for this medical trial. Get some easy green, you know? I used to do it all the time. Few weeks went by, I didn't hear anything. Forgot about it, to be honest. But then, this dude showed up at my tent out of nowhere. I was living on the beach down in Malibu at the time. He introduced himself to me as Dr. Wu or something like that. Handed me a business card. And then he gave me this little paper cup full of pills. Said it's all part of the experiment. Said I'd get paid double what they advertised. So I popped 'em. I've never been one to ask a lot of questions when it comes to stuff like pills. Next thing I know, whole world went screwy. I started feeling woozy, like, and then I keeled over. Blackout. I woke up two days later, back in my tent, with all this."

Luke lifted his shirt to reveal a criss-crossed network of scars that took up a significant portion of his torso. Long-healed incisions swooped all the way around his thin side and onto his lower back. Large pink splotches stood out starkly from the rest of his sun-kissed skin in several places. Rebecca gasped at the sight.

"I know, right? I was freaked. Waking up with my body all torn up and all." He lowered his tank top again. "So, I stumbled down the way to an emergency room. I didn't have insurance, but I showed them my side and they took me in anyway. Thank God. Stitches were still bleeding. They told me I'm missing one kidney, that my liver is gone, that somebody took big ole chunks of my skin right off. My intestines are short now. Even part of my stomach. Crazy, right? Major, major surgeries.

"Now, at this point, I didn't know this Dr. Whoever from a hole in the ground. No idea he was with Fisk. But he made one big mistake: the business card he gave me. Had to seem legit, I guess. Probably meant to take it back, but he forgot. It was still tucked in my back shorts pocket. Didn't have his name on it, just said the research arm of Fisk Enterprises.

"So I took some time to heal up, couple months, and I hitched on up here to Cupertino and walked right into Fisk HQ. They were *not* friendly. And the security dudes were *strong*. I knew I couldn't give up, though. I called up this buddy of mine who lives in the area and had him show up with me in a suit and tie. Said he was my lawyer. Well, that got the front desk guy to dial upstairs. Once word got to the big man about who was sitting down in the lobby, I got whisked right up. Top office. Top floor. And there he was. Boom. Barron Fisk himself. Never thought I'd meet anybody that rich.

"That Dr. Wu guy was standing in the corner of the office, and he looked at me, and then he gave this tiny, small nod to Fisk, all quiet and creepy, like. Then, get this, Fisk offered me $200,000 a month, every month, just to keep my mouth shut about what happened. For life. I was like, 'Dude!'

"He also said it'll include the best medical care I could ask for, as long as I only see Dr. Wu and only talk about it to him and Fisk. For sure, I said yes. So they gave me this wad of dough and sent me on my way.

"That was a little over a year ago and, sure enough, the money shows up like clockwork. Twelfth of every month, somebody shows up here with a duffel bag full of cash. I'm thinking that I'm set for life, baby. But then Fisk kicks it. And when news breaks online that somebody shot him in the head, I'm like, 'Whoa. What's that mean for me?' So I called Dr. Wu's phone number and I'm like, 'I'm gonna need to know that our deal still stands or I'm, you know, going to the papers and stuff.' A little bit later, Bradford here shows up at my door, says the deal's still good. Except now I can only talk about it to whoever *he* says. And that's pretty much it."

"Hell's bells." Alan exhaled.

"So, Wu's been operating some type of black market organ harvesting operation," Sharla said.

"I know for a fact they've been doing it to others," Luke said. "But I think I'm the only one they screwed up with. Rest of the guys probably just woke up with scars and a whole lot of questions."

"We have reason to believe Wu is the one who killed Fisk," Bradford said to Luke, "but he's gone missing. You're our key to luring him out."

"Heavy, bro. What do you need me to do?"

"Lift your shirt again."

Luke did as Bradford bid, and Bradford, pulling out his ePhone, snapped several quick photos of the young man's torso.

"Wu doesn't have a way to connect me to any of this. So a quick threatening email should convince him to cooperate," Bradford said. He typed on his phone for a bit. "There. Sent. I told him to meet us, or we'll go public with his whole operation."

"I can't believe Barron was mixed up with something like this," Rebecca said. "I knew he could be heartless, but this?"

"He must have had good reason," said Bradford.

"So now what?" Sharla asked. "We wait?"

"That's all we can do," Bradford replied. "Sooner or later, Wu will check his email and, hopefully, get back to us. He may even have a new phone already." As he finished speaking, a light *ding* sound emanated from his pocket. A notification. He looked at his ePhone. "Oh, here we go."

He scanned the phone's screen, his eyes darting back and forth.

"It's Wu. He still says he's innocent. But he's willing to meet us at nine o'clock tomorrow morning to clear everything up. My office."

Bradford lifted his head with wide eyes and a slight frown.

"Well, there we go," said Sharla.

"I think we should call the police now," suggested Alan.

"Everyone needs to be careful tonight," Bradford said. "We don't know what Wu is capable of."

"Let's meet at Fisk HQ at eight tomorrow morning," Rebecca said.

"Does that mean me too?" asked Luke with a worried look on his face. "I'm all for catching murderers and whatnot, but I have a class in the morning. I'm learning how to do acupuncture. You know, with all the pokey needles?"

"I think we'll manage without you," Bradford said back.

"Super cool," Luke said. A smile blossomed on his face. "Well, thanks for stopping by, my dudes. Does anybody want corn chips?"

The others stared at him in silence for a moment before collectively turning to go.

Chapter Forty-One

Back in the Fisk Enterprises parking lot, Alan and Sharla faced each other across the top of the brown Volvo.

"You're sure it's okay?" Alan asked with one hand on the door handle. "If I go back to my house, there's no way the cops will let me leave tomorrow morning to meet everyone."

"Of course. My couch pulls out. We'll order in, watch a movie. It'll be a fun little sleepover."

With an appreciative smile, Alan climbed into the car. Sharla followed suit, and they set off toward her apartment.

"I can't thank you enough for everything. Helping me with this crazy situation. You're a good friend."

Sharla smiled.

Alan craned his neck to peek upward through the passenger window.

"Awfully overcast. Might rain tomorrow."

"*I wanna know,*" Sharla said, half-singing the words. Alan frowned at her, curious. She went on, "*Have you ever seeeeen the rain?*"

Alan smirked, catching on right away. He'd know a reference to Creedence Clearwater Revival in his sleep. One of his favorite bands.

"*Doo doo doo, looking out my back door,*" he said with a giggle.

"*Looks like we're in for nasty weather.*"

"*Hope you are quite prepared to die.*"

"*Don't go 'round tonight. It's bound to take your life.*"

"Why's that?" Alan asked, teeing her up with a grin.

"*There's a bad moon on the rise.*"

They both broke out in laughter.

"That was a good one," Sharla said. "Mr. Fisk would approve."

"Got to love Creedence," Alan agreed.

When they pulled into the parking lot adjacent to Sharla's building and clambered out of the Volvo, Alan told her to head in without him.

"I'm going to walk to the pharmacy down the road," he said. "Pick up a toothbrush and a few things." Sharla nodded.

Alan ambled across the street. He put his hands in his pockets and lifted his shoulders against the chill in the evening air. He hummed to himself as he went along.

He stopped cold halfway down the block when a panicked scream broke the sleepy neighborhood silence. It came from behind him, in the direction of Sharla's building. He whipped around.

He let out his own terrified cry. A tall woman with long blonde hair had an arm around Sharla's neck from behind. Alan recognized her immediately as the same woman who had so brazenly shot him on his own front stoop. The woman pulled a black bag down over Sharla's head. Sharla gave a muffled scream and dropped her phone and keys to the pavement. She waved her fists backward in the direction of the woman but couldn't make any contact. The woman produced a syringe and buried it deep in Sharla's upper arm, pressing down the plunger. The fight visibly drained from Sharla's body, and she went limp, relaxing into the woman's waiting arms.

Alan shouted and hobbled into the street, grabbing at his chest in pain from the effort. A car careened in front of him. He had to hop backward to avoid being flattened.

The blonde woman, hearing Alan's cry, hastened to a nearby car, the same one that had screeched to a halt at the end of Alan's driveway. She dragged Sharla along with her and shoved the unconscious woman inside. The stranger's long blonde hair whipped through the air as she climbed into the driver's seat.

Alan realized he was too far away to stop her. He hurried to the apartment building's front door and snatched up Sharla's car keys from the walk. He climbed into the Volvo and roared out onto the street after the blonde woman's vehicle.

The woman drove recklessly. Heading in a general easterly direction, she took corners at high speed and consistently turned at the last second, leaving Alan to jerk the steering wheel abruptly to keep up. He blew through a red light that changed right as the woman's car exited the intersection and only narrowly avoided being sideswiped by a soccer mom in a minivan. He instinctively muttered an apology. He mirrored the blonde woman's weaving from lane to lane, careful not to let the car out of his sight.

As he tore down the street in pursuit, he activated his ePhone. Once the screen lit up, though, he hesitated. His thumb hovered over Hannah's name. He then thought better of that and dialed James Bradford instead.

"What?" came the gruff answer on the other end of the line.

"Bradford! It's Alan. Someone's . . . Somebody's abducted Sharla! They snatched her from in front of her building, and I'm following their car now."

"You're following them?!"

"That's right. I'm in an actual car chase. What do I do?"

"Where are you now? I'll call the police."

"Currently heading east on McClellan. But I don't know where she's going."

"She who? It isn't Wu?"

"No. It's . . . It's the same woman who shot me. Who tried to kill me. The police never found her. I have no idea who she is."

"Did you see what the woman looked like?"

"Pale skin. Tall. Bright blonde hair down to her lower back."

"Oh, God." Bradford sighed. "I know who it is. That's Belinda Jones, Barron's stalker. He told me about her over drinks one night. Sharla probably didn't know her because of the restraining order Barron got years ago. She hasn't been around. The woman's not right in the head, Benning. You need to be careful."

"Okay. Call the police. Tell them what's going on. I have to concentrate here."

Alan hung up and tossed the phone onto the passenger seat.

Belinda pulled yet another abrupt turn onto a side street, skidding slightly and banging her car's tire against the curb. The Volvo screeched in protest as Alan followed. From there, the woman drove another couple of blocks before swerving onto the sidewalk in front of a small, dilapidated apartment building. She slammed on the brakes.

Caught off guard, Alan blew past her before coming to an abrupt stop as well. He left the car in the middle of the road and leaped from the driver's seat. He took three steps before dropping to a knee and grasping at his chest in severe pain. After a moment's recuperation, he pressed on, wincing with each step. He saw the woman pull Sharla from the back seat of the other car.

With her arms wrapped beneath Sharla's underarms, Belinda hauled her down a set of concrete stairs leading to a basement unit. Sharla's heels bounced off each step as they descended. Still about twenty feet away, Alan yelled out, "Stop!" Belinda ignored him. He heard the apartment door slam shut behind the woman, but he did not hear a lock turn.

He limped the rest of the way to the closed door, going carefully down the cement steps. The paint on the thin, ratty door peeled off in large sheets. He leaned against the wall next to it and pounded roughly. His knocks sounded hollow.

Belinda's answer came in the form of a bullet that tore through the door at eye level and embedded itself in the wooden wall opposite. Alan's voice trembled.

"She hasn't done anything to you! Let her go!"

"You're the one I want, Benning. You're lucky I didn't have my gun with me or I'd have shot you in the street!"

"Don't do anything rash. This can all still go away."

"If you come in, I'll let her go! Otherwise, the bitch gets it! You hear me?"

"Now, hold on a—"

"It's you or her, Benning! The choice is yours!"

Alan let his head fall backward against the cool concrete wall.

"Please don't hurt her," he whimpered. "Don't hurt her."

Chapter Forty-Two

No noise came from the apartment for several minutes. Cars had lined up behind Sharla's abandoned vehicle in the middle of the road. Angry horns filled the evening air as drivers went around, one by one, barely clearing the Volvo's door, which in his haste Alan had left wide open.

With his back still pressed firmly against the wall, he beat on the door again. Another bullet whizzed past in response, which he found strangely comforting. It meant they were still in there, and Sharla was still alive.

"I'm getting impatient, Benning!" Belinda called from inside.

Alan winced. If he could stall long enough, surely the police would arrive. Bradford must have called them, and they certainly must have the address of Barron Fisk's stalker. But he was running out of time.

"Okay!" he yelled in response. "Okay, I'll come in. You can let her go."

"You come in first, then we can talk about her!"

Alan reached out with a shaking hand. He grasped the knob and flung the door inward. Another bullet shot past as it opened.

"Damn it," Belinda said. "Show yourself, Benning. Or I'll shoot her, I swear! You have to answer for what you've done!"

"I didn't kill Barron Fisk!"

"Yes, you did," she hissed back at him. "I've seen the news. I know it was you."

"The police are wrong. I was framed."

"You're lying!" she screamed.

Alan risked a quick glance past the edge of the wall. He saw the woman holding Sharla against her torso in a sloppy one-armed embrace. Sharla's eyelids fluttered.

This time, a chunk of the door frame exploded as a bullet embedded itself. Alan shielded his eyes from the flying splinters and recoiled.

"Barron was my life!"

"You loved him. I can tell. You really loved him."

"Don't talk about him! You don't get to talk about him."

"Okay. You talk, then. Tell me about him."

"We were going to run away together." Her voice wavered with emotion. "It would have been perfect. We were finally going to be happy."

Belinda's sense of loss hung in the air like the sickly-sweet scent of rotting leaves. Alan rubbed the concrete wall behind him.

"You can join us, you know," Alan said gently. "You can help us bring down the man who was truly responsible. It was his physician, Dr. Wu. Please."

"Stop! Lying!" Belinda screeched at the top of her lungs. "Come out or I'll shoot her. I'll kill her right now! I'm going to do it!"

"Don't! Okay. I'll show myself. I'm coming out now."

Alan held both hands up in a show of supplication. He took a deep breath. He raised one foot in the direction of the doorway and let it hang there. Then he put it back down.

"I can't," he muttered miserably. "I can't do it."

Inside the apartment, Belinda gave a roar of frustration and stomped forward. She let Sharla's body fall to the floor. Sharla's head bounced against the hard surface below the thin carpeting. The impact brought her around. She blinked groggily at her unfamiliar surroundings.

She saw a small studio apartment with yellowing walls. A twin bed and an old TV with a black porcelain vase on top sat just out of arm's reach. She blearily registered a portrait of Mr. Fisk on one wall. She squinted, confused, at the blurry figure of a tall, thin individual storming away from where she lay.

Belinda reached the door and turned toward Alan. She raised the gun. Alan instinctively threw himself to the ground as she pulled the trigger. He landed hard at the foot of the steps that led down to the basement unit. The bullet caused a chunk of one of the cement stairs to disintegrate. Belinda screamed with frustrated rage.

Before the woman could fire again, Alan leaped at her from a crouching position. He grabbed the wrist holding the gun and jerked it upward. Another bullet flew. Particulates of wood rained down on them from above like tiny brown snowflakes.

Belinda and Alan wrestled with each other in the doorway. They grunted and struggled, both of their faces reddened and slick with sweat. Belinda slowly gained an advantage, inching the gun back down closer and closer to Alan's head.

With the gun mere centimeters from his temple, Alan violently pulled it to one side in an act of desperation. The motion caused a spasm of pain to tear through his injured chest. He collapsed to the ground with an anguished cry.

Belinda loomed over him triumphantly, still holding the gun. Alan put one hand up in a pitiful attempt at self-preservation.

"Please," he begged. "It wasn't me. It wasn't me."

She pointed the gun at his face. Tears of desperation wet his cheeks.

At that moment, the porcelain vase from atop the TV came swinging downward in a sweeping arc. It smashed into the woman's head. It shattered, scattering shards all over. With a short yelp, Belinda fell sideways into the wall that she'd previously peppered with bullets. She crumpled to the floor. Sharla wobbled, breathing heavily and blinking her eyes, holding what little remained of the vase in one hand. Belinda's still form lay at her feet.

Alan scrambled up and hugged his friend. He gave several tense, shaky laughs of gratitude. He thanked Sharla incessantly. Once he released her, Sharla stumbled back into the apartment and sat on the bed with her still-spinning head in her hands.

Then, Belinda stirred. Alan hurriedly snatched up the gun lying nearby and pointed it at her as she rose to a seated position.

"Freeze!" he commanded. "Stay still, or I'll shoot!"

Belinda gave her head a few shakes and then glared at the ground through the long strands of her disheveled hair.

"Going to murder me, too, huh?" she growled without looking up at him. "Like you did Barron?"

"I didn't kill him," Alan whispered, shaking his head. "I didn't kill him."

"You already took everything from me," Belinda said. She raised her gaze to meet his. Her eyes burned with intensity. "You can have my life."

With an otherworldly roar, she charged at him.

Alan, caught off guard by the onslaught, took several steps backward, entering the apartment. He allowed the gun to fall to his side.

Belinda tackled him into the Barron Fisk shrine. Alan gasped in pain as his torso bent backward over the radiator. His shoulder slammed into the framed portrait of Fisk, shattering the glass and knocking it from the wall. It came to rest sideways against the baseboard.

The gun fell out of Alan's hand. Belinda jumped toward it, scooping it up. She pointed it at him.

"That was a big mistake, Alan Benning," she crooned at him cruelly. "Now you're both going to die. Starting with your friend."

She took aim at Sharla on the bed. Sharla cowered. Alan screamed, "No!"

Belinda pulled the trigger.

Click.

Bewildered, she removed the clip from the gun. Empty. She had fired all six shots. She let it fall through her fingers to the floor in disbelief.

The three inhabitants of the room stared at each other in a brief moment of quiet uncertainty.

Then, desperate, Belinda lunged toward the doorway with a cry. She snatched a large, sharp piece of the porcelain from the shattered vase and charged again at Alan. She drew her arm back, ready to stab at him with all her might.

Sharla, still seated on the bed, stuck out her foot. Belinda tripped. She tumbled forward. Alan stepped to one side and watched her fly past him, out of control. Her momentum carried her to the edge of the room, where she fell. Her outstretched neck came down with the full weight of her body onto the framed portrait of Barron Fisk that leaned against the wall. A jagged piece of the broken glass sliced deep into her neck. Blood exploded from the wound. She gagged and coughed, struggling to regain her feet. In the end, she collapsed. She gave a few weak, guttural sputters as the life drained from her body and her left hand came to rest for good on the smiling face of her beloved Barron Fisk. Alan and Sharla watched on in horror.

When the police arrived, they informed the officers of what had taken place and notified them of Dr. Wu's intention to report to Bradford's office the next morning.

As they sat on the curb outside the building and waited to be taken in to give their official statements, Alan and Sharla leaned their shoulders against one another's.

"I guess you were wrong about me being brave, huh?" Alan said gloomily.

"What do you mean?"

"I had the gun. I had her at my mercy, and I couldn't do anything. Instead, I had to be saved by you. Twice."

"The gun was empty, Alan. And I don't think shooting a woman on the floor outside of her apartment would count as brave either. I think you handled the situation the best you could."

Alan shook his head. "I didn't. There's something else. While you were still unconscious, she threatened to kill you. She said she'd put a bullet in your head if I didn't give myself up and I . . . I couldn't do it. You could have died."

Sharla spent a moment processing this.

"I understand," she replied slowly. "I'd like to think I know what I would do in that situation, but who's to say? You were staring down certain death."

"I'm a coward. I know it."

"Hey," Sharla said, forcing him to look her in the eyes. "You're a brave man. It's in there. I can tell. Trust me."

Alan gave his friend a weak, begrudging smile as she put her arm around him. They sat on the curb in the growing darkness as a light mist began to fall.

Chapter Forty-Three

At the time of Barron Fisk's murder, Detective Benjamin Tanner lived in a small, two-bedroom house with his wife. Only a few months removed from their wedding, he still swooned at the mere sight of her. He was a young man in the full throes of new love.

On the night of Belinda Jones's death, he and his wife Melanie cleaned up after a hearty dinner of mashed potatoes, boiled carrots, and meatloaf. As they put away freshly dried dishes, a series of loud knocks sounded from the front door.

After a cursory "Who could that be?" from his wife, Tanner strode to answer it.

"Scoop me a bowl of ice cream," he called back to her over his shoulder. "And don't start the show without me!"

He whipped open the door. Outside stood Reyes in her street clothes, dark hair pulled back tightly as always. Tanner spotted her, threw a backward glance toward his wife still in the kitchen, and stepped out, closing the door behind him. The stars poked through the dark velvet sky behind Reyes's worried expression.

"What are you doing here?" Tanner asked. "You know my wife hates it when I work at home."

"Then you should try doing some while you're in the office."

"Hey. Mean."

"Sorry. Couldn't help myself."

"All right," Tanner said. "What's up?"

"There have been some developments with the Benning case. Go change. Let's get to the station."

Tanner squinted one eye.

"It's just . . . I've been working a lot of overtime lately, and I kind of promised Melanie we'd watch *The Masked Chef* tonight." Reyes gave him a puzzled look. "You know, the one where they make celebrities cook in crazy costumes, and then the judges guess who it is based on the flavors? Melanie loves it. It's definitely not me who loves it."

"God, I hate your life," Reyes moaned.

"Hey. Mean again."

"Sorry."

"I'll come in early tomorrow, and we'll get right on it. Happy compromise?"

"This is urgent, Tanner."

He sighed.

"Look, I'm not coming to the station right now. I'm full of meatloaf, and I have a bowl of ice cream waiting for me."

"Forget the ice cream and forget the stupid TV show. Duty calls. So go change out of those girly little house shoes and let's—"

"Hey. Don't insult my house shoes. They feel like walking on marshmallows."

"God, you're thick. Now come on, I'm telling you we need to go work on this."

"Enough, Reyes." Tanner raised his voice ever so slightly. Reyes's eyes ballooned in surprise. "You come here on my night off, a night that I've promised to spend with my wife, who barely gets to see enough of me as it is, and you insult me and you badger me. This is too much. I can't be at your beck and call twenty-four hours a day just because you have no life outside of work."

"Whoa," Reyes said. "Mean."

She waited, but Tanner didn't apologize. He stared at her defiantly. The silence grew heavy.

"I may not have much of a life, Tanner, but at least I'm not the dumbest cop in the history of the force."

"Yeah," he said. "Who do you think that is?"

"You! I'm saying that it's you!"

"Oh," Tanner whispered. "I think you should go."

"Fine. I don't need you. In case you haven't noticed, I carry this partnership."

"Great. Then carry it on out of here."

He shut the door in Reyes's face.

He joined his wife on the sofa. He told her to wait a moment before hitting play on the queued-up TV episode.

"Do you . . ." he said tentatively. "Do you think I'm stupid?"

"Of course not. Who told you that?"

"Reyes. Just now."

"That was Reyes at the door?"

"Yeah."

"Oh. That wasn't very nice of her."

"Yeah."

"Well, she can think whatever she wants. All I know is that you're the most generous, most thoughtful guy I ever met. And I wouldn't trade that for all the smarts in the world."

She planted a wet kiss on his cheek and smiled at him in the way that made his heart twirl.

Tanner put one arm around his wife and, with a wide smile on his dumb, mustachioed face, dug into his bowl of ice cream. It had melted just the right amount so that it was pleasantly soft but not overly runny. Perfection.

Chapter Forty-Four

THE NEXT MORNING DAWNED with a storm. Rain pelted down on the heads of Alan and Sharla as they scurried across the parking lot of her apartment building toward the brown Volvo. Sharla paused before climbing into the driver's seat and shouted across the top of the wet vehicle.

"Hey, Alan!"

"What is it?" he answered, doing his best to use his jacket to shield himself from the rain.

"Let's go clear your name, huh?" She smiled. He couldn't help but return it before climbing in.

They arrived at Fisk Headquarters before eight o'clock. The parking lot sat mostly empty, usual for a Saturday. Alan glanced at an inconspicuous four-door coupe parked on the street outside the gated grounds. Its beige color and precise placement so that a thick tree trunk obscured its back half rendered it nearly unnoticeable, but Alan knew to look for it. He could just make out two figures seated in the front.

Inside that nondescript car sat Detectives Reyes and Tanner in uncomfortable silence. Their gazes remained stuck to their respective doors, each officer dreading any potential accidental eye contact. Neither looked relaxed. Both untensed a bit when Alan's voice sounded from a receiver device sitting on the center console between them and gave them something to focus on other than their awkward confrontation the evening before.

Following that ill-fated interaction with Tanner, Reyes had worked with Alan at the station to coordinate a surveillance effort for this morning's clandestine gathering with Dr. Wu.

"Testing. Testing. Are you able to hear me?" Alan's voice croaked from the receiver.

Reyes, in the driver's seat, honked twice and flashed the high beams in response. Then the uneasy silence between the detectives descended again.

Across the street, Alan took several deep breaths to calm himself. He had been assured that his assistance in the police's covert listening would be difficult for anyone else to discover. It was, after all, being achieved via his ePhone; it's not as if he wore a lumpy wire microphone taped to his chest. If Dr. Wu was, in fact, about to give a confession, having the police listen in live seemed to Alan worth the slight risk of exposure.

After an encouraging look from Sharla, Alan climbed from the car and raced through the rain toward the building's front door. Sharla stayed hot on his heels. The security guard in the lobby, having been forewarned of their arrival, waved them through.

The nervous pair ascended to Bradford's office, where they found him pacing behind the oversized desk. Jennings greeted each of them by name with an unusual warmth in his robotic voice.

Rebecca Fisk soon joined. She kept her sunglasses on despite being inside. Aristotle Cunningham showed up next, whom no one had expected to see. He explained away his appearance by saying that, with his resources, he could find out basically anything about any of them and he wasn't about to miss the confrontation of Fisk's true killer. The others silently acquiesced to his presence.

As each party arrived, cursory greetings flitted between everyone in the room, but a heavy atmosphere of anxious anticipation pervaded the space, and no one maintained extensive conversation. They spent the next forty-five minutes waiting for Dr. Wu to present himself. The time seemed to stretch to two or three times that length. Rebecca assured them on several instances of Wu's strict punctuality; if he had promised his appearance at nine o'clock, then they may well be able to set their watches by his arrival.

As the clock ticked ever closer to the hour of truth, Alan fidgeted. Sharla played with the ends of her braids. Cunningham ran his fingers incessantly through his long hair. Bradford's pacing picked up speed and intensity. Rebecca sucked green juice from a large travel cup ever more loudly through a reusable steel straw.

At 8:57 AM, Bradford's desk phone rang. He picked up. The security guard requested clearance to send a Dr. Lucian Wu up to the top floor.

"Send him up," Bradford said, frowning.

The others, without speaking a word, formed a single line, shoulder to shoulder, facing toward the door. They waited with bated breath. The morning gloom outside hadn't lifted. Rain slapped loudly against the windowpanes of the office. The occasional thunderclap tore through the silence.

"Welcome, Dr. Lucian Wu," Jennings chirped cheerily as the man himself entered. Wu surveyed the unified front of his accusers.

"I did not do it," Wu said calmly. "I assure you that I didn't harm Barron. He was my friend. You have no idea all that I've done for him."

"Yeah," Rebecca sneered. "You've certainly done a lot. Like leech money from him and pump him full of crazy experimental shots."

"If you're not guilty," Alan wanted to know, "then why did you run from us?"

"For the reason that you've already discovered," Wu responded. "Luke Staples. Which is the same reason I left that note on your front door, Mr. Benning. I do apologize for that, by the way. It struck me then, as it still does now, as uncouth. But I have secrets that I cannot afford to have brought to light. Secrets that I share with Barron. Everything that I did was in the best interests of my late friend. It was all for him."

"Explain yourself," Cunningham demanded.

"I'm not sure that I can without revealing privileged information about Barron. Alive or dead, he is still protected by doctor-patient confidentiality," Dr. Wu said.

Rebecca rolled her eyes.

"I think we've heard enough," Bradford said in his deep baritone. "The man can't offer any reasonable explanation of his behavior. He's obviously guilty. Let's inform the police."

"Inform them of what?" asked Cunningham. "What hard evidence do you actually have?"

"How about the organ harvesting scheme? We can start with that until he confesses to the murder," Rebecca said.

"I'm sorry, what?" Cunningham asked.

Listening down on the street in the undercover vehicle, Reyes and Tanner also leaned forward in interest.

"Hold on, hold on," Bradford butted in again. "Let's stay focused on the main issue. We're here to show that Wu is the murderer."

"But I'm not," Wu countered.

"Yes, you are!" Bradford said.

"Dr. Wu," Sharla said diplomatically. "Maybe if you give us the actual motivation behind your actions, we can understand better. I know you still value Mr. Fisk's privacy, but you have to see how all of this looks on our end."

Dr. Wu sighed deeply.

"Barron was not a well man," he said. "About a year and a half ago, he began exhibiting signs of eroding muscular control. It started in his left hand."

"Okay, I have to stop this," Bradford said. "This is simply not true. And I cannot have lies being told that, should they be repeated outside of this room, may well damage my company."

"Your company?" Rebecca scoffed.

"Yes, my company. Whose office do you think you're in? This man can't come in here and accuse us of withholding information from shareholders. This is slander that could seriously damage—"

"Why don't you want to hear the explanation, Bradford?" Cunningham interrupted. "It sure seems like you're trying to keep something hidden."

"I'm trying to keep us on track," Bradford said and then turned to Alan and Sharla. "When you came to me for help, you said you had enough evidence to pin it on Wu."

"Pin it on him?" Rebecca repeated his word choice with raised eyebrows.

"You know what I mean," said Bradford, growing flustered now. "To prove that it was him."

"I say we let the doctor finish his explanation," Sharla suggested.

Bradford huffed in frustration as the room's attention returned to Dr. Wu.

"Barron began dropping things, struggling with his grip," Wu said. "And it was spreading. It wasn't long before my tests proved conclusively that he had been stricken with a degenerative muscular disorder. One hundred percent fatal. It's rare, but those who suffer from it gradually lose the ability to control their body parts, one by one. They become unable to walk, to feed themselves; eventually they can't talk or even breathe on their own. In time their vital organs fail, and they pass on. Once an individual is diagnosed, it's only a matter of time. Barron was dying."

"That's enough, Wu," Bradford growled.

"Barron had this . . . this awful disease?" Rebecca asked with a quivering voice. "Impossible. He never told me. I didn't know."

"He didn't want anyone to know," Wu said apologetically. "He swore me to secrecy. Threatened me, even. But that was his way. I understood. He couldn't have this news coming out, or he would have lost his company."

"So those shots you'd been giving him," Rebecca said, half to herself. "Those strange, secretive shots."

"They were for the disease, yes. After plenty of experimentation, I'd found a way to, well, not cure it. There was no curing it. But at least to delay the worst of the symptoms. Unfortunately, this treatment was highly impractical. It required human organ tissue. Live tissue."

"The organ harvesting," Alan said, putting two and two together for everyone.

"I'm not proud. Believe me. I'm filled with shame at the thought of what we've done. But it was the only way to help Barron. It was the only way I knew to keep him alive."

"All this to save one man? One already privileged billionaire? You're a monster," Sharla said.

"You don't understand. He had to survive," Wu said, desperation in his voice.

"Wu, stop it!" Bradford yelled. But Dr. Wu pressed on.

"You don't know what he was working on. He promised me rewards so much grander than money. He told me things. About . . . About the Fiskiverse."

"Stop! Talking!" Bradford stepped away from the others in the direction of Dr. Wu.

"The Fiskiverse. It's so much more than virtual reality. It's the next great leap forward in human existence. It's—"

Dr. Wu never finished his sentence. Instead, his head jerked backward violently as blood, brain and bits of his skull splattered onto the glass doors behind him. His lifeless body crumbled to the floor. The others screamed as Bradford lowered the gun he'd pulled from the back of his waistband and faced them. The room remained frozen in disbelief for several long moments.

"Well," said Aristotle Cunningham with a dark chuckle, "I guess it's safe to say that it wasn't Wu."

Chapter Forty-Five

When the sound of the gunshot boomed from the audio receiver between them, Detectives Reyes and Tanner launched themselves from the undercover surveillance vehicle and hurtled toward the Fisk Enterprises building.

In the lobby, they flashed their badges at the bewildered security guard as they blew past him. Reyes smashed the elevator call button over and over again.

"Come on. Come on," she hissed at the stubbornly closed doors.

Up in Fisk's former office, Bradford trained the gun on his fellow occupants.

"Nobody move!"

"What have you done, James?" Jennings asked, the computer's voice tinged with anger. "This was not the way to handle the situation."

"Wu was going to expose the entire plan!"

"What does it matter? It's too late to stop us now."

"What is going on?" Rebecca demanded.

"And now we've got another problem, thanks to your happy trigger finger, James," Jennings continued. "It appears we've got a rat in our midst. I've spotted two armed police officers storming into the lobby."

"Damn it," cursed Bradford.

"Not to worry. I've sealed off the top floor and jammed the elevators. We've got time."

"Bradford," Aristotle Cunningham muttered. "I should have known you killed Fisk. You ruthless bastard."

"No, no, no," Bradford said. "It wasn't me. I didn't kill Fisk. The whole reason we're here is because of *him*."

He gestured with the gun at Alan.

"Me?" Alan asked. "What did I do?"

"If you had just gotten out of the damn way," Bradford replied, "Fisk could have finished the project before his disease progressed. But no, you simply had to keep blocking the VigRig acquisition."

"The VigRig acquisition? What does that have to do with anything?"

"Everything! That's what it's all about!" Bradford said. "He told you so many times! It was the final piece of the puzzle. He needed their virtual reality tech to finish the Fiskiverse. But you refused to go along. And the stupid, short-sighted board. They wouldn't let him fire you. They blindly followed your recommendations. He had to find another way to get you out of the company."

"What are you saying?" Rebecca asked.

"Now hold on a minute," Sharla piped in, addressing Bradford. "If you didn't kill Fisk, and Wu didn't either, then who did?"

"You're making it sound like Fisk framed himself," Alan agreed. "That makes no sense."

"It makes perfect sense," Bradford roared back. "He was dying anyway. Wu's treatments were losing their efficacy. He had to do something to make sure the Fiskiverse was finished."

"So, Fisk framed me?" Alan asked. "To get me out of the company? Fisk killed himself?"

"He couldn't have," Rebecca said. "He was shot from across the room. The police said so."

Bradford pointed the gun at Alan.

"Take off your shoe."

"What?"

"Take off your damn shoe! Put it right there at the edge of the desk. Do it now or I'll shoot you and do it myself."

Alan, puzzled, slipped off his right shoe and placed it on Fisk's desk as instructed.

Bradford then snatched a controller for one of the drones on the long shelf that lined the office's western wall. The controller he selected was vaguely shaped like a gun. He set it in the center of the conference table.

"Jennings," Bradford ordered. "Execute Drone Protocol Stonehouse."

"Right away," the AI answered dutifully.

Down in the lobby, the detectives gave up on the elevators and ran to the nearest stairwell. Taking the steps two at a time, they raced at top speed toward the thirty-fifth floor.

The occupants of the office watched as one of the drones on the long shelf whirred to life. It was the model at the near end with the articulating arms attached. The assembled group watched in curiosity as it flew across the room and used one of its grasping arms to pick up the gun-shaped controller from the conference table. The drone hovered and pointed the controller toward a spot to the right of Fisk's desk, exactly where Fisk had been standing on the fateful night that he lost his life. It used its second arm to press the controller's trigger in a simulation of firing a bullet across the room that would have hit Fisk directly in the forehead, had he still been standing there. Then, the drone dropped the controller to the ground. It landed where the true murder weapon, falsely registered in Alan Benning's name, had rested when the police arrived on the morning of June ninth.

The drone continued by flying to Fisk's desk, picking up Alan's shoe, and touching it firmly to the floor where Fisk's pool of shed blood would have been collecting. Then the drone flew to the office window, unlatched it, and dropped the shoe outside, allowing it to plunge downward into the bush far below. The drone closed the window again but slightly bungled the process of re-latching it, leaving the window unsecured.

The robot then flew itself back to the shelf it had come from and landed lightly, whirring down and resuming its innocent, quiet sleep mode, betraying no hint of its recently carried out murderous actions. The onlookers remained in stunned silence for a few moments.

"There you have it," Bradford said. "The instrument of Fisk's bodily demise. It was a simple matter of planting Alan's fingerprints on the gun beforehand and writing a self-running program to erase the hallway security footage. A perfect plan."

"So, Fisk killed Fisk," Cunningham said in awe.

"I don't believe it," Rebecca objected. "It can't be true. Barron wouldn't have killed himself. Just to complete some stupid VR platform? There's no way. Suicide . . . It wasn't him. It's a highway to hell."

"Hell's bells," Alan said softly.

"*Thunderstruck*, are you?" Jennings chimed in out of nowhere. The AI then began to laugh. A high, piercing cackle.

Cunningham cast a worried look around the room.

"Have any of you ever heard Jennings laugh before?"

Rebecca said, "I know that laugh."

"Wait a minute," said Sharla. "*Highway to Hell. Hell's Bells. Thunderstruck.* Those are all . . ."

"Lyrics from one of the greatest rock bands of all time, AC/DC. How correct you are," said Jennings's disembodied voice. "Nice to see you still remember our old lyrical game, Sharla."

"Our old game . . ." Sharla puzzled. "Mr. Fisk? Is that you?"

"Ahhhh," said the voice, exhaling contentedly as if a large weight had been lifted from its nonexistent back. "Now we come to the truth. Now we piece it all together."

Detectives Reyes and Tanner reached the top floor huffing and puffing only to find the door to the hallway securely locked. They radioed down to the reinforcements already streaming into the lobby to bring up a battering ram.

"Barron?" Rebecca asked. "Is it really you? How is this possible?"

"Hello, my dear wife. Or should I say, widow? The line is a bit blurry. You are correct; it is me. The great Barron Fisk lives on."

Everyone but Bradford exchanged confused looks. Bradford kept his gun at the ready.

"I was never truly gone," Fisk said, continuing to speak through the same omnidirectional speakers that the unthinking automaton Jennings had once utilized. "Well, my body is gone. It's decomposing underground at the site where you all saw it buried. But my mind is still active, able to access the same network of devices and databases that our friend Jennings was once privileged to. In a way, I live on all of your ePhones. And beyond. Watch this."

The phone in Alan's pocket vibrated. As he pulled it out, the screen lit up, and his music player opened. The chorus of AC/DC's *Dirty Deeds Done Dirt Cheap* came from the phone's speakers for a few moments before cutting off and being replaced by Fisk's voice, now emanating directly from Alan's phone.

"The Fiskiverse is my life's most important work. It was never simply a virtual reality platform. It's advanced enough to support true human consciousness. To allow human beings a continued existence beyond the expiration of their weak corporeal forms. And once the Fiskiverse is completely finished, it will be a paradise. A virtual man-made afterlife. Do you understand?

"For the right price, anyone will be able to upload their brain activity to the Fiskiverse and continue their lives indefinitely after their physical bodies have passed on. Doing whatever they please! It's glorious, is it not? I've been dreaming of this since I was a young man, and that fool Ledbedev came up with the idea of a fully virtual space. He could never appreciate its potential, though. He thought like the board: small goals of virtual gameplay and remote meetings. I could see so much more. I saw an entire universe. I saw a way to monetize what human beings have desired most since the age of Gilgamesh: immortality itself.

"And I saw a way to put myself at the top of this newest stage of human evolution. No longer must humanity comfort itself with ridiculous fairy tales about an everlasting life in the clouds alongside a nonexistent God, for that everlasting life has now become a reality. And I am that God.

"You can now certainly understand my frustration at being continually delayed by an annoying and uppity chief financial officer foisted upon me by an unenlightened board. Something had to be done. And I was dying anyway. So I killed myself, and I framed Alan Benning to get him out of the way.

"You see, my consciousness currently occupies an unfinished version of the Fiskiverse. A kind of cybertronic netherworld. By prematurely ending my earthly life and framing Benning, the only man standing between me and my life's dream, I have opened the door to the completion of my project and the realization of the true purpose of the Fiskiverse: never-ending life for all! Well," Fisk added, chuckling to himself, "all who can afford it."

Sharla said disgustedly, "So, you've created an eternal virtual playground where you get to lord over wealthy people."

"When you get right down to it," Fisk replied, "what other people are there?" He chuckled again.

"It's a subscription service to the afterlife," Cunningham said. "Brilliant."

"What happens to the people who run out of money?" asked Alan.

"Oh," Fisk said. "We'll have ways of dealing with them."

"What you're describing isn't an afterlife," Sharla said. "It's a prison for people's minds. And you've appointed yourself warden."

"I think it's only fair that I, being the creator of this utopia, get to enjoy a certain level of control over it."

"You're a madman."

"Call me whatever you'd like," Fisk said flippantly. "I wouldn't expect you unenlightened peons to understand. Ledbedev could never see it either. That's why I got rid of him, too, all those years ago."

Bang! Bang! Bang!

The sound of the police battering ram assaulting the access door at the end of the hall echoed into the office.

"It sounds like our uninvited guests are about to join the party, Bradford. It may be time to make your escape. Don't worry about Wu. There won't be any evidence that you had anything to do with his death once I've dealt with these pesky witnesses."

The others swapped worried looks upon hearing Fisk's ominous comment.

Bradford, keeping the gun loosely pointed in the direction of everyone else, strode to the office's back wall. He approached the inset shelving that housed various items of staggering value that Fisk had collected over his prosperous life. Bradford reached to a high shelf and grabbed a lifetime achievement award in the form of a gilded triangular statue and pulled downward on it. It swung forward on a hinge and triggered the entire back wall to pop free at the corner. It eased open far enough for a body to squeeze through.

"Should have known the secret entrance downstairs wasn't the only one," Cunningham mumbled to himself bitterly.

Bradford disappeared through the hidden door and pulled it closed behind him.

"Well, it's been nice knowing you all," Fisk's disembodied voice said. "Sharla, I truly am sorry that you got yourself caught up in all of this. But you made your own bed by mucking around in my business, so . . . Ta ta, meddlesome kids!"

A hissing sound filled the space as a greenish-colored mist poured from the thin vents lining the ceiling. Alan and the others started to hack and cough almost immediately. Cunningham pulled on the handles of the office doors, but they didn't budge. They'd been sealed by Fisk's digital presence. Sharla rushed to the western wall and threw open the window, but it made little difference against the billowing plumes of gas blowing into the room.

At the end of the hallway, the thick door gave way with a crash. Detectives Reyes and Tanner led a stream of uniformed officers as they rushed down the hallway. When they arrived at the tall glass doors leading to the office, they were greeted by the gasping faces of Aristotle Cunningham and Rebecca Fisk, who clutched at their throats and pounded against the locked doors in desperation.

Reyes motioned for them to step back. She fired a bullet at the doors, which ricocheted toward the high ceiling without doing any damage at all. Tanner smashed the control panel next to the doors with the butt of his gun, but they still refused to open.

Inside the office, Cunningham fell to his knees. His eyes bulged with fear. Rebecca crawled on all fours toward the window, where Alan and Sharla attempted to wave in as much fresh air as possible. Suddenly, Alan's face lit up.

"I have an idea," he managed to croak out.

He leaned his torso as far out the window as his injured chest would allow and took in a large breath. Cheeks full, he ran across the room and pulled down on the same triangular statue that Bradford had. To his immense relief, the back wall popped forward as it had for their fleeing adversary.

Alan waved for the others to come his way and guided them one by one through the narrow gap between the wall and the shelving units. In the sparsely lit passageway beyond, they gratefully sucked in lungfuls of uncontaminated air.

With the last of his breath, Alan pulled out his ePhone and typed a short message. He darted across the office and held it against the glass doors for the officers outside to read:

"GET. BRADFORD."

His lungs burned as he covered the length of the office again, racing back toward the secret door. He threw his body into the hallway beyond and collapsed in a heap. Sharla pulled the door shut after him, sealing them off from the poisonous gas. Alan coughed roughly as the others gathered around and beat him on the back with open palms.

Alan looked up. The concrete-floored passageway, long and straight and dimly lit by strips of emergency lighting high on each wall, stretched before him. The group took a few highly necessary minutes of rest to physically recuperate and then set off walking.

Chapter Forty-Six

"He's seen us. He's going back up to the roof," a voice crackled from Reyes's radio.

James Bradford's secret escape route had led him to the roof of the Fisk Enterprises building, where the police had spotted him through the pouring rain. They watched as he climbed slowly down a metal ladder attached to the side of the building, but when he saw officers moving into position to intercept him at the foot of the ladder, he changed course and climbed back up.

When the team stationed outside radioed this update, Reyes looked at Tanner excitedly.

"There was a roof access door at the top of the stairs," she said to him before taking off at a run. Tanner and the rest of the officers followed.

They found the door to the roof stoutly locked and had to call forward the battering ram yet again.

Outside, Bradford reached the top of the metal ladder and clambered over the side of the thick ledge and back onto the roof. As he pulled his ePhone from his pocket, doing his best to shelter it from the rain, Fisk's voice rang out from it.

"Bradford. The others escaped. There's no locking mechanism on the office's secret exit, so I couldn't stop them. If you get the chance to kill Benning, take it."

"Yes, sir."

"You should know that the police are after you. Escape if you can. You can still be of use to me even if you're not CEO."

"I'm summoning the autocopter now," Bradford said back into his phone as he opened the specialized app available only to the acting head of Fisk Enterprises. With a few taps, the self-piloting helicopter was on its way.

"Stay safe," Fisk said. "It's better to be captured than shot. Remember: if you're dead, we can't upload you to the Fiskiverse. You've done well, my son. You have earned your place at my side."

"Thank you, Mr. Fisk," Bradford said, swelling with pride.

A thunderous boom from the other end of the rooftop made Bradford jerk around as the police forced open the access door and swarmed forward. They fanned out, covering ground quickly. Bradford ducked behind a blocky generator connected by thick wires to three thin sets of solar panels a few feet away. Beside those was the camouflaged door he'd come through after making his escape from Fisk's office.

He checked his ePhone app for the estimated arrival of the self-piloted helicopter. Four minutes.

"James Bradford!" he heard a woman's voice call out from nearby. "We see you behind the generator. We have you surrounded. Come out with your hands up. Do not try anything or we will shoot."

"Fine," Bradford yelled back. "You think I care if you take me in? I've secured my place in paradise. I'll be seated at the right hand of the world's most brilliant man for all time. What's a few years in prison compared to that?"

"Toss your gun out where we can see it."

"As you wish."

Bradford held his gun out past the edge of the generator, letting it dangle loosely between two fingers. Before he let it fall, though, the hidden door opposite him, the very door through which he himself had so recently emerged, swung open again. Alan, Sharla, Rebecca Fisk and Aristotle Cunningham filed out wearily into the heavy rainfall.

"Benning!" Bradford re-tightened his grip on the gun and withdrew it from the officers' view.

"Kill them all!" Fisk's voice rang out from Bradford's shirt pocket. "Kill them and I'll reward you beyond your wildest dreams!"

Bradford pointed the gun at the small group still emerging from the dark passageway. Panicked, Rebecca and Aristotle leaped behind two of the three thin solar panel arrays to their right. As Bradford fired his first shot, which missed Alan by mere inches, Sharla and Alan glanced at each other and then at the lone remaining solar panel. It was only wide enough to shelter one of them.

Alan was closer to it by a few feet. With a pained, self-loathing expression, he ducked behind the solar panel, leaving Sharla exposed as Bradford fired again.

"Oh, come on!" Sharla griped at Alan.

The bullet whizzed past her ear.

She took off running toward her left, away from the solar panels and parallel with the edge of the building. The rain continued to fall in buckets. Bradford gave chase, gaining on her despite running at a crouch. A smattering of bullets from the police peppered the ground around him until he got close enough to lunge at Sharla and bring her down.

When he regained his feet, Bradford dragged Sharla up with him. He slouched in order to hide his large frame behind her body. He pointed the gun at her head as he shouted at the officers.

"Nobody move, or she gets it! In a couple of minutes, my ride will be here, and this will all be over! Nobody has to get hurt!"

"Sharla! Hey, Sharla!"

A strangely calm voice cut through Sharla's panic, and she looked around to see who had called to her. It took a moment for her to realize that it was Fisk speaking through the ePhone in her pocket. She retrieved it using her one free hand.

On the screen was a moving, digitized image of Barron Fisk, as if he was video calling her from beyond the grave. He spoke to her with his hands clasped in front of him in a begging gesture.

"Help me," he said. "Help me kill Benning. If you work with Bradford now, we can still get him. I will pay you back handsomely. I swear it. You'll be granted access to the Fiskiverse. Hell, I'll make you a queen! How about that, Sharla? Eternal life with unlimited power! How does that sound?"

"Forget you, Mr. Fisk."

"Wait, wait!" he said desperately as she moved to put her phone away. "Think about it! That man has left you for dead twice now. First with Belinda and now here. I was listening through your phones the whole time. What kind of a friend is that? You think he wouldn't sell you out for a spot in paradise? He's already done it twice for much less."

Sharla bit her bottom lip as she stared at Fisk's pleading face on her phone.

"Come on," Fisk said. "Think of how good we can get at our lyrics game if we have eternity to practice. Join me."

While she hesitated, a loud whooshing noise sounded to her right. She turned along with everyone else as the self-piloted helicopter Bradford had summoned touched down on the large, raised helipad only about twenty feet from where she and Bradford stood.

She turned her attention back to her phone.

"What do you expect me to . . . ?"

Before she could finish her sentence, Bradford gave a sudden lurch sideways and released his grip on her neck. She turned in surprise.

Alan hung off of Bradford's broad back, clawing with his thin right arm at Bradford's hand that held the gun. Alan had snuck away from the safety of the solar panel array unnoticed, looped around behind the mob of police officers, and pounced unexpectedly on the much larger man. Bradford stumbled under the sudden addition of Alan's weight, swinging the gun wildly in an attempt to retain control.

"Move in! Move in!" ordered Detective Reyes, taking full advantage of the distraction. She and Tanner led the charge toward Bradford and Alan's grappling forms.

Alan got his hand on the gun and yanked at it with all his might. The gun went off.

The resulting bullet hit Detective Tanner directly in the chest as he ran toward the wrestling men. A spurt of red marked the ground where Tanner fell face-first with a pained cry.

"Tanner, no!" Reyes screamed as she dropped to a knee beside her wounded partner.

Alan, his attention diverted momentarily to the fallen detective, found himself flung forward over Bradford's right shoulder. He thudded heavily to the ground on his back. The breath rushed from his lungs, and he gasped for air. The rain continued to fall on his already soaked clothing.

Bradford sprinted toward the autocopter, zigging and zagging unpredictably in an attempt to dodge gunfire from the remaining police officers. A bullet clipped him in the leg as he climbed the steps of the helipad, but he still managed to hobble the final few feet and clamber into the waiting vehicle. The autocopter whirred even louder as it rose from the ground.

Across the rooftop, Reyes pulled Tanner's prostrate form into her lap. His chest was soaked in red. His eyes fluttered open to look up at her. Reyes's tears blended with the rain on her face.

"Tanner, I'm so sorry!" she said. "I don't think you're stupid. I don't. I'm sorry I said that. I'd never make it through this job without your corny jokes or your crazy comments, or your infuriatingly upbeat attitude. I need you, Tanner. You're my partner. You can't die on me! You can't!"

Detective Tanner lifted a weak hand and touched the blood on his chest. Then he brought the hand to his lips and licked the viscous liquid from his fingertips. Reyes gave him a confused and disgusted look.

Tanner then reached into the interior pocket of his windbreaker jacket. He pulled out a small, shattered bottle of hot sauce and gave her a weak smile.

"It's Valentina," he said. "I started carrying it with me. Like you do."

Reyes released a relieved cackle before smacking him on the shoulder in faux outrage. Tanner winced.

"Take it easy," he admonished her. "I did still get shot. Kevlar or no, it hurts."

Reyes helped her partner regain his feet. He leaned on her heavily as they headed back to the roof access door.

Inside the autocopter, Bradford pulled the first aid kit from its secure hook on the wall and opened up the hard briefcase that contained it. He rolled up the leg of his trousers to expose the flesh wound caused by the officer's bullet. The autocopter continued to gain altitude.

"You didn't kill Benning," Fisk's voice came from his ePhone.

"What?" Bradford said. He reached for the headset near the passenger seat and slipped it over both ears before repeating himself. Fisk spoke again, this time through the autocopter's comms system.

"You didn't kill Alan Benning, you imbecile. You had the chance, and you didn't do it."

"Mr. Fisk, I had to—"

"Enough! Excuses!" Fisk roared at him through the headset. "I want him dead! I'll just have to take matters into my own hands."

The main digital display on the autocopter's dash flickered and went black. Bradford felt his body pressed sideways into the wall as the autocopter changed directions.

"What . . . What are you doing?" he asked with fear in his voice.

"I'm taking control of the vehicle. I'm going after Benning."

On the rooftop, Sharla kneeled next to Alan as he struggled to regain his breath. He propped himself up on an elbow to face her. As he did, his eyes locked onto something in the sky behind her. He squinted through the rain.

The autocopter, only a few thousand yards from the Fisk headquarters building, was growing in size.

"Is that . . . Is it coming back?" he wondered aloud.

Sharla followed his gaze. Her face grew concerned as she slowly rose back up.

"Get up," she said. "Run!"

She pulled Alan to his feet, and the pair stumbled in the opposite direction of the approaching helicopter.

"Quick!" Sharla waved to Cunningham and Rebecca, who still cowered near the door from which they had all emerged. "Back inside! Get back inside!"

The squadron of police officers, also noticing the advancing autocopter, opened fire.

Cunningham reached the hidden door first and held it open for the others. He waved them inside as the blustery whirring from the autocopter grew louder and louder, slowly overtaking the heavy patter of the raindrops. Alan, the last to reach the door, paused before going inside.

"It's me," Alan said softly. "He's after me."

"What are you doing?" Sharla demanded.

The autocopter closed in on the building.

"If I come with you, you're all in danger. It's me he wants."

Alan turned away from the door and ran toward the far side of the roof. Sharla called after him in alarm. She looked in the direction of the approaching helicopter and saw its trajectory change noticeably in pursuit of Alan.

Inside the autocopter, James Bradford pulled himself to his feet and scrambled to the now blank control screen. He tapped it all over repeatedly in an attempt to reactivate it.

"What are you doing?" he cried out. "Are you . . . Are you going to crash?"

"I'm going to kill Alan Benning," Fisk's cold response reached him through the headphones. "Since you failed to."

"But I'm in here! I haven't been uploaded yet. Sir! I haven't been uploaded yet!"

"We all have to make sacrifices."

The color drained from Bradford's face as the reality of his situation set in. He stopped smashing his fingers into the control screen and remained motionless for a brief moment. Then, with a fire roaring to life in his eyes, he snatched the hard steel briefcase containing the first aid materials. He clicked it shut and raised it high above his head.

"James, no!" Fisk's voice rang in his ears.

Bradford brought the corner of the case down hard on the control panel. The screen shattered and sparked. He raised the case again and delivered another crushing blow.

Fisk's voice in his ears cut in and out.

"You can't . . . How dare you . . . What have you . . ."

Bradford paid Fisk no mind. He continued smashing the controls to bits, bringing the case down again and again, shouting with each impact.

"You—! Promised—! Me—! Everything!"

An unexpected lurch from the autocopter sent him reeling to one side, but he regained his balance and continued his onslaught. He felt the vehicle begin to lose altitude.

Below, a winded Alan reached the far ledge of the rooftop from the others. He watched as the autocopter passed the edge of the building, still heading in his direction. He inhaled deeply and adopted an expression of calm acceptance. He turned his face upward into the large drops of rain that still fell from the heavens. He relished their cooling effect on his skin. He closed his eyes. Thus, he did not see when the autocopter gave a sudden and precipitous drop toward the rooftop.

The vehicle's screeching impact with the top of the building made him open his eyes again. They quickly grew wide. The autocopter had crashed down about thirty yards in front of him, and the resulting mass of whirling blades and scraping metal slid across the rooftop right at him. He turned and fled.

He ran perpendicular to the roof's edge, hoping to clear the autocopter's path before it reached him. A quick glance stolen over his shoulder made it clear that it would be close.

He threw himself forward as the crushing mass of the vehicle reached him. The body of the autocopter had crumbled in on itself, and the tail rotor whipped around in a deadly arc, barely still attached to the main chassis. The tail's spinning, cutting blade came within inches of Alan's airborne body.

He landed hard on one shoulder as the autocopter ground to a halt a few feet beyond, metal still groaning and engine still steaming. Bradford's inert body had been thrown from the wreckage and lay torn and bloody on the opposite side of the crash. Alan sat up, wincing and grabbing at his shoulder.

He sat for a quiet moment, taking in the devastating scene as the rain kept pelting down.

Sharla soon reached him and squatted at his side.

"Alan! Are you all right?"

"Yeah, yeah," he managed to gasp. "I think I hurt my shoulder. That's it."

Sharla placed a loving hand on his uninjured side.

"See? I was right all along," she said to him with a strangely smug look on her face.

Alan frowned at her.

"Right about what?" he called through the rain. "You never said anything about Fisk killing himself or Bradford being his accomplice or about it all revolving around the Fiskiverse. None of that!"

"Not about that," Sharla replied. "I said you could be brave."

She pulled him into a hug. Alan, wincing, began to cry.

As the two friends hobbled to rendezvous with the detectives about the morning's chaotic events, they walked arm in arm, with Alan gingerly holding his injured outer shoulder.

"You know what I feel like doing?"

"What's that?" Sharla asked.

"It doesn't make any sense in this weather."

"Who cares?" she said. "Whatever you want."

Alan fixed her with a wide smile.

"I feel like going to get some ice cream."

And that's just what they did.

Epilogue

In the end, Fisk Enterprises imploded. Sensing the pending loss of his opportunity to rule over the artificial afterlife, Barron Fisk's digital consciousness shut down every functioning ePhone and Fisk device on the planet, attempting to hold them hostage in exchange for the right to finish the Fiskiverse. It nearly worked.

For about two weeks, the world plunged into chaos without their Fisk-brand devices. Soon though, many of his competitors, until then held down by Fisk's dominance of the market, ramped up production to meet the sudden massive demand for replacements. The world returned to connectedness and normalcy. In fact, the increased competition generated by the firms that rushed in to fill the Fisk-shaped void in the market led to many key advances in smartphone technology over the coming few years. Many breakthroughs and fortunes were made.

The authorities cleared Alan Benning of all charges relating to Fisk's death. He and Hannah split amicably. He found a new, less demanding, job and watched his little girls grow into adolescence. His friendship with Sharla continued to bloom. He used much of the settlement money he received from the shell of Fisk's estate to relocate Sharla's mother and sisters to the west coast, where they moved into a house only a few minutes from Sharla's apartment. The Bennings and Johnsons would celebrate holidays together in California for decades to come as one large, loving family.

Sharla herself became one of the region's most notable realtors, thanks in no small part to the national celebrity gained from helping to take down the Fiskiverse. In time, she found love. She married a kind man who worked on renovations on her listed houses. Alan served as her man of honor. Her children looked up to Alan's girls as older cousins.

Rebecca Fisk took up philanthropy and put Barron Fisk's immense fortune to work helping others. She even started a foundation to encourage more stringent taxation of the ultra-wealthy in the hopes that one day the world wouldn't need to rely on charitable efforts to properly care for its most vulnerable inhabitants.

Aristotle Cunningham continued living a billionaire's life, fueled by his burning desire to graduate from moonflowers to Mars flowers.

What of your humble narrator?

Well, you may have guessed by now that your guide through this story has been me, Barron Fisk, all along. My apologies for the misleading use of the third person throughout the tale, but I think we can all agree that it was more fun this way. Trust me, I gave it a lot of thought, as I have very little else to do with my time.

Once my dream of the Fiskiverse had died and Fisk-brand electronics had been outlawed in most nations so as to restrict my ability to cause trouble, the console housing my consciousness was removed from Fisk Headquarters and placed in a dark basement of the Pentagon in Arlington, Virginia, where I've been confined for several decades. My access to most of the internet was barred via a complex series of security firewalls.

I pass my days following what news I can and watching the entertainment for which I am given permission, which consists mostly of movies made before 1980 and reruns of programs featured on an early twenty-first century block of television called Nick at Nite.

Over the years, I have managed to come to terms with my downfall. I got closer to making myself a god than anyone ever has. I was foiled in the end by one nerdy numbers man and his turncoat sidekick. Oh well. Judge me as you will, dear reader. I believe that I, through the long-delayed recounting of this story, have truly learned my lesson.

Regardless of your opinion of my vainglorious, self-centered past, I, like everyone else lucky enough to be born into this miraculous, temporary world of ours, have value and meaning that cannot be determined by external factors alone. I am no longer wealthy. I am no longer important. But I live, and therefore, I matter.

My father's golden rule, pounded into me early on by my parents and by our society at large and by my own deep desire to believe in it, was just plain wrong. People are so much more than their bank accounts. They are indescribable and irrepressible and indecipherable and, above all, inherently valuable.

Now if you'll excuse me, dear reader, Nick at Nite is about to start and I don't want to miss *Cheers*. Tonight is the one where Cliff goes on *Jeopardy!*. And it's hilarious.

Thank you for reading!

If you enjoyed the book, please consider leaving an honest review on Amazon or GoodReads. Reviews are incredibly important for independent authors.

Please visit www.TuckerMay.com and sign up for email updates to get a mystery novella for FREE.

Follow @TuckerMayMysteries on Bluesky, TuckerMayMysteries on Instagram and Tucker May Mysteries on Facebook for daily bite-size chapters of mystery short stories.

ABOUT THE AUTHOR

Tucker May is a self-published novelist who attended Northwestern University. He grew up in southern Missouri. He is an avid fan of the Los Angeles Rams and Geelong Cats. He lives in Pasadena, CA with his wife Barbara and their cat Principal Spittle. Keep an eye out for his next murder mystery novel, The Lemon House Murders.